A TIME WITHOUT SHADOWS

He smiled. 'Do you want to dance?'

She laughed. 'I wish we could.'

He shrugged. 'Why not?' And with his arms around her he waltzed her slowly, their feet scraping on the gravel pathway. As the music came to an end they stopped and she laughed up at him. 'He's bowing to us, the bandmaster.'

And as he turned to look the stout *Kapellmeister* with his traditional waxed moustache, bowed and kissed his hand in their direction.

They walked on to the far end of the gardens and there with their arms around each other they'd kissed and said goodbye. He stood watching her walk away until she was out of sight. It was a short walk to the Métro at Concorde and half an hour later he was on the train to Melun.

He was alone in the carriage with his eyes closed as he tried not to use up his happiness too quickly. It had to last a long time. But it was like shaking up a kaleidoscope and finding a beautiful pattern. He was glad that he hadn't been sensible. Glad that he had taken the risk.

About the author

Ted Allbeury rose to the rank of Lieutenant-Colonel in the Intelligence Corps during the Second World War, and went on to success in marketing, advertising and radio before he turned to full-time writing in the early 1970s.

All his recent novels have been national best-sellers, and his books have been translated into seventeen foreign languages. He has turned three of his novels into popular and highly acclaimed radio series, and several are optioned for television and films. His most recent novel is *Deep Purple*.

A Time Without Shadows

Ted Allbeury

NEW ENGLISH LIBRARY
Hodder and Stoughton

British Library C.I.P.

Allbeury, Ted
   A time without shadows.
   I. Title
   823'.914[F]

ISBN 0-450-53060-4

Printed and bound in Great Britain for Hodder and Stoughton Paper-backs, a division of Hodder and Stoughton Ltd., Mill Road, Dunton Green, Sevenoaks, Kent TN13 2YA. (Editorial Office: 47 Bedford Square, London WC1B 3DP) by Clays Ltd., St Ives plc, Reading, Berks. Photoset by Rowland Phototypesetting Ltd., Bury St Edmunds, Suffolk.

To Barbara Wright with love from us all.

Ted Allbeury

This book is about France, but it began in Ethiopia.

I lived for a time in a house on a hill just outside Harar, an almost biblical town, in Ethiopia. The house was covered with bougainvillaea and I shared it with another army officer. We had a portable gramophone and were both madly in love with Josephine Baker. We had a record of hers that we played a dozen times a day. On my side she sang *J'ai deux amours – mon pays et Paris* and on my friend's side she sang *La petite Tonkinoise*. His ambition for after the war was to live in Saigon. Mine was to live in Paris. For France to have been defeated and occupied by the Germans seemed incredible and obscene. When, eventually, Germany was defeated and I was part of the occupation, the lesson that has stayed longest in my mind is that in occupied countries life has to go on. It doesn't make much difference whether you are French or German, the same indignities and human virtues and vices still apply. Occupiers and occupied are just men and women, like the marriage service – for better or worse, richer or poorer, in sickness and in health. I wrote this novel mainly for those who didn't live in those times – to show how it was. My friend never made it to Saigon. He died in Auschwitz. And I've lived in many places but never in Paris.

Prologue

Marcus Price was the Member of Parliament for one of the West Midlands constituencies. An excellent constituency MP but an infrequent speaker in the House. It was only because it was a Friday afternoon and most MPs had already left for their constituencies that he caught the Speaker's eye.

'Mr Price.' The Speaker called, and Price took one last quick glance at his single page of notes before he stood.

'Will the Prime Minister inform the House of the circumstances that led to the betrayal and deaths of British officers in Special Operations Executive during World War Two. I refer to the deliberate betrayal by the then Prime Minister, of the SOE network code-named "Scorpio" who were callously sacrificed to placate Soviet demands for a Second Front in Europe. Can the House also be informed as to the compensation paid to the relatives of the officers concerned?'

When Price sat down there was some conferring on the government front bench. Neither the Prime Minister nor the Foreign Secretary or the Minister for Defence were present and it fell to the Minister of Health to respond.

'I feel sure that the whole House will regret the incredible and unwarranted slur on a brave man and war-leader – the late Sir Winston Churchill – unsubstantiated innuendo is not the currency we deal with in this place. I deplore the wild accusations promulgated by the Honourable Member

And the Minister sat down.

Marcus Price stood up and said, 'I equally resent this evasion of a reply and the cavalier attitude to a serious question by my Right Honourable friend. I shall pass my information through the usual channels and will look forward to receiving a considered reply to my question after the recess.'

There were a few desultory cries of 'Shame' from the scattering of government supporters and silence from the handful of Opposition MPs. It seemed a sour note on which to end proceedings when there was the long summer recess to look forward to.

Several lobby correspondents tried to persuade Marcus Price to give them details of what his question was all about but he refused to be drawn as he made his way to the Opposition Whip's office. Even there his reception was frosty. Thirty-year-old events and casting aspersions on popular war-heroes were not vote-getters whichever way you looked at them. The public wouldn't like it. No matter what the historians said, for the general public, old Winnie was the man who had won the war.

It was midnight before Crowther and Travers had been able to get together in Crowther's office. Crowther sat in his shirt-sleeves, his tie unknotted and hanging loose.

Travers said quietly, 'Are the PM's office at panic stations?'

Crowther shook his head. 'No. Seem to be taking it all with a pinch of salt. Asked for something they can use in rebuttal if it comes up again in the autumn. What about the media?'

'Interested, but Price wouldn't give them anything. They'll ferret around for the Sundays but they've got nowhere to start. No names, no dates – nothing.'

'What did he pass to the Whip's office?'

'Nothing much more than he said in his question in the House. Nothing any outsider could latch on to.' He smiled and shrugged. 'Nothing most insiders could latch on to either.'

'But he's obviously referring to the Masson business, isn't he?'

'There's nothing else that would fit.'

'Are there any SOE archives anybody could get to?'

'No. They were officially destroyed in September 1945 by SIS.'

Crowther sighed. 'You know better than that, don't you?'

'I've heard rumours that they were spirited away to some place in Wales.'

'They're down a mine-shaft of an abandoned mine near Builth Wells. Sealed off so that you'd need mining equipment to get at them.'

'Why did we do that with their records?'

Crowther shrugged. 'That was friend Palmer's doing. He was obsessed with hatred of SOE from the moment it was started. Some say he worked actively against them. He probably wanted to make sure that there was nothing on file that could be used against him.'

'So why didn't he have them destroyed?'

'I guess he didn't dare go that far.'

'What do you want us to do?'

'Put somebody on it. Somebody reliable. Just one man. And make clear that he doesn't talk to the media, nor to Marcus Price. Just let him find out what actually happened. There's no hurry. He's got plenty of time. And meantime the PM can say that a full investigation is under way if there are any more questions that have to be answered. There'll be the usual bull-frogging from the media for a few days but it'll die away. Just stonewall them. No comment all the way. All calls to you. OK?'

'Yes.'

As Travers was leaving Crowther said, 'Keep me in touch.' Travers opened his mouth to speak, changed his mind and just nodded as he opened the door.

Part One

1

Both families, the Duchards and the Macleans, had always spent the summer in Provins. The Duchards owned both houses but the smaller of the two was rented permanently to the Macleans. Their homes in Paris were in different *arrondissements* and apart from the summer months they met less frequently. But as the years went by M. Duchard, who was not fond of the English, came to accept Maclean as a Scot. A countryman of his much-loved Mary Queen of Scots. The friendship was cemented by their weekly game of bridge where Maclean always diplomatically allowed his opponent to win a small amount.

The Duchard family consisted of the couple and their only daughter, Anne-Marie. The Macleans had a daughter and two sons. Adèle Maclean was French from the Seychelles and M. Duchard only recognised as French those born and raised in Metropolitan France. But Adèle Maclean was both beautiful and vivacious and she could do an imitation of Josephine Baker singing *La petite Tonkinoise* that endeared her to M. Duchard despite her origins.

Anne-Marie was fifteen and Philip Maclean twenty when he first realised that he was in love with her. They had walked together down to the field at the edge of the woods. A field full of pale red field-poppies and a scattering of marguerites and buttercups. He had set up his easel and by mid-day he had finished the basic painting and made colour notes on his cartridge paper block. When he turned to show the girl what he had done he saw her opening the small basket of sandwiches and fruit that his mother had packed for them. And for the first time he realised how beautiful she was as she raised her head to look at him. The big, brown, heavy-lidded eyes, the neat nose and the dimples at the side of her mouth as she smiled up at him.

'Beef or ham. And there's two tomatoes each.'

For several moments he didn't answer and then he said quietly, 'I ought to have been painting you, not the poppies.'

She blushed. 'Come on. Say which you want.'

He smiled, reaching out his hand to touch her hair and said, 'Let's have one of each.'

He was conscious of a constraint between them as they ate but when they walked back along the bank of the river she made no move to stop him when his arm went round her waist.

The next day both families had driven down to Fontaine-bleau and while the adults did the tour of the palace the young people were allowed to explore the forest. Philip's elder brother Tom had tactfully taken his sister for a long walk as Philip and Anne-Marie sat together on one of the wooden benches. Tom had recognised long before the couple themselves that they were a natural pair. He was also aware that M. Duchard would not have approved of even the mildest affection towards his daughter. He was a lecturer on German literature at the Sorbonne. Old-fashioned in his views and he would have been something of a domestic tyrant if his pretty wife had not learned early on how to tease him into relaxing his penchant for rules and regulations where his family was concerned. She and Adèle Maclean often laughed together at some of his antics that had been subverted. The two women were close friends and fond of their young people.

By the end of the summer everyone except M. Duchard knew that Philip and Anne-Marie were a couple. They had been seen walking hand in hand, smiling happily at each other and everyone was happy for them and hoped it would last.

In late September the families had moved back to their homes in Paris. Anne-Marie to study for her *bachot* and Philip to art school. There had been some talk that Philip should widen his experience by a year at art school in Edinburgh, the Maclean family city. But already the young man was selling his paintings, providing him with enough income to be independent.

In September the following year Philip had asked M. Duchard if he and Anne-Marie could become engaged. Her father had angrily refused and despite protests from their mothers he had insisted that they didn't see each other any more. A week later the Munich agreement had been signed but it had gone by unnoticed by the two young people. It seemed irrelevant in their misery. With the connivance of their families, they usually managed to spend a few hours together every week. But between the young man's anger and the girl's feeling of guilt their time together was never long enough or relaxed enough to satisfy them. The mounting political pressure in Europe and in France itself, they barely noticed.

The tensions were increased when Andrew Maclean decided to take the family to Edinburgh for Christmas and the New Year. Philip refused to go until his mother persuaded him that he was being unreasonable. They would only be away for two weeks, his Scottish grandparents were eager to see him and his father felt that his son was being selfish. Smiling but with tears in her eyes she said that she thought his father was right. She understood why he wanted to stay in Paris but a love that couldn't sustain a two-week absence must be rather fragile. She hated saying something that she didn't really believe for she understood her son's temperament all too well. She wasn't being fair but he was being selfish.

In fact he enjoyed his time in Edinburgh, meeting his grandparents and distant relatives and there were parties and visits that kept his mind occupied. He had arranged with Anne-Marie to phone him when her father was out and he was rather ashamed that he felt so happy when she sounded so sad. There had been no parties at the Duchard home. But he would be with her in two days' time. It was then that he decided to buy her the ring. His mother had gone with him to the jeweller's in Princes Street and had approved his choice of an opal in a gold Victorian setting. It seemed expensive at £25 but it was very beautiful and as his mother pointed out the opal was the birthstone of both of them.

Anne-Marie and her mother had met them in from the boat-train and for a couple of hours they were all happy to be back. And Paris was their home again.

But the elation didn't last. There was an uneasiness sweeping through Paris. Threats against France and her African colonies from Mussolini. The Germans taking over the last remnants of Czechoslovakia and then in March the French Assembly gave Daladier wide powers to speed up rearmament. That had been the final signal for Andrew Maclean. Slowly and discreetly he made arrangements to transfer his business to Edinburgh. It would be just as easy to use his expertise and contacts to import silks and rayon from Lyons as to export them to Britain.

When von Ribbentrop and Stalin signed the German·Soviet non-aggression pact in August and Neville Chamberlain warned Hitler that Britain would stand by Poland it was the last straw.

When Andrew Maclean told his family that they were leaving France and moving to Edinburgh there was a kind of relief all round. It looked now as if war was inevitable and if there was to be war they wanted to be in their own country. And Paris was no longer the Paris they loved. There were constant rumours of corruption and subversion amongst the politicians, vague talk of an accommodation with the Germans. And underlying it all was a mixture of panic and euphoria. Fear of what was going to happen and relief that the uncertainty, the guessing, was soon to be resolved one way or another.

* * *

Philip could see the concern in his father's eyes but he was adamant. He was going to stay.

'You realise that there's going to be a war with the Germans, Phil? It's inevitable now. Just a matter of time.'

'If there is a war, father. Then I'll probably come back.'

'The French are in no mood for fighting, boy. You can tell. It's in the air. All the chest-beating and defiance doesn't mean a thing. The people at the top are totally corrupt. The army is unprepared and the people don't believe in their leaders any more.'

'It's the same in England, father.'

Maclean shook his head. 'It isn't. It looks the same but it isn't. It's an island and that makes a difference. It always has and it always will. They don't want war any more than the French do but they've learned the lesson of appeasement. The French haven't.'

'I'll come back if it gets bad.'

'If you leave it too long it won't be easy. There'll be conscription as soon as it starts and if you don't report you'll be committing an offence.'

Philip smiled. 'In that case I'll have to join the Foreign Legion.'

'It's not a joke, son. I've been through it all. If things go bad for the French you'll find that foreigners, especially the British, will get the blame. Fighting to the last Frenchman and all that rubbish again.' He paused. 'Where will you live?'

'I've got myself a room on the Left Bank.'

'Already?'

'Yes, father.' He smiled. 'I can look after myself.'

As the clouds gathered over Europe Marie Duchard had insisted on inviting her best friend's son to the house. It would be shameful not to do so when he was on his own in Paris. And Duchard had reluctantly agreed. After a few weeks there was no need for formal invitations and Philip visited most days for a meal or to take Anne-Marie for a stroll. It was the most beautiful summer that anyone could remember.

Philip had tuned the Duchards' radio to the BBC and they all sat listening to Neville Chamberlain announcing that Britain was now at war with Germany. Later the same day the French government announced that France too was at war with Germany.

Philip and Anne-Marie had walked to the Tuileries Gardens to get away from the gloom of the Duchard household. When they got back there had been a telephone call from Philip's father, but when he tried to return the call all unofficial overseas calls had been temporarily suspended.

A telegram from his father arrived at his room the next morning. Urging him to return home immediately. Three days later he was able to phone home and spoke to his mother. His father was very worried about him and when he told her that he intended staying on unless the situation grew more serious, she said that even she felt that he was being reckless, and stubborn.

Two weeks later he got a letter from home to say that his brother Tom, who was a lieutenant in the RNVR, had lost his life when HMS Royal Oak had been sunk at her home base in Scapa Flow. But life in Paris seemed virtually unaffected by the war and from reading the English newspapers it seemed to be much the same at home. People were calling it the 'phoney war' and there were editorials in the French papers suggesting that the war would be over by Christmas.

He had almost decided to return home at Christmas but discovered that transport to the UK was virtually impossible without some sort of official blessing. In the case of civilians that approval would have to come from the Paris Embassy. The consular official at the Embassy had pointed out rather frostily that he was overdue for call-up and should have returned as soon as war was declared. Despite the admonitions he was told that he would have to make his own way back, there was no assistance the Embassy could offer.

He was overcome by indecisiveness, seized by a strange lethargy, and even after Christmas he felt no urge to make his way home. Neither could he justify in his own mind why he stayed. He knew that leaving Anne-Marie was part of the problem but it was more than that. He wanted his life to go on as it had for the last six months. Painting, seeing Anne-Marie almost every day. He didn't feel that he was involved in the war in any way. And England and home seemed like something from the past. A different life, and he was no longer part of it. He had his own private and pleasant limbo and was determined to ignore the outside world. He sensed that he was less welcome now at the Duchards' house. He saw Anne-Marie every day but he was seldom invited in for meals and their meetings had an air of conspiracy about them now. Their feelings towards each other were even more intense but the cloud of unexpressed disapproval gave them an irrational feeling of guilt at being so happy and uninvolved with the war news.

2

Only two days earlier he'd arranged to meet her at their favourite café on the Champs Elysées. And now he couldn't even cross to the other side because the German troops were marching down the Champs Elysées. It didn't seem possible but there they were. It was Thursday, June 14, 1940.

The whole city seemed to be suspended in time. Three million Parisians had already fled the city. There were shutters up on all the shops and no traffic in the streets. Just a handful of people watching in silence as the Germans marched by. There had been no radio, no newspapers that day. A few statues had been protected with sandbags and far away black smoke rose from burning fuel depots darkening the sky in one last pathetic act of defiance of the Germans.

He could see now that like the rest of the shops and cafés theirs was boarded up. It was going to be difficult to contact her again. He was British and they blamed the British for the French surrender.

As he walked back slowly to his room he wondered what he ought to do. Rumour said that all the British would be rounded up and sent to prison camps, but despite that he was reluctant to leave. He was only twenty-two and he was madly in love with Anne-Marie Duchard. It would take time for the Germans to track down several thousand Britishers. And he wasn't sure how he would get back to England anyway.

There were lights on all over the Hôtel Crillon and a

line of German staff cars outside, it looked as if it was already some kind of German headquarters. It was an hour before he got to his room off the Rue du Bac. There was no electricity and he stumbled up the rickety staircase to the third floor. As he sat on the edge of his bed in the darkness he suddenly felt incredibly tired and deeply depressed. And for the first time in his life he knew that he was scared.

It had taken him nearly a month to get to Marseilles. Cycling most of the way on small back roads, avoiding big towns, sleeping in barns and woods, buying food in country markets. Eating raw fruit, cheese, butter and bread. A few shrewd shopkeepers had obviously realised from his accent that he was English. Some refused to serve him, others gave him fresh milk and bread from their own kitchens. For the first part of the journey the roads had been crowded with refugees but gradually the roads emptied and the country people seemed almost unaware of the war and the German occupation. There were few signs of the Germans, and the French police had given up trying to check documents. Too many people genuinely had no means of identifying themselves. The checks were mainly to discourage refugees from trying to settle in villages where food and accommodation were short.

There was an American consulate in Marseilles and although they had questioned him suspiciously for over an hour they had given him a name and address that they said might be helpful. They had also agreed to notify his family in Edinburgh through the Red Cross that he was safe. They warned him that there was a newly-arrived detachment of the Gestapo already operating in the city. They said that at the moment the Germans were more concerned with registering French Jews than security. He wondered why they were so interested in Jews.

The Frenchman whose address they had given him had stared at him for long moments and then had refused to let him in the house. But he had given him another name, a man who ran a small garage just outside the city. Two weeks later he was on a Panamanian-registered freighter with a cargo of hides from Jibuti destined for Liverpool. He had been given forged papers and been signed on as crew.

At Liverpool he had been interned and sent to a camp at Aintree where he had been interrogated daily for two weeks on how he had escaped from German-occupied France.

In the middle of the third week an army captain in battle-dress had sat in on the interrogation, listening but not speaking. The following day he had been taken to a different part of the camp and in a small office the captain had smiled and waved him to the wooden chair on the other side of a small table. Maclean noticed a file with his name on the cover alongside a clip-board.

'Mr Maclean, my name's Mathews, I'm sorry all this rigmarole has taken so long but I'm sure you'll understand that everyone who arrives in the UK from France is not as straightforward as you are. And in your case we had a special interest. You speak fluent French, you know Paris very well and you showed a great deal of initiative in getting back here on very slender resources.' He paused, smiling as he looked across at Maclean. 'I wonder if I could interest you in joining the army?'

'Does that mean that if I don't join I'll be kept in this camp?'

'Good heavens, no. We've notified your parents that you're sound in mind and limb and that they can expect to see you in the next couple of days or so.'

'Wouldn't I be called up anyway?'

'Yes. But you'd be able to opt for the Royal Navy or the RAF. I'd like you to make it the army. We need people with your qualifications.' He paused. 'You'd be given fourteen days' leave before you went to the depot. Time to sort yourself out and all that.'

'Where's the depot?'

'Are you interested?'

Maclean smiled and shrugged. 'I suppose I feel slightly flattered that I've gone from being a prisoner to a useful human being.'

'Not a prisoner, Philip. An internee.'

Maclean grinned. 'It feels the same. Do I have to sign anything?'

'How about we have a sandwich together in our local pub?'

'I'd rather get straight back home, sir, if that's OK.'

'Of course. Let me tell you a bit about what you'll be doing. Because of your French you'll be in the Intelligence Corps, but before you do your Corps training you'll be doing three months' basic infantry training at the Royal Sussex depot in Chichester.' Mathews smiled. 'The War Office felt we ought to learn which hand to salute with and all that. When you've finished that you'll be going to Winchester and get your training as an NCO in Field Security. After that – a lot of doors are open.'

He had been given a rail-warrant, clothing coupons and ration cards for two weeks and his army record and pay-book, and had taken the train to Edinburgh. It was a slow journey with long hold-ups because of air raids, and the train was crowded, mainly with servicemen, all strangely silent in the unlit carriages and corridors. In the darkness he closed his eyes and thought about Anne-Marie, wondering what she was doing and how they were coping with the Germans. Maybe they had moved from Paris to the house at Provins.

Captain Mathews and the other interrogators had made him describe watching the Germans marching down the Champs Elysées again and again. It was only when describing it to them that he realised that he had seen a piece of history in the making. But it still seemed incredible. The collapse of the French armies had seemed inevitable. The French had been in no mood to fight, but somehow nobody had actually envisaged what that meant. That the Germans would occupy Paris, and control the whole of France. Even the Germans must have been amazed that it had been so easy.

Mathews had said that because he spoke fluent French and knew Paris so well that he could be useful to them. He would do anything they asked if it meant the chance of seeing her again. The British seemed to feel that the French deserved what they were getting because they had been so weak and demoralised. And Mathews and the others had seemed faintly amused when he had made excuses for the French. It was hard to explain to people who hadn't been there what it was like. Like a party that had gone on too long and where the last stragglers had been interrupted by a gang of hooligans. But the British didn't see it that way. They had been left to fight it out on their own, and they barely concealed their contempt for their former allies.

The two weeks' leave with his family were a strain. They were so obviously still mourning the death of his brother Tom. He spent a lot of time with his mother who was eager to hear of his experience in Paris after they had left. She tried to reassure him that Anne-Marie would be safe with her parents. Duchard may be a hard, unbending man but he had influence and that sort of man would know what to do to see that his family survived.

His sister was in London, working as a clerk at the Admiralty and his father was now an Air Raid Warden. No longer the decisive man that he had been, he had become withdrawn, his thoughts seemingly far away. There had been a few moments of pride when he had taken Philip down to the Air Raid post and introduced him to the other Wardens.

He was ashamed that he was relieved when the time came for him to go to the Royal Sussex depot at Chichester. Only his mother had gone with him to the station and as they stood there on the platform she had tears in her eyes as she said, 'It'll be better next time, my love. It takes time to adjust.'

He kissed her and said, 'Don't worry, *Maman*, I understand. Take care of yourself and Father.'

She looked a frail figure as she waved a chiffon scarf to him as the train pulled out.

For three months Philip Maclean had done foot drill, weapons drill, boiled out a Lee Enfield rifle, stripped and assembled a Bren gun and learned how to use the back of a toothbrush to burnish the toecaps of his boots. And one other thing had happened. He had been taken in front of the depot commandant and offered immediate promotion to WOII – Company Sergeant Major in the Royal Sussex Regiment. It had been suggested obliquely that he was too good a soldier to spend the rest of the war with a bunch of wets from universities. And Maclean *was* a good soldier. When he was on guard duty there was no dossing down for a nap in the guardroom in the early hours of the morning. Private Maclean was on guard for King and Country. He was also ambitious enough to want that quick promotion. Private Maclean actually liked the army and the army liked him. With the proviso that he should grow a moustache to give him an air of maturity in his new role the deal was done.

At least they thought it was done. But three days later a major with green Intelligence Corps flashes on his battle-dress sleeves had spent ten minutes in the commandant's office. But his voice had been heard way past the company clerk's office, the adjutant's office and as far as the cookhouse. There were no obscenities, no cursing, no blasphemy, but people had listened and tried to remember the words that were uttered for future use.

Private Maclean had been given a rail warrant and his AB64 Part 2 and packed off with a flea in his ear on a train to the Intelligence Corps depot in Winchester. The training staff at the depot were Intelligence Corps NCOs or officers but the so-called permanent staff who were responsible for administration were all from Guards regiments who enjoyed their short spell of harassing professors of history and a flock of soldiers who could speak between them every language from Serbo-Croat to Swahili. It was an offence of dumb insolence to look an officer in the eye unless he spoke to you. If the Commanding Officer was not in his office when you entered you saluted his empty chair. The contempt of the Intelligence Corps recruits for the Guardsmen was obvious. To most of them it was incredibly childish and rather pathetic, but Maclean had had a foretaste of the military at their devotions on his infantry course.

The intelligence training covered advanced map-reading, survival training, unarmed combat, small-arms and automatic weapons, the administrative structure of the British Army (how to obtain rations and supplies to which you were not entitled) and finally the basic elements of security of persons and premises. After a short course in motorcycle rough-riding Maclean was posted for more advanced intelligence training to an establishment in the Derbyshire hills, in what had formerly been a luxury hotel.

He was subsequently posted to a Field Security Unit in his home town – Edinburgh. He had been back from France almost nine months when he was recruited into Special Operations Executive and was sent for further specialised training at a country house in Surrey. At Wanborough Manor he learned how to run a network in enemy occupied territory. Coding, operating a radio, parachuting, surveillance, how to use explosives, and the organisation of the various German intelligence organisations and how to resist interrogation. And finally he did a parachute course at Ringway.

When he was briefed that he would be leading a small network in the Dordogne he was flattered by their faith in his competence. Two weeks before he was due to be dropped he was told that he now had to take over a network that had lost its leader. A network just south-east of Paris based near the small town of Melun. It would be a temporary command until an experienced leader could be found. He would only be there for two or three months. New maps and different aerial photographs had to be studied. He would go by Hudson and be dropped further south below the small town of Sens. It was more a village than a town but there was a good dropping ground in parkland west of Sens.

Twice the drop had been aborted because of heavy cloud over the dropping area but on the third attempt there was a clear sky and an almost full moon.

There was a last minute final check of his clothes and equipment and then they walked in the darkness to the vague white shape of the Hudson. Mathews had come as his directing officer and had wished him luck as he took one last look around before he entered the plane.

They were taking a dog-legged route. Down to the Iles Chausey and across the Baie de Mont Saint-Michel to cross the French coast just south of Granville. Then south-east almost to Le Mans before the final leg due east to Sens.

The navigator gave him the ten minute warning then a minute-by-minute countdown until they were over the area. They saw the marker lights clearly on the first pass and he was to drop on the return, the supply canisters going first.

As one of the air-crew turned the levers on the hatch and lifted it back on its hinges there was a noisy rush of cold air into the body of the plane. Maclean leaned back to keep his balance as he swung his legs into the opening and seconds later the crewman's mouth by his ear said 'Jump'. Maclean was tempted to pull the release before he had finished counting but he knew that if he did he could easily be caught up in the plane's slipstream. When he pulled the ring the canopy snapped open seconds later and his body swung so that for a few moments the marker lights disappeared. As he steadied the parachute lines the sound of the plane was very distant and all was silent except for the rush of air past his face, as he dropped slowly.

Then there was that last rush of the ground towards him and a sudden vision of a ploughed field before the shock of landing, rolling sideways, clawing at the parachute lines as he was dragged along the ground. Then the disciplined routine took over as he slipped out of the harness and collapsed the canopy. He saw the figures of two men running towards him, one took over folding the 'chute and the other, panting said, '*Qui vive?*' and Maclean said softly '*L'arc en ciel*'. The man gripped Maclean's hand in both of his and put a hand around his shoulder, leading him towards a line of trees at the edge of the field. He said softly, 'The canisters are already loaded and on their way. Pierre will take care of the parachute. Can you ride a cycle?'

'Yes.'

'It's not far. About five kilometres.'

They had spent that night in the barn of a small arable farm on the outskirts of Sergines, a small village off the main road about half-way between Sens and Melun. Even on the short cycle ride and their arrival at the farm he had been aware of several lapses of security. It wasn't the right time to comment but he was determined to make them more secure in future. They had very little sleep that night. Georges Loussier who had led the reception group had told him about the more important members of the network which covered a wide area almost up to the outskirts of Paris itself.

'What have you been doing in the last six months?'

'Training on weapons and explosives. Identifying targets. Recruiting in special areas like the railway workers, power station technicians, civil engineers, radio repairers and so on.'

'How many people do we have?'

The Frenchman shrugged. 'About twenty who are really important. At least a hundred who will actively take part and a lot more who will give us information and tip-offs who are on our side but have obligations to wives or families that limits what they will do.'

'What was Fayolle like as a leader?'

'A good, solid man. Didn't want to take risks. Said it was a time of preparation. Action would come later when London gave the signal. Very strict but much liked.'

'What happened?'

'He had a small farm. He was killed when his tractor overturned when he was on a steep slope.'

'And you've been running the network since his death.'

The Frenchman smiled. 'Not running it. Just holding it together.'

'You've got a room for me in Melun.'

'Yes. A good-sized room over a bakery.'

'Who owns it?'

'The widow of the baker. She still runs the place. Very reliable. She hates the Boche. They took her son. Sent him off to forced labour in Germany. Just rounded up men in the streets, stuck them on a train and that was the last anyone heard of them.'

'What's the general attitude to the Germans?'

The Frenchman hesitated then sighed as he said, 'Most people ignore them and get on with their lives as best they can. See them as a fact of life – like the weather. Some actively collaborate. Think the Germans will bring discipline and get rid of the bad influences in French life.' He shrugged again. 'Depends on their experience with the Germans.'

'And Vichy? What do they think of Vichy?'

'The old Marshal is popular. War hero, father figure. But people see the rest of them as just typical politicians with their snouts in the pig trough. The people who lost the war for us.'

'Do people expect France to be liberated?'

Loussier smiled wryly. 'Not really. It's like winning the lottery. A nice thought, but not taken seriously.' He paused and looked at Maclean, hesitating before he spoke.

'I don't want to discourage you but most people if they spoke the truth would rather things went on as they are. Liberation means war again. More Frenchmen killed. More families destroyed.'

'So why do we have so many supporters?'

'They are the proud ones. The ones who care about being free. They won't rest until the Germans are defeated. Patriots who put France above all other things. Families, loved-ones, the easy life.'

'What do they feel about the English?'

'Most feel you let us down. They know it's not really true but it saves some guilt feelings.' He grinned. 'But the same people hope against hope that the English throw the Germans out. Even if they only do it to suit their own reasons. They respect the English.' He laughed grimly. 'They have to. They're our only hope.'

'Is it safe to sleep here for a while?'

'Yes. You didn't meet them but there are two men on watch around the buildings. I'll wake you in a couple of hours.'

'Did you get me the painting things?'

'Yes. They're in your room at the bakery.'

They had taken the bus into Melun, walked to the baker's shop and had been given the key to the large attic room on the third floor and Loussier had gone off to buy food for him.

The son had been training to be a graphic artist and a designer, and the walls were covered with posters and labels from household products. Labels of La Vache qui Rit, Le Petit Marseillais, a pure olive soap, and a Camembert label with a portrait of Napoleon. A poster for Byrrh tonic wine and a poster advertising Maurice Chevalier at the Olympia.

There was a single bed along one wall and a long workbench under the gabled window. One wall was shelved from top to bottom. Most of the shelves were empty apart from a dozen or so Livres de Poche and two or three *objets trouvés*. The bark of a tree, a smooth stone from a beach and a piece of purple pyrites.

A drawing board and a T-square were upright against the wall beside the door and there were two comfortable-looking cane armchairs with cushions. A small curtained-off section was a toilet and wash-place and a small gas hob stood on a marble-topped set of drawers with hooks above and cups and other crockery ranged in line. An easel and four canvases were propped against the wall by the window. And the paints and charcoal were in a cardboard box.

And suddenly the pressures of the last twenty-four hours took over and he walked over to the bed and sat down, his head bowed. It all seemed unreal. It had appeared so straightforward in training but now it seemed crazy. Sitting in a strange room in German-occupied France with grown men who assumed he could lead them in defiance of the Germans. He felt a wave of anger against the people who had so calmly arranged for him to be there, fifty kilometres from Paris where the Gestapo, the *Sicherheitsdienst* and the *Abwehr* with all their men and resources were ranged against him. Why the hell had he got himself involved in such a ridiculous and dangerous pantomime? He lay back on the bed and closed his eyes. A few moments later he was asleep.

3

Henri Georges Masson was born in September 1909 in a decaying cottage on a farm estate just outside the town of Evreux, west of Paris. The cottage was one of several on the sprawling estate housing farm labourers and their families.

His father had been a labourer on the estate until a minor heart ailment forced him to look for other work. He was considered fortunate to have got a job in the local post office. He was a humble man without ambition and his wife had to work as a servant at the estate-owner's mansion. There were two older sons whose temperaments were very different from that of Henri. They were to become respected craftsmen when they grew up.

Young Henri often accompanied his mother to the big house, being given small tasks in the kitchen to pass away the time. In these almost daily visits the boy saw the vast difference between his own home and the style of living at the rich man's house. It was to become both a spur to his own ambitions and part of the fantasy he wove around himself in later years. He came to despise his father for his submission and lack of ambition but he relished being his mother's favourite. She was doing her best to make ends meet and took all the household decisions that a husband would normally take.

When Henri was 16 he sat for his baccalaureat. Frustrated by failing the exams and angered that he had needed his despised father's influence to get him the lowest grade of job with the PTT, the authority for postal and telephone

26

services, he started work in Paris. He was eventually promoted to the grade of clerk, still angry at his own humble circumstances.

The big change in his life came when, with thousands of others, he saw Charles Lindbergh land his plane at Le Bourget after his non-stop flight across the Atlantic. For the first time in his life he knew exactly what he wanted to be. An aviator. A flyer. Respected by everybody, even by the President of France himself.

Henri's mother recognised immediately that this new enthusiasm could be the saving of her youngest son. She had asked her employer how she should go about helping the boy and, as a reward for her long years of conscientious work, he took over the problem. He solved it by sponsoring Henri himself to a course at a flying school just outside Paris that specialised in training young men as pilots for the French Air Force.

To everyone's surprise Henri Masson turned out to be an exceptionally good pilot. But a probable clue to his future lay in his choice of flying career. He joined a flying circus that toured the country giving displays of aerobatics, parachuting and short pleasure trips. It was during that time that people noticed that Henri Masson had another speciality – charm. A charm that gave credibility to the picture he painted of his background. The scenarios were varied to suit the listener. From being the son of a rich merchant, to the illegitimate son of a count, to being an officer in French intelligence. With girls the charm alone was enough and his conquests made him the envy of his fellow pilots. Those who had heard several different versions of his background were amused at his audacity but took it as no more than what any young man might do to charm a girl into his bed.

The depression killed off the flying circus and Henri Masson was forced to take a job as a salesman. Faced with the realities of selling, the charm didn't work. But fate always seemed ready to save Henri Masson. A new air-line called Air Bleu was formed to transport mail inside France.

Masson was a pilot again. The new air-line had a chequered early history and sometimes its employees, including pilots, received no pay; but it gradually established itself.

As if someone had heard one of his romantic background stories, he was contacted early in 1936 by an officer of the *Deuxième Bureau*. It started with payments on the side for delivering letters and packets to contacts in the places Masson flew to. Then, using hired planes, Masson had flown his contact over military sites in neighbouring countries. The ports of Livorno and La Spezia in Italy, and the Siegfried Line in Germany. Masson seemed to have a taste for danger and an ability to deal with those moments of stress that flying in all sorts of conditions inevitably created. There was double pay for night flying and as there were only the crudest navigational aids this meant following roads and rivers in the moonlight. But Henri Masson was sure that he would always survive. He was a natural survivor.

It was from that secret service contact that Masson met two other men. The first was an Englishman named Carlton. Roger Carlton whose father was something important at the British Embassy in Paris. Masson and Carlton had much in common. Charm, a desire to be involved in intelligence work and a liking for the high-life. The second man was a German, Kurt Westphal, an officer of one of the Nazi intelligence organisations. He took letters and packages for the German too. With his pay from Air Bleu, from French intelligence and the German, Masson was making good money.

When France declared war on Germany Masson was testing a new plane for one of the small aircraft manufacturers. Day after day he flew the plane and then waited for its faults to be corrected. He was totally absorbed in his work and when the German armoured columns were sweeping through Holland and Belgium it all seemed as if it was going on in some other world.

On the day when the French Prime Minister phoned the

newly appointed British Prime Minister, Winston Churchill, to say that it was all over for France, Masson had taken the plane up for two test flights.

On the night when the Germans marched down the Champs Elysées Masson and his colleagues got blind drunk, cursing their army, their generals and their government.

To the relief of the pilots and ground staff of Air Bleu the company continued to operate on the instructions of the French government in Vichy. The company's contract was to carry mail and official passengers in Metropolitan France, and the countries in the Mediterranean and Near East.

Masson was bored by the routine but glad that he was still flying.

Much to the surprise of his friends and colleagues he married a divorced young woman he had met in Marseilles. It was hard to imagine Masson tamed at last and domesticated.

4

Masson had made two return flights from Marseilles to Vichy that day and although he was tired he walked from the hangar to the pilots' mess. He enjoyed the company of pilots and the drinks and food were both plentiful and cheap.

He cheered up as he opened the door and heard the sound of voices and laughter.

He had been there for nearly an hour and by then there was only one other pilot at the bar. He knew André Delors and he saw Delors grin and raise his glass. For a moment he hesitated and then he walked over to the other man.

'Haven't seen you for some days, André. Where've you been?'

'Supposed to be secret. A couple of generals delivered back safe and sound from Syria.'

'I thought that we and the Germans had been kicked out by the English.'

'There's still a few hanging on. What about you? What have you been doing?'

'Just the bloody milk-run to Vichy.'

'I was in Athens and Aleppo a couple of weeks ago. While I was there the British Army took over Aleppo and something funny happened.'

'You found a new girl.'

'No. A very senior British chap interviewed me. Said they were very interested in recruiting Air France pilots for the Free French.'

'He was probably some Boche testing your loyalty. And

if you'd been interested you'd have been blacklisted by the Gestapo or tried for treason.'

'No. I'd seen the chap before in the Spanish Civil War. I did a couple of delivery flights for him at the time. Paid well.'

'Let's go over to a table.' Masson smiled. 'The Boche poster says "The enemy listens too" – and they're right.'

Masson had ordered two beers and had taken the bottles and glasses to where Delors was sitting at a table in the far corner of the room.

As he sat down Masson said, 'Tell me more about this chap who tried to recruit you.'

'When I met him in Spain he was calling himself Lord Granar, but now he's an RAF Wing Commander and he calls himself Arthur Forbes. There was a chap named Maxwell from BOAC who took me to see him.'

'What did you say to him?'

'I said I was interested but I'd have to come back here to Marseilles to clear up my personal things. I think he knew I hadn't decided one way or another.'

'So how did you leave it?'

'He gave me the name of a contact in Marseilles who would pass the word back to London.'

'Who is he?'

Delors smiled. 'He's someone at the US Consulate here.'

'What's his name?'

'Why d'you want to know?'

'Because I'm interested.'

'They said they were looking specifically for Air France pilots.' He smiled. 'And this circus we're flying for ain't Air France by a long way.'

'That's no problem, they won't know the difference. I'll go and see this chap and find out what's on offer if you like.'

They had talked until midnight, Masson trying to convince Delors of his sincerity.

They had gone the next day to see the American in the Visa Division of the US Consulate and Delors had listened as Masson used all his charm. Claiming that they were both Air France pilots eager to go to England to fly in any capacity for the Free French or the RAF.

Despite Masson's persuasive powers the American seemed in no hurry to take up the offer but arranged for him to contact an official at the US Embassy in Vichy. And even at that level there seemed to be no hurry. But he was given a long interrogation about his experience and the official was obviously interested, asking about his routes and what he had seen at the various airfields. For several weeks he was given packages when he was in Vichy to take to the US consulate in Marseilles and packages back to the US Embassy in Vichy.

Uncertain of his future, he still operated in the black market and from time to time carried messages and packages for Westphal's local people. He wanted to make sure that whichever way things went he had resources to fall back on. Although he wasn't aware of it his name had been passed back to London, to Clive Palmer.

All contact was broken when the Americans declared war on the Germans but before the Embassy closed the Americans had put in one final recommendation to London on behalf of Masson and Delors. Part of London's problem had been that the SIS escape line run by Palmer's men in Marseilles was strictly confined to helping British agents and servicemen. No foreigners had ever been allowed to use it.

One thing that had always surprised and puzzled the people who knew Masson was his relationship with the woman he called Toto, Sabine Cortot, who had met him first when she was a shop assistant at a local jeweller's. Three weeks after meeting him she had moved into his room. Married, and at best described as 'jolie-laide', she was not Masson's normal type of woman but they had lived together ever since the surrender. He wasn't faithful to her, always finding it easy to pick up girls, which his job and life-style made easy. People wondered what the rather plain woman had that kept him with her for so long. When her divorce came through and they married few people expected it to last.

Masson had not told Toto of his contacts with the American or of his courier activities for them, and the German, Westphal, and the French *Deuxième Bureau*. When word finally came through that would get him and Delors on to the escape route, he went to see her immediately where she worked and told her that he would be away for longer than his usual trips and also told her that he had left money for her at their rooms.

That night Masson and Delors had met at the Gare St Charles, Marseilles' central railway station, and Delors had been disturbed and surprised by Masson bursting into tears as they got on the train for Narbonne. He was distressed about leaving his wife and it disturbed Delors because it was out of character. Masson's attitude to his women had always been entirely selfish and ruthless.

5

Loussier had taken him to the doctor, a Belgian who had been settled in France for ten years. The doctor had given him a signed note to say that Philippe Benoit was suffering from a chronic heart condition that had been caused by rheumatic fever when he was a child. He had also given him six small tablets. If for any reason the Germans were going to check his heart he was to take one tablet and there would be no problem. The effect would last for about six hours and on no account should he take more than one tablet in forty-eight hours. He now had all the document-ation he needed. Identity card, *permis de séjour*, *permis de conduire* and the medical certificate.

The following day he had spent the morning with Janine, his radio operator. She operated out of an attic room in one of the back streets of the town. Loussier had intro-duced them and left them alone.

He sat on the edge of the ramshackle bed and watched her as she took the radio set from under a pile of hats on the top shelf of an open wardrobe. It was a B2 suitcase transceiver. It had obviously been carefully looked after but he noticed the mains wire with its plug attached.

'Do you need to use the mains? It's not really safe in a town. The D-F men can cut off the supply and if your traffic stops they can get a rough idea of where you are.'

The girl smiled. 'I know, but I had a vibrator for back-up battery power and the original one is *kaput*.'

'There are spare vibrators in the cylinders that came on my drop. See Loussier about them.'

'OK.'

'Tell me about you.'

'I'm twenty-four. Mother French. Father Welsh. Bilingual but brought up in London. Worked in Woolworth's. Answered an ad. Did my radio training on the top floor of Peter Robinson.' She shrugged and smiled. 'And here I am.'

'Any problems?'

'Only men.'

He laughed. 'Well, you're very pretty so you must know how to deal with those you don't fancy.'

'Some of them aren't that easy.'

'If anybody pesters you just let me know.' He paused. 'How did you get on with Fayolle.'

'Fine. No problems.'

'How many Biscuit receivers have we got?'

'Four.'

'Who's got them?'

'I've no idea.'

'So who listens for our *messages personels*?'

'I don't know.'

'Who's reliable enough to do that properly?'

'I think Georges Loussier could tell you better than I can.'

'OK. Give him the sets and he'll tell you who's to have them. You give them out and you give them proper instruction how to use them.' He paused. 'By the way – what's your cover?'

'I sew on buttons for a dressmaker.'

'Enough money?'

She smiled. 'Loussier gives me food. I get by.'

As he walked back to the bakery he knew what he had to do. If he spent his time going to see people after he'd once met them he'd never have time to think and to plan. He needed a small group as his immediate staff. Reliable carriers and good junior commanders.

'We've got to plan for when we get more weapons and more explosives, Georges. How many men have we got who can give instruction on Sten guns and how to use plastic?'

'Most of the group leaders can handle rifles and pistols but they couldn't teach people. They use guns by instinct.'

'OK. I'll give up two weeks and you and I will visit all group leaders and talk with them. Put them in the picture.' He paused. 'I want two reliable couriers who know the countryside really well. Who shall they be?'

Loussier thought for a moment. 'An old man named Pierre. He's got a bad leg but he can ride a bike. And he's one of us. All the way. Then there's a young woman, Lisa, her family are farmers in a small way. She delivers produce all around. She's got a licence for a *gasogène*. Her fiancé is a Resister. He's a *gendarme* in Champeaux.'

'OK. Get them both in this evening at my place. And, Georges – you're my deputy from now on.'

Maclean had liked Pierre. The so-called old man was in his early fifties but his white hair and his limp made him seem older. He was the gardener at a small local château and both he and his employer were solid supporters of the Resistance, helping out with both money and food.

Lisa Perrier was 24, a pretty, blonde girl who ran a delivery service for several farms to the street market in Melun. Her father was a sergeant in the French Army who was now a prisoner-of-war in Germany. Once a week she took fruit and vegetables to Paris. Her permit allowed her to use her truck as far east as Chaumont and as far west as Le Mans.

Maclean questioned them at length about the procedures the Germans used at road blocks. He also made notes of their suggestions of sites for parachute drops of arms and explosives.

That night there was a signal from London that informed him that he could expect a visit from an SOE man who would be in charge of all drops and receptions in future. No details of the man or how he would identify himself were given. It was good news because London had told him that the RAF had been threatening to restrict their flights because of bad sites and careless handling of drops and landings by Lysanders. Previous supplies had been lost and in some cases planes had been damaged by the stumps of trees on a landing strip and at least one plane's landing gear had sunk axle-deep in mud. London were determined not to send more than basic necessities until reception had been improved everywhere.

By the end of five weeks he had not only visited all the groups in his network but had assessed the strengths and weaknesses of their leaders and had gone with them to check possible drop-sites and strategic points for future sabotage.

In the course of these meetings he had become aware of problems that London had not seemed aware of. For even some totally committed Resisters there was a barely veiled resentment of being led by a man they called 'an English'. It wasn't aimed particularly at him but he got the impression that there was a veil being drawn over some of their thinking and attitudes that excluded him. The second problem was politics. He had been warned that in those networks that were more concerned with *Maquis*-type groups, more concerned with military-type skirmishes with the Germans, there would be a strong communist influence. But Maclean found that there were not only communists in his network but that they were bitterly resented by the non-communists. He was determined not to be involved in any aspect of French politics. But in a strange way it was a sign that all sides were obviously expecting to be liberated. The politics were the preliminary rounds of the political struggles to come when France was free again.

6

When Masson and Delors arrived in England they were separated. Delors was taken for interrogation at a camp on Epsom racecourse and Masson to the Royal Victoria Patriotic School, a high-security interrogation centre in Wandsworth.

Delors was interrogated for three weeks but after a week Masson had been taken to a hotel in London and was left with a man who introduced himself as Clive Palmer.

Palmer waved Masson to an armchair and when the Frenchman was seated Palmer said, 'Tell me about yourself.'

Masson smiled and shrugged. 'What do you want to know?'

'Tell me about your flying experience.'

'I've discussed every detail with your people at the interrogation unit. What more can I say?'

'You can tell me the truth.'

'But . . .'

Palmer spoke sharply. 'Don't waste my time, Masson. Why did you claim to the American in Marseilles and to my people that you were currently flying for Air France.' He paused and said coldly. 'You've never flown for Air France, have you?'

'Well, Air Bleu was part of Air France.'

'Rubbish, they have no connection with Air France. And you know it.'

'That's what they told us. We were a subsidiary of Air France.'

'Who sent you over here, Masson? Was it Sturm-bannführer Westphal?'

For long moments Masson was silent and Palmer knew that the Frenchman was scared.

'I just sold him things on the black market. You have to do that to survive. One needs ration cards, permits, gas and all the other things.'

'How often did you see him?'

'Sometimes once a week. Sometimes not for months.'

'And the packets and letters you delivered for him. Who did they go to?'

'It was just a mail service. Mostly to Vichy or sometimes to friends of his.'

'German friends?'

'Most of them, yes.'

'You were acting as a courier for the German intelligence organisation – the *Sicherheitsdienst*? You knew that, didn't you?'

'I didn't ask who he was.'

'You didn't need to ask. He told you and sometimes he was in uniform. SS uniform.'

Masson shook his head slowly. 'They all wear some kind of uniform. You don't notice it after a time. They're just Germans. They've got money. That's all.'

'But you knew the Frenchman was *Deuxième Bureau*, didn't you?'

'Yes. He told me so. So what?' He shrugged. 'He's a Frenchman, so am I. He's the legal government as far as I'm concerned.'

'They both paid you?'

'Yes. It all helped.'

'Tell me about your background. Your childhood.'

'My father farmed six hundred hectares. We were well off.'

'Education?'

'I passed my *bachot* with honours in three subjects. I was offered a place at university but I wanted to earn money.'

'Which university?'

'The Sorbonne.'

Palmer sighed but said nothing for several moments. Then he said, 'The RAF and the Free French Air Force wouldn't take you but there are other things I might be able to arrange for you.'

'I'll do anything you want.'

'Do you know any Frenchmen in the Resistance?'

'No. I've heard rumours but that's all.'

'Would you be willing to go back to France and work for the Resistance?'

'Yes. Of course.'

'You'd be in charge of parachute drops of supplies and personnel. And sometimes landings. Do you think you could do that successfully?'

'No problem at all. I'm used to flying at night. I know what's needed.'

'You realise you could be tortured or killed if you were caught.'

Masson's smile was confident again. 'I'd never get caught.'

'Well, we'll talk again tomorrow. We've booked you a room in this hotel and we've brought your things here. There's some cash for you as well. You're free to go out tonight but I warn you if you talk one word about our conversation you'll regret it bitterly. I warn you that you'll be under surveillance. You must be back here by midnight.'

Palmer tossed two keys on a ring on to the coffee table.

'Those are the keys to your room. Enjoy yourself.'

Masson had spent three weeks with an officer from the RAF unit at Tempsford that was used for dropping agents and supplies in France, and had been taken down to the airfield at Tangmere that was sometimes used for their flights. Squadron Leader Scott was a dedicated man and he and Masson got on well together.

Masson went as passenger on a Hudson drop and an

actual landing near Angoulême and at the meetings afterwards to discuss the operations Masson had been able to suggest several improvements in operational procedures. He was both liked and respected by everyone in the unit.

Back in London for two days there were further meetings with Palmer. Meetings that probed his background again and his contacts with the German, Westphal.

In the evening of the first day Palmer had taken him for a meal at a flat in St James's Street and after they had eaten Palmer had waved them to facing armchairs.

'Now, let's talk, Masson. And depending on your responses I'll have to decide what to do with you, OK?'

'Of course.'

'Right. Now let's get one thing clear. From now on don't ever feed me that bullshit about your background. I'd had it all checked out before you even got here. It may impress your women but it doesn't impress me. You're a natural liar, Masson, you know it and I know it. So be it. But you don't ever lie to me from now on, understand?'

'Whatever you say.' He paused. 'Can I ask you something?'

'Ask away.'

'Who are you exactly?'

'I'm a senior officer in British intelligence. That's all you need to know. When I say British intelligence, I don't mean some war-time organisation but the real thing. And that brings me to a vital point. You will be responsible to me. You will carry out my orders. I emphasise that because I shall be recommending you to another organisation called SOE, Special Operations Executive. They are only a war-time organisation and are responsible for organising resistance in various countries, mainly France. My organisation has its own agents overseas, including France. They are not there for sabotage or armed resistance, they are there to gather intelligence. They are professionals. SOE are war-time amateurs with different objectives to my people.

'So you'll be working for SOE networks, identifying

41

dropping sites, supervising and organising landings and drops. Sometimes you will be doing the same for my agents. You will have radio contact with SOE but any instructions from me will come from my people on the ground.'

'Will the SOE people know that in fact you're my boss?'

'No. That's just between you and me. Nobody else will know. Not even people in my organisation.'

'What if the SOE people find out?'

'There's only two people who know about the arrangement. You and me.'

'Can I ask why you want it done this way?'

'I want to know what SOE are doing in France. You'll be my man inside. You'll have all my weight behind you all the time.'

'Does this mean I'm accepted?'

'Do you want what I've discussed?'

'Yes. Definitely.'

'OK. I'll introduce you to the SOE people tomorrow. They desperately need somebody to look after their transport problems and you've already got the backing of the RAF people. There'll be no problem.'

Masson had spent two weeks at the Baker Street HQ of Special Operations Executive, being interviewed by several officers and then long briefings on the networks in France for which he would work.

Despite what Palmer had said, there had been a problem. And there had also been a surprise.

The problem had been a woman officer. For once Masson's charm didn't work. He couldn't understand why. She was young and attractive but she sat there stony-faced and unresponsive as she listened to his answers to her questions. He knew instinctively that she disliked him.

The surprise was to find that his old drinking and gossip friend from Paris, Roger Carlton, was now what he had always wanted to be – involved in intelligence. He was an officer now in SOE. A desk officer, not a field officer, but content with his role as an administrator. Carlton had filled him in on the backgrounds of the top brass of SOE and had told him in advance of the official decision that SOE had accepted him and were delighted that at last they had an expert who was approved of by the RAF at Tempsford. It seemed that the RAF had promised more flights when he took over.

Carlton had taken Masson to the clubs and bars of Soho and was amused to find that the Frenchman was even more successful with the local girls than he was in France.

Masson was put up at a pleasant flat in Mayfair and after the day's briefing with large-scale maps of France he always went over for a drink with Carlton. On that particular day they had gone to a pub in Victoria and when they were waiting for a taxi Masson saw André Delors. They had gone back together in the pub for another drink and a chat. It seemed that Delors was staying in a run-down boarding house near Victoria Station and was very unhappy. After his interrogation he'd been receiving a small weekly sum and his accommodation paid for. He had been told that the RAF were not interested but the Free French Air Force were considering him. But he had heard nothing so far. Speaking almost no English he was already bitterly regretting coming to England.

Carlton had suggested to SOE that Delors should go back to France as an assistant and courier for Masson and after several interviews with the RAF people at Tempsford Delors had been accepted.

As neither Masson nor Delors had ever had parachute training and Tempsford were anxious to get Masson in place it was decided to arrange a landing by Hudson. The landing took place at full moon in a field near Tours.

7

Maclean and Loussier were eating at a small café near one of the bridges over the river. The Café de la Paix provided black market meals. It was simple food and the prices were only a little over the odds. That night there was a choice of a quiche or omelette au jambon with a good house soup to start.

They were sitting alone at a table near the door when a man came in, looked round the room and then walked over to them, pulling out a chair and sitting down. He looked at Maclean, smiling as he said, '*Il pleut dans ma chambre.*' Then he held out his hand and said softly, 'Masson. Henri Masson. I came in four days ago. I've got some packets for you from our friends. Did you get the signal about me?'

Maclean hesitated for several moments before he replied. 'Yes,' he said. 'When are you ready to start?'

Masson laughed softly. 'You're my main network but I've got two others to service. Can we do some planning tomorrow?'

'Of course. Where are you sleeping tonight?'

Masson grinned. 'I've got a girl-friend who's going to give me a bed for a few days. Where can we meet tomorrow?'

'At the bakery. On the top floor. Say nine o'clock.'

'OK. I'll put your envelopes on the empty seat alongside your colleague.' He leaned forward before he stood up, smiling as he said, '*Soyez sage,*' and walked to the door.

When Masson had left, Maclean said, 'What did you think of him?'

'Is he the one who's going to control the drops? The pilot?'

'Yes.'

'Seems very self-confident.' He shrugged. 'If he can get us more supplies he's very welcome. Do you want me to pass the word around?'

'OK. But no details and no promises.'

Maclean sat on his bed reading the contents of the two envelopes by the light of a candle. There had been an electricity cut at 10 p.m.

There was a letter from his mother, in French, just family gossip, amusing and comforting but from a faraway world. Baker Street would have briefed them on what they could write, and although the letter bore no signs of censorship he knew it would have been censored. There was no home address on the letter.

There were coded messages from Baker Street on availability of supplies. Cancellation in two weeks' time of their current radio code and a new code enclosed. There were frequencies listed for weather reports and a brief message saying that he might be recalled in about six weeks' time. And finally an extract from Part II orders confirming his appointment as captain.

He burnt everything, including his mother's letter, that he didn't need to keep, and powdered it to ashes before washing it down the sink.

As he lay in his bed he was aware of the change in his attitude from the day when he arrived, when he would have jumped at the chance of going back. And now he resented the possible recall. This was where he belonged, with his people and their lives.

Maclean had spent a whole weekend with the nine group leaders. They had assembled at a farm about fifty kilometres east of Melun and just north of the small town of

Sens. They sat in the big barn at a long table that was used for feeding the extra staff at harvesting time when peas, beans and early potatoes had to be picked and dug in a few days.

The couriers and Masson had also attended. As Maclean looked around at his oddly assorted team he was impressed by their patriotism and their discipline. But there were things that had to be said.

'Gentlemen. Later today I shall talk with you about our plans for the near future and tomorrow Georges will give you instruction on new weapons and new explosives. But first of all I want to talk to you about security. Some of the things I have to say will not be welcome but you are experienced enough, I think, to recognise the good sense of the rules I am making. They are to save your lives and the lives of your neighbours. So let me start.

'On my travels I have been shown two safe-houses where there are children in the family. I will not accept any safe-house where there are children. It is unfair on their parents no matter how patriotic they may be.' He paused. 'All my orders today apply immediately.

'I come now to contact with safe-houses. No house is ever safe from the Germans but I have been with senior men who just stroll up to a safe-house without any checks. This can be fatal for you and fatal for the loyal people who cooperate with us. You will arrange a sign that indicates if there are unfriendly visitors at the house. A simple sign. Drawn curtains in a certain room. A geranium in a window. A bucket outside a door. And it has to be a negative sign. If the sign is there the house is clear, if not you have been warned. It is not always possible to move around if Germans are there and maybe not possible to arrange the sign. It is less suspicious to open curtains or use a bucket or water a plant than the other way round.

'When there is a telephone contact to arrange a visit or a meeting the same principle applies and you should instruct your friends accordingly. If you telephone and all is clear at the other end they should say that it's not convenient

46

for you to visit them. If there are Germans or unfriendly people there they should say, "We should be delighted to see you."' He looked around the table. 'Understood?' There were nods of agreement from most of them.

He went on. 'And right now all group leaders have got to sever all contact with their families. Don't put them in danger. Move out of wherever you live now. When our new supplies come through in the next few weeks we shall have things to do. All the waiting will be over. And if we're going to fight the Germans we do it as professionals not just patriotic amateurs.'

For two hours he went over all the standard procedures that would provide maximum security for the groups.

During the next four weeks Masson had arranged three successful supply drops and two Lysander landings that brought another radio operator and a weapons officer and allowed a group leader to be sent to London for training. Maclean felt that the month without a man would be worthwhile if he came back with his respect for security reinforced. There was no lack of courage and eagerness throughout the network, but eagerness without training could easily bring disaster. There was still time to prepare, but as yet there had been no real contact with the Germans. A few probes that brought routine responses but no real venom.

When the signal came for him to be picked up on the next Lysander landing in a week's time he knew as he walked in the woods to the arms cache with Loussier that he was going to do what he had been tempted to do many times. In the early days he had thought about it almost daily but as his responsibility pressed on him it had only been a fleeting thought in a tired brain in the few seconds before he slept.

The next morning he cycled out of the town to Machault and used the public telephone by the post office. A woman answered but he didn't recognise the voice. It wasn't

Anne-Marie or her mother. He hesitated and then hung up. But instead of teaching him caution the failure only fed his impulse, over-riding his own commonsense, and his training.

He cycled back to Melun and chained his cycle to the railings with the others and caught the next train to Paris. As if to bring home his foolhardiness there was a *Wehrmacht* check on the train and a full-scale Gestapo check at the Gare de Lyon, in Paris. It was the first time his documents had been subjected to a thorough and expert inspection and it was a salve for his guilt at his impetuosity that there had been no problems.

He took the Métro to Palais Royale and walked to the Rue du Jour. The café was still there and open and he sat with an ersatz coffee without milk or sugar and tried to collect his thoughts.

Paris was quite a shock. The streets were full of Germans in uniform. Some on leave, wandering around in groups like pre-war tourists but most of them obviously on business. Despatch riders on BMW motorcycles. Officers in confiscated Citroëns and Peugeots. Steel-helmeted guards outside occupied buildings. Some in *Wehrmacht* and some in SS uniforms. The streets were littered with signposts in German with directions to various military units, military barracks and hospitals and to the *Kommandatur* in the Place de l'Opéra.

The French people in the streets looked pale and tired but the girls in their worn clothes, despite everything managing to add some touch of chic with a bright scarf or gloves. There were still people sitting at the tables of the street cafés and there were still luxury goods in shop windows. It certainly wasn't the old Paris but it all looked more settled and normal than he had expected.

He had come with no plan and he had no idea how he could contact her. Maybe they didn't even live in the same place now. Maybe she was away in the country. He hadn't told Loussier where he was going and if anything happened to him they would have no idea where he was. He had that same feeling of isolation and unreality that he had felt the first day after he'd been dropped.

With the same impetuosity that had brought him there he bought a sheet of paper and an envelope from the *patron* and scribbled her a note, sealing it in the envelope and addressing it to her.

It was 5 p.m. and the unsigned note said that he would wait for her in the Café Latour until 8 p.m. Then he walked to her house and pushed the letter under the door, ringing the bell before he hurried away. She would recognise his handwriting he was sure.

He had ordered a cheese sandwich and a tomato with half a carafe of the house red, eating slowly to make the time pass. It was barely half an hour later when she walked in looking around the café. And then she saw him, hurrying over to his table.

'Philippe,' she whispered. 'What on earth are you doing here?'

He laughed. 'Sit down and I'll tell you. And don't look so worried.'

She sighed as she sat down. 'You look different.'

'So do you. You used to be pretty and now you're beautiful.'

'You look old. Tell me what's happening. Why are you in Paris after all this time?'

'It's better I don't tell you very much. The less you know the better.'

'You look bigger and different. Kind of aggressive.'

He laughed. 'I don't mean to be. Tell me about you.'

'It's pretty awful. You'll hate it. Daddy works at the *Kommandatur*. He's chief assistant to a colonel who is in charge of Franco-German cultural cooperation. He didn't have any choice.'

'I'm more interested in what you're doing.'

'I did my *bachot* and had a year at university and then they reduced the staff and they closed down my faculty. I had to get a job.'

'Go on.'

49

'I work in a photographic studio as assistant to the photographer.'

'What does he do?'

'Mainly portraits.'

He smiled. 'For soldiers to send home to Germany.'

She nodded and said, 'Yes.' And then very quietly, 'I guess you won't approve.'

He smiled. 'It seems a sensible thing to do. Your boss wouldn't get chemicals and paper if he wasn't of some use to the Germans. I shouldn't worry about it. And certainly don't feel guilty.'

'Does this mean you never got back to England?'

'No. I got back. With some difficulty.' He grinned. 'But I came back.'

'And you're in Paris. Isn't that terribly dangerous?'

'No. I'm outside Paris. I just came here in the hope of seeing you.'

'You're crazy.' But the smile and the look in her eyes belied the statement.

'Are you married or anything?'

'No. Of course not. Neither married nor anything.'

'Am I still your fellow?'

She smiled. 'It looks like it. Am I still your girl?'

'You never stopped being my girl.'

'Will I be able to see you sometimes now?'

'I'll be away for a few weeks but after that it's possible. How can I contact you?'

'You can contact me at work. I'll give you a card.'

'If I phone who shall I say I am?'

'Just Philippe, *accent seizième*, my boyfriend.'

'How's your mother?'

'She's well but unhappy. She and father don't speak to one another any more.'

'Why not?'

'Because he works for the Germans. She despises him.'

'He's too old to be independent. He probably doesn't like doing it himself.'

'I'm afraid he does. He spends a lot of time with them, socialising.'

He laughed. 'I can't imagine your old man socialising.'

'You'd better believe it. It's Maxim's and the Ritz every night and he's totally defensive about them. More German than the Germans.' She paused and looked at his face intently. 'Is there anything I can do to help you?'

'Just think about me before you go to sleep and I'll do the same.'

She smiled. 'Let's have a set time. Say midnight.'

'I love you my love but midnight isn't sleeping time for me. I'm roaming around with other people.'

'Why did you come back?' she said softly.

'A little bit for *la belle France* and a lot for you,' he said softly. And then said, 'Will you marry me when it's all over?'

'Of course I will. I'll marry you now and go away with you if you want.'

'I want very much but I love you too much to do that. I'll happily wait.'

'So will I. Not happily. But I'll wait.' She frowned. 'Right now I can't believe it will ever end.' She looked at him. 'Do you think it will?'

'I know it will.'

'You're very different.'

'In what way?'

'You're not young any more. You're a man.'

'And you're still a girl. A bit taller. A lot more beautiful. And I wish it was all over now.'

'Can I tell *Maman* that I've seen you?'

'No. Nobody.'

'How did you get here?'

'By train.'

'I wish I knew where you are so that I can imagine you there.'

'Think of Fontainebleau. It's not there but think of me there. And then think of us when we were there together.'

She smiled and shook her head slowly. 'I can't believe

I'm sitting here with you. It's so wonderful. Almost like we'd never been apart.' She reached out to touch his hand where it lay on the table. 'Do you have friends who look after you?'

He laughed. 'I'm here to look after them, my love.'

'Do you get enough to eat?'

'Yes. Probably more than you do.'

She smiled. 'Your clothes are terrible. You look like some country-bumpkin up in the big city for the day.'

He grinned. 'I am, honey. I am.'

'How long can you stay?'

'About half an hour. Shall we go for a walk?'

She smiled. 'In the Tuileries Gardens?'

'Yes.'

They had walked hand in hand along the terrace by the river, across to the pond and then to the Jeu de Paume, where a German military band was playing to a scattering of onlookers.

She smiled as she said, 'Can you hear what they're playing?'

'I know the tune but I don't know the name.'

'It's the waltz from *La Veuve joyeuse* – the Merry Widow.'

He smiled. 'Do you want to dance?'

She laughed. 'I wish we could.'

He shrugged. 'Why not?' And with his arms around her he waltzed her slowly, their feet scraping on the gravel pathway. As the music came to an end they stopped and she laughed up at him. 'He's bowing to us, the bandmaster.'

And as he turned to look, the stout *Kapellmeister* with his traditional waxed moustache bowed and kissed his hand in their direction.

They walked on to the far end of the gardens and there with their arms around each other they'd kissed and said goodbye. He stood watching her walk away until she was out of sight. It was a short walk to the Métro at Concorde and half an hour later he was on the train to Melun.

He was alone in the carriage with his eyes closed as he

tried not to use up his happiness too quickly. It had to last a long time. But it was like shaking up a kaleidoscope and finding a beautiful pattern. He was glad that he hadn't been sensible. Glad that he had taken the risk.

8

Maclean stood on the stone bridge looking at the river as Masson talked.

'Unless the weather changes the pick-up will be the day after tomorrow. I'm afraid I couldn't find anywhere nearer than Villeneuve. There's an SS division moved in just south of your area and they're spread out right across the Ile de France. But I've got a good flat field and a co-operative farmer and I've rehearsed the reception team thoroughly. Should go very smoothly.'

'There's another radio operator coming in on the plane. He's English but he speaks good French.' He turned to look at Masson. 'Is there anything you want from London, Henri?'

'One of the other networks has got a ground to air telephone. It's called an S-phone. That could be a great help for landings and drops.'

'What does it do?'

'I could talk to the pilot as he's coming in to check that he's on a correct flight-path or even abort a landing if something on the ground makes it necessary.'

'OK. I'll see what I can do.'

'I've arranged for Lisa to take you down. She's fixing a delivery down there as a cover.'

'That reminds me. The mail packet that comes on the plane. Hand that to Georges as soon as possible.'

'OK.'

'One more thing.' He turned again to look at Masson as he spoke. 'Lay off Lisa.'

Masson grinned. 'Why, for God's sake? She rather fancies me.'

'I don't care whether she fancies you or not. Sexual relationships inside a network always cause trouble. People get jealous or envious and if the affair ends in a quarrel that can be a security problem. Find your girls out of my area in future.'

Masson was still smiling as he said, 'If that's how you want it, OK. Are you sure you're not jealous yourself?'

'I don't understand.'

'The pretty Lisa's madly in love with you. Thinks you're a real hero.'

Maclean laughed. 'I'm sure she doesn't. But no, I'm not jealous. But several others might be. Anyway, it's an order.'

There had been unusual anti-aircraft fire and they had had to take a dog-legged route that had left them short of fuel and they had landed at Tangmere in Sussex instead of at Tempsford in Bedfordshire. But the RAF had been asked to supply a car and driver to take him on to London. Mathews was stuck at Tempsford but would be back in London in time to receive him at Baker Street. The welcome had been typical, low-key but warm and concerned and Mathews had taken him to the Hyde Park Hotel where they had booked him a room. Mathews had gone up with him to check that the room was comfortable and had given him a phone number to ring if there was anything he wanted. After that there had been no questions. They could wait until he'd had a good night's sleep.

Mathews made sure that Maclean had a non-ration breakfast. Porridge, bacon and eggs and toast with butter and Cooper's coarse-cut marmalade.

'What's the food like in France?'

'Not bad if you've got money, or influence, or something to trade. Most people get by.'

Pouring himself a coffee Mathews said, 'Our people are very pleased with you.'

Maclean shrugged. 'I've done very little. Just made them more security conscious. Organised them and trained them.'

'That's all we asked you to do.'

'When can I give them something to do? They're impatient for action. They want to feel that they are fighting the Germans.' He paused and looked at Mathews. 'They hear of other networks who are killing Germans, not just learning how to do it.'

'If they hear that, Phil, then they'll hear that those networks are being wiped out. They're no good to us, the wild men who ignore our orders. A few more months and you'll all be getting all the action you want. We'll talk about that. That's one of the reasons we brought you back.'

'What are the other reasons?' He smiled. 'You're going to replace me with someone more experienced.'

'Quite the opposite, in fact. We want you to take over an additional network and combine it with your own.'

'Where are they based?'

'In Chartres.'

'Who's doing it now?'

'A man named Proctor. One of the wild boys. We've recalled him, and we've stood his network down for the moment. So you'll have to put the bits together again.' He paused. 'That's if you're willing to try.'

'I'd like to hear a bit more before I say anything.'

'Of course.' Mathews looked at his watch. 'How about we go over to HQ.' He smiled. 'There are several people who are eager to talk to you and to hear what you have to say.'

'When are you planning for me to go back?'

'There'll be moon enough for another four days.'

'I'd like to see my parents. Just a brief visit.'

'We'll get the RAF to fly you up and back. Have you phoned them?'

'No. I'll phone when I know when I'll be there.'

The rest of the day had been spent in de-briefing, with Maclean giving details of his groups and their leaders, marking on large-scale maps where there were arms caches and safe-houses. Going over long lists of supplies that he wanted.

He was driven to Northolt the next morning and flown up to Edinburgh where a car was waiting to take him home. It was Mathews who had called it home and it had seemed strange and disturbing when he said it. Home was the room over the bakery.

As he walked up the path to the house he realised that he never thought about it. It was a Victorian house built solidly from stone, four-square to the world as if it was built to resist invasion. His eye caught the movement of a net curtain and the door was flung open, his mother standing there tears pouring down her cheeks.

'Hello, *Maman*. How are you?'

And for five minutes the words had been equally banal on both sides. But slowly they relaxed although his parents and his sister were obviously aware that the questions they really wanted to ask were out of bounds.

They talked about themselves, the trivialities of their daily lives, longing to hear about his life too so that they could have something to think about, some setting they could imagine him in.

Both parents had contrived a few minutes alone with him. He sat in the living room with his father who looked just the same, but much older. Still subdued, but calm and solid.

'Is it what you expected?'

'Not really. In a way it's more mundane, more normal than I expected. People have to get on with their lives despite losing a war.'

'And the Germans?'

'In general they're well-behaved. But the bad ones are

57

very bad. But the bad ones would be bad wherever they were.'

'Are you scared at all?'

He smiled. 'No. There isn't time to be scared. There's too much to do. And they trained me well.' He shrugged. 'Sometimes it seems very strange giving orders and caring about men who are much older than I am.' He smiled. 'One of them reminds me of you. Looks before he leaps and thinks before he speaks.'

'How long before we see you again?'

'I don't know. It risks the lives of a lot of people when people come and go.'

'We think about you all the time. And worry of course. They contact us sometimes just to say you're OK. Nothing more.'

His mother called him from the kitchen and he walked in and sat at the table where they had all sat when they were children. Tom and Mary and him.

She was leaning against a cupboard as she looked at him and said, 'Have you seen Anne-Marie?'

For a moment he hesitated and then he said, 'Just once, *Maman*. I don't want to involve her in what I'm doing.'

'How is she?'

He smiled. 'Just the same but beautiful instead of pretty.'

'And her parents?'

'Old man Duchard is working for the Germans and he and Madame don't talk any more. She despises him.'

'My God. So she should.'

He smiled. 'He always was rather Germanic. *Sturm und Drang* and all that.'

She smiled. 'Your father always said he would make a good Prussian.'

'He would too.'

'Do you still love her?'

'Yes.'

'Does she still love you?'

'Yes. When it's over we shall marry.'

She closed her eyes. 'I can't wait for that day.'

'*Maman*, don't worry about me. I'm fine. It's much the same as here. Just one day after another.'

The car came for him at four and he was surprised that he felt sad at leaving them. He thought it must be like that when you had to leave your children with strangers.

He had talked with Morton about the Chartres network, read their files and signals traffic. It was a very different kind of network from his own. Businessmen, lawyers, minor officials and the owner of a night-club. They had provided a lot of intelligence on the Germans. Economic and political intelligence. But that wasn't what SOE was set up to do. And they weren't the kind of men who could fight Germans.

'Why did you let him recruit these people?'

'We thought that because they were well placed strategically and with a good inside knowledge of what was going on inside the German organisations they could feed information or get information that would allow a more normal network to be guided to really significant targets for sabotage in due course.'

'Do you still think that?'

'Yes. They know where the Germans are really vulnerable.'

'What do you want me to do?'

'Check the safe-houses, contact the people. Try and keep them going – organise them. Those that are left.' He paused. 'They could be really useful. Vital. When things come to the boil.'

'When will that be?'

'I don't know.'

'Does anybody know?'

'I expect so, but there'll be no second chance. This time it's got to be seen right through to the bitter end. You don't plan that sort of operation in weeks or even months. But there are signs for those who can recognise them. Straws in the wind and all bending towards people like you in France.'

59

'How about a compromise?'

'Like what?'

'I take these people over for six months. Dust them off and put them back on the train lines and then you send someone else to take them over.'

'But why?'

'They're not my kind of people.'

'They're patriots, willing to take risks for France.'

Maclean smiled. 'I'll look them over but it'll be a long time before I trust them. So do we compromise?'

'I'm sure we will. I'll let you know tomorrow.'

There had been more talking. The compromise was agreed to. They'd asked him about Masson. Was he satisfied with what he was doing? Was he conforming and doing what Maclean ordered him to do? The RAF people were glad that someone who knew what he was doing was at last in charge of drops and landings.

He bought a few things that were hard to get in France and the same night he was on a Whitley bomber heading for a drop near Chartres.

Masson was there, and Loussier. It felt like coming home.

They all slept that night in the office of a small cinema and next morning Masson and four men loaded the two canisters that had been dropped with him on to a farm cart pulled by two horses. They were going to a cache in Dreux for another network.

It was two days before he got back to Melun. There were road-blocks on all the main roads and random patrols on the minor roads. They were looking for able-bodied men to ship to Germany to work in the factories. A doctor's note would cut no ice with them. They'd say he could sort that out at the transit camp with the Gestapo. He had travelled only at night perched uncomfortably on the pillion seat of a motorcycle that one of the local men had stolen.

*   *   *

Back in Melun Maclean's first move was to meet the new radio operator. He was based at a garage on the outskirts of the town at La Rochette. It was a garage that specialised in the repair and servicing of farm tractors and farm machinery. The new man was in his thirties, a Welshman from Birmingham. Alwyn Williams. He had worked in France before the war and spoke reasonable French. He knew more about the technicalities of radios than Janine and could service the radios competently.

One of the problems with radio operators was that it was best if they were confined to radio and did nothing else. Which was fine in the early days of SOE when the German detection vans were very scarce and SOE traffic could occupy three or four hours a day. But once the German DF groups were built up radio operators were tracked down and arrested in great numbers. With the new orders laying down that ten minutes transmission a day was the maximum it left radio operators with long hours of boredom. But Alwyn Williams was a trained engineer and could help out with the servicing of farm machinery.

Maclean had taken his new man into the small orchard at the back of the garage. They sat on a small grassy tussock.

'I'm Philippe. Welcome to the network. Any problems?'

Alwyn's freckled face and red hair gave him a cheerful look that was typical of his actual temperament.

'No problems at all. But plenty of things to do.'

'Like what?'

'Now we've got two operators I'm going to build the girl's set into a normal domestic radio. You'd have to take the back off and be an expert to discover that it's not just a household set. She doesn't need to keep moving the set from place to place, we can use mine for that.' He grinned. 'She needs a bit of a lift, but she's OK.'

'Who have you met?'

'All the group leaders and Georges Loussier, the couriers and Masson.' He smiled. 'He's a bit of a lad that

Masson. Got the black market sorted out. But I wouldn't buy a second-hand car off him.'

'Why?'

'He's too fly. The kind of guy who stuffs the gear box full of sawdust so you can't hear the crunching noise from the broken metal. But he's real professional on the drops and landings. They've got to be just how he wants 'em or there's trouble.'

'Where did you learn your French?'

'I was working in Paris before the war, servicing electrical goods. Cookers and the like.'

'I'll see you again tomorrow.'

The winter came early in 1942 and Maclean sent urgent signals to London to get all the supplies in before snow left the tell-tale signs that showed up the tracks and footmarks of landing sites quite clearly to the Luftwaffe reconnaissance planes that cruised slowly but methodically over the area. But it was a good time for training and planning. Bridges, telephone exchanges, factories making spare parts for German tanks and field guns, and marshalling yards, were all pin-pointed and listed.

By December a complete network had been built up that covered the whole of the railway system in the area with people in place who passed on details of troop movements and strategic freight. Even the main roads were reasonably monitored for *Wehrmacht* and SS convoys of troops and supplies.

There was less tension in the network as people realised that they were not wasting their time but being prepared for action when the time was right. Sooner or later there would have to be an invasion if France were to be liberated. Even the Germans recognised that. All those fortifications on the Channel coasts. The huge concentration of troops. They didn't need those to hold down the French population. France was like a boxer conserving his strength in the early rounds, fending off the blows, ready for the final burst of energy that would lead to victory.

It was an opportunity to go to Chartres and check on the other network. See who was still willing to go on and who had had enough.

9

Whenever he could find the time he had painted. Landscapes, the back streets of Melun and the cathedral, scenes by the river and a few still-lifes. A small gallery near the Hôtel de Ville had bought them and was eager to take all the work he could produce. He no longer found any pleasure in painting, it was just a source of income and provided his cover. It also provided him with an excuse for travelling around the countryside. It seemed ironic that most of his paintings were bought by Germans.

The middle-aged woman who owned the gallery had been introduced by Loussier. He surmised that she knew or guessed that he was to do with the Resistance but she made no attempt to probe his background. Neither did she attempt to force down the prices she paid for his pictures because of anything she knew. She paid a fair price and the relationship was friendly but businesslike.

He had brought in two paintings of the Eglise St Aspais that day. The larger canvas showed the evening sun reflected in the church's beautiful stained-glass windows. She had propped the canvas up on the mantel-shelf in her small back office and had stood looking at it for a long time.

Then she turned to look at him.

'You know, Monsieur Benoit, I could sell this picture ten times over. Why don't you do more like this?'

He smiled. 'What's so different about it?'

She looked at him intently and then said, 'May I be quite frank?'

'Of course.'

'There is an unkind phrase we gallery people use about some paintings – *oeuvres alimentaires* – your usual pictures are in that class. Competent, but stylised. Painted in a hurry to earn your daily bread. Don't mistake me, people like them. But this one is different.' She smiled. 'It has a little love in it. And that makes the difference. I can offer you a lot more for this one.' She paused. 'But I shan't sell it. I shall keep it for myself. Not for investment but for pleasure. Shall we say five thousand francs?'

Maclean smiled. 'You've been very kind to me, madame, I give you the picture with pleasure. With great pleasure.'

She shook her head. 'Oh, no. I insist on paying. These are hard times for all of us.'

'Not so hard that a lady can't accept a small gift.'

For long moments she looked at him in silence and he saw tears at the edges of her eyes. Her voice quavered as she said quietly, 'You make a very *galant* Frenchman, Monsieur Benoit.'

He knew then that she knew. 'I'll remember that, madame.'

She paid him for the other picture and as she handed him the notes she said softly. 'Count me as a friend. A friend in all your enterprises. Not just your painting. Count me as a fellow patriot. Ready to help whenever you need it.'

Maclean hesitated before replying and then said, 'Thank you, madame. I'll remember that. How long have you known?'

She smiled. 'I didn't know. Just guessed.'

'How?'

'Perhaps a mixture of observation and feminine intuition.'

'Tell me.'

'Your manner didn't match your humble clothes. You were always too polite to be a country bumpkin – *un paysan*.'

He smiled. 'I must remember that. You're very observant.'

'Just a woman, Monsieur Benoit. Just a woman.'

He went on to meet Loussier at a café near the main bus stop. Loussier was already there with a half empty glass of beer. He grinned as Maclean sat down.

'I've got us each a beef sandwich.'

'How d'you manage that?'

Loussier smiled. 'The *patron* gets his supplies from Lisa.'

'I'm going to be away for about three days. Will you be OK on your own?'

Loussier shrugged. 'I suppose so. Can I ask where you'll be?' He paused. 'Not in Paris again, I hope.'

For long moments Maclean was silent as he looked at the older man. 'Tell me about Paris.'

'Louis, the man in the ticket office, saw you and heard you ask for a return ticket to the Gare de Lyon. And old Pierre saw your bicycle chained up to the railings. It was still there late that night but gone in the morning.' He paused. 'You were crazy not to tell me where you were going. For our sakes as well as yours.'

'I apologise, Georges. It was irresponsible.'

'Tell me something. Was it the girl from Provins?'

'What girl from Provins?'

'I don't know her name. But I know you lived there in the summer when you were a kid and I heard you were in love with a young girl.'

'What makes you so interested in these things?'

'A very simple reason.'

'Tell me.'

'We have a good set-up in Provins. Good people in the right places. You've never been there. Not even once. I suggested a visit several times. You always made some excuse. It's the only one of our places that you've never visited or asked about. I wondered why. Then Jean-Pierre our gendarme friend down that way was up here for a meeting with Pierre and he saw you with me. He thought he recognised you but didn't know where from. I told him to think about it. A week later he said he remembered you and your family renting a house by the river. I told him to make some enquiries. All he found out was your father's name and talk of you being in love with a neighbour's daughter. He was told that both families lived in Paris.'

'Why did you want to know all this?'

'Are you offended?'

'Yes. And angry. So answer my question.'

'At first it was curiosity. But something else he found out worried me.'

'What?'

'It seems the girl's father works for the Germans at the *Kommandatur*. He's a collaborator. Did you know that?'

'Not until I went to Paris.'

'So it *was* the girl?'

'Yes.'

'You're still in love with her?'

'Yes.'

'And she with you?'

'Yes. We'll get married when this is all over.' He looked at Loussier. 'At least you've taught me one lesson.'

'What's that?'

'In training they always said – "Don't trust anyone absolutely."'

'So now you don't trust me?'

'Not absolutely.'

'And the girl. You trust her absolutely?'

Maclean hesitated for a moment, then laughed, the tension eased. 'You bastard. You ought to have been a lawyer.'

Loussier put his big paw on Maclean's hand. 'Nobody but me and Jean-Pierre knows what I told you. It was only the Paris trip that started me worrying. We need you, my friend. We can't afford to lose you. So where are you off to?'

'You'd better come with me. I'm going to Chartres.

There's a *réseau* there that's come apart. London want me to put it together again.'

'Don't go, my friend. Don't go.'

'Why not?'

'I've heard rumours about them. Ten killed and many arrested. Crazy attacks on German troops and no security. Everybody did what the hell he liked. Whoever was the boss was a fool.'

'He's been taken back to London.' He paused. 'They need help, Georges. We can't just let them go down.'

'And you want me to join you in a suicide pact, yes?'

'So?'

Loussier burst out laughing. 'When do we go?'

'Tomorrow.'

And then the sandwiches came. And a jug of milk.

10

Maclean wasn't sure why he decided to contact the night-club owner first but instinct told him that a man who ran a night-club would at least be shrewder than the average businessman. The kind of man whom his predecessor had recruited.

The club was in one of the poorer streets of Chartres, at the back of the theatre. It had once been a livery-yard for travellers' horses, had then become a warehouse for electrical goods and had been converted by its present owner, Charles Picquet, encouraged by the local German commander, immediately after the surrender.

It was 4 p.m. when Maclean arrived, alone, uncertain as to what his reception would be. There were two large main doors and a small side door with a bell. He pressed the bell and heard it echo inside the building. It was several minutes before the door swung open. The man who opened it was well dressed and in his middle thirties. Handsome in a coarse way like actors who play gangsters in American films. A neat moustache and a scar from his ear to his jaw.

'I'm looking for Monsieur Picquet. Charles Picquet.'

'What about?'

'Some friends asked me to contact him.'

'Which friends?'

'They told me to give him a message.'

'What's the message?'

'It's for Monsieur Picquet personally.'

'I'm Picquet. Go on.'

'The message was "*Redites moi des choses tendres*."'

For a moment the man looked surprised as if he didn't understand and then Maclean saw comprehension dawn slowly on his face. He nodded. '*Comme un oiseau qui s'enfuit vient chercher le nid.*'

The man glanced into the street and then opened the door wide and signalled Maclean to go inside. He heard a key turned in the door and a bolt pushed home and then he followed the man down a dimly lit corridor and up two sets of iron staircases. The man unlocked a door and waved him inside a room.

'What's your name, my friend?'

'Benoit. Philippe Benoit. I'm a painter.'

'What can I do for you?'

'I came to talk about 'Merlin'.'

'They disbanded us. Told us that we're not wanted.'

'Who told you that?'

'The Englishman who ran the network. He's back in London already.'

'London have asked me to see if it can be re-organised.'

'Sit down. Would you like a drink?'

'I'd like a coffee if you have any.'

Picquet smiled. 'I've got anything you could want.' He walked over to a telephone and pressed two buttons. 'Sylvie. Two coffees in my room please.' He laughed. 'No, my love. I've got a friend here . . . good.' He hung up and turned to Maclean. 'No more talk of these things until she's brought the coffee.'

'Tell me about the club.'

'I started it up with money from an insurance policy and a few loans. I contacted the German military before I plunged. They were much in favour of it.' He laughed. 'Thought it might keep everybody from missing the last train from Paris every night.' He shrugged. 'It's successful in a modest way. I make a living.'

There was a knock on the door and Picquet walked back and took a tray from a very pretty girl.

When the coffee was poured Picquet said, 'How much do you know about 'Merlin'?'

'I know it was badly led, with almost no security and most of the people were unsuitable. They tried playing games with the Germans and paid the usual price.'

Picquet grimaced. 'That's about it. They asked for trouble and they got it.'

'Not worth starting up again?'

'Do you have a network?'

'Yes.'

'Where?'

'That's my business.'

'Tell me something. How many men have you lost?'

'None.'

'How many Germans have you killed?'

'None.'

'So what do you do, for God's sake?'

'My people are trained on weapons, sabotage, surveillance and strategic observation. They are ready for action when the time comes for action.'

'And when will that be?'

'When London says so.'

'Sounds pretty tame.'

'It is.'

Picquet laughed. 'I like you, Philippe Benoit. You seem like an honest man. A safe man too. Not a man who thinks that defeating the Germans is playing cowboys and Indians.' He looked at Maclean's face. 'Why did you come to me? Why not one of the others?'

'I'm not sure. Instinct maybe. A feeling that a man who ran a night-club and was on good terms with the Germans and still chose to be in the Resistance must have a lot of guts and be a genuine patriot.'

'Why a patriot?'

'Why should you take the risk? I'm sure you make a lot more than just a living out of this place? You could just sit back and enjoy it.' He paused. 'Why do you take the risk?'

'I could be working as an informer for the Germans for all you know.'

'I had that in mind when I came to see you.'

'And?'

'And I'm sure you're not.' Maclean laughed. 'Don't ask me why. Just instinct tells me so.'

'So what do we do?'

'Tell me about the members of the *réseau* who could be trained and properly organised. And your views on whether they would be willing and disciplined.'

'There are a few. But I'd have to think about it carefully. How long can you stay?'

'Just tonight but we could meet again. Say in a week.'

'Where are you staying tonight?'

'I haven't fixed a place yet.'

'You can stay here if you want.'

'I have one of my men with me.'

'Is he reliable?'

'He's my second-in-command.'

'There's room for you both. It'll give you a chance to see how the other half lives.'

'I know how they live.'

'Knowing is one thing. Seeing is another. It sickens me.' He leaned forward. 'We serve better food than they get in Germany and better wine. We have a three-piece band that plays good jazz but has to end up playing oompah music for the Boche. But all that is merely the outward appearance. This place is just a bordello. What they really come for is the girls. I employ fifteen so-called hostesses, French girls who earn their living opening their legs for Germans. Mirrors on the ceilings and chains and whips for those who like that stuff. It was only 'Merlin' that kept me sane.'

'It must be a wonderful opportunity of finding out what the Resistance needs to know.'

'It is. But it was wasted on your predecessor. He was gun crazy and wouldn't have been interested in the order of battle of this command. He was a fool.'

'London pulled him out as soon as they realised that.'

'So why recruit people like that in the first place?'

'Just wrong timing. He'll be very useful at the right time with proper direction.'

Picquet nodded. 'You've got a big mind, my friend. We're going to need big minds to throw those bastards out. And we'll need big minds when it's all over too.'

'Show me where we can sleep.'

'Where's your friend?'

'He's hanging around the Place du Théâtre.'

'Go and get him. Can you mend a fuse?'

'Of course.'

'If there's any questions asked you're electricians looking over the electric system here. OK?'

'Fine. His name is Georges.'

They had travelled back to Melun on different buses but they had met in the evening at a farmhouse near Chatillon-la-Borde, one of the emergency safe-houses. The family had gone to bed early and left them alone with the luxury of logs burning in the fireplace.

'What did you think of him, Georges?'

'At first I didn't much like him. He reminded me of our friend Masson. A bit too smart and a bit self-important. But after talking with him I was impressed. I think the other was part of his job, running a night-club.'

Maclean smiled. 'Masson does a good job too. What are Picquet's weak points do you think?'

'His obligations to the Germans must make him vulnerable.'

'Dangerously so?'

'No. But he might have a need to compromise.'

'We all do that, Georges.' He smiled. 'But we don't admit it.' He paused. 'Let's see how it goes.'

11

It was two days before they met after the visit to Chartres. Loussier had had to go down to Provins to talk with Brieux and Mendes about a local family who had offered their help. They owned a large park-like estate and lived in an old manor house with a number of cottages nearby. Near-aristocrats and respected but not much liked by the locals, they could be of great help to the network not only as a landing and dropping zone but as an emergency safe-house. Despite some prejudice on the part of Mendes, Loussier had decided to take them into the network. Maclean had spent all his time on administrative work which he hated. He had made a coded list of every arms cache, its contents and location, including a drop while he was in Chartres. When he totted it all up he knew that he needed more *plastique* and detonators.

They met mid-morning on the island in the vestry of the church of Notre Dame. The priest in charge sat reading the Bible on a chair outside the vestry door.

'What did you finally decide about our friend Picquet, Georges?'

'I liked him. Tough, shrewd, and a patriot.'

'And the lawyer?'

'I don't know. He said all the right things. Obviously doesn't like the Boche even though he gets most of his business from them. Could be very useful. But I still don't know.'

'Don't know what?'

'He's a desk man. I don't see him standing up to any

74

pressure from the Germans. Not physical pressure any-way.'

'I've decided not to re-form the network over there. I'll just take over Picquet and limit their operation to Chartres.'

'That's up to you, you know what's best.'

'It can wait. It's two weeks before Christmas and I want us to visit all our sections and organise them properly. Not just one man in charge. When we go into action we're going to need a properly organised set-up at every point. So I want to spend the day tomorrow going over the present leaders with you to make sure we've got the right man. OK?'

'Are you expecting something? Some action?'

'I think it's the end of the time of consolidation. We're nearly in 1943. It must be time for the start of real resistance.'

'Our people will be glad to hear it. They've been patient for a long time.'

'Where shall we meet?'

'The cheese place by the Château de Blandy. I'll let them know today.'

Maclean smiled. 'I know this is the home of Brie, and it's a lovely cheese but my God, Georges, the smell's terrible in that place.'

Loussier laughed. 'The Germans have got all this year's Brie from them. They've been clearing it out. And it's safe.'

'OK. What time?'

'Say eleven?'

'OK.'

It was snowing heavily as Maclean put his cycle in the barn and then walked across to the long low building where the cheese was prepared and matured. The big main door where the cheese was loaded was closed and locked and he made his way to the far end of the building that housed the offices. The door opened on to a narrow corridor and there was an open door at the far end that led into a small office. Loussier was sitting at the table looking at a map. He looked up as Maclean walked in.

'You're early, Georges.'

Loussier smiled. 'I cheated. I slept here last night because of the snow.'

As Maclean sat down he said, 'I think we should limit our centres to eight places including Melun. I don't think we're capable of controlling more than eight. D'you agree?'

'Depends on the places. Apart from Melun we certainly need Nemours as the southern limit and Troyes as the eastern limit. After that I'd go for Provins, Sens and Fontenay Trésigny. That leaves two more.'

'I think Montereau and Nogent-sur-Seine should be the two. They're well placed and we've got good people there.'

'OK. Let's talk people. At Fontenay Trésigny we've got Duras and Estang. Who takes over?'

'I had in mind Estang.'

'Why?'

'He's a doctor. He's used to organising. He can travel around freely and he's got useful contacts everywhere.'

'But he's not a leader like Duras. Duras is a born leader.'

'He's the big fellow with the beard, yes?'

'Yes.'

'Fill me in on him.'

'Ex-sergeant in the Chasseurs Alpins. Wounded in the leg. Strong as a horse. Works as a ganger on the railway. And intelligent.'

'You prefer him?'

'If I was in a fight I'd prefer him to the good doctor.'

'OK. We make Estang local commander and Duras operations commander. Would that work?'

'Yes, I think it would.'

'Any other problem areas?'

'Yes. Provins and Troyes.'

'Tell me.'

'In Provins we've got two good men. Brieux and

Mendes. Not much to choose between them but Mendes is political. He's a communist.'

'I'm not interested in anybody's politics, you know that, Georges.'

'Maybe not but it matters locally. Brieux is a strong Catholic and he resents Mendes trying to influence people's politics when they join us.'

'Are they influenced?'

'The young ones are.'

'But at least it shows that Mendes thinks that France is going to be liberated some day. His politics are wasted while we're occupied.'

'And then we get taken over by the commies.'

Maclean laughed. 'I can't see it happening, Georges. Anyway there would be elections.'

'And the best organised party gets the votes. Especially if you can say that commie candidates were all in the Resistance.'

'The picture I got in London was that the communists were concentrated in the *Maquis*, not our kind of operation. They want to slug it out in weapons.'

'So London does at least think about these things.'

'Of course. But we definitely want the French to decide what they want when it's all over.'

'That's fine, but if the commies go on trying to win votes right now that's not what the rest of us are fighting for.'

'I'll talk to Mendes.'

'You want him to take over in Provins?'

'Yes. I had a talk with him a few weeks back when I was in Nogent. He was delivering bricks from the brick-works in Provins. I was impressed. And I liked him. He's intelligent and it was obvious that he had absorbed everything I had tried to put over to them.' He paused. 'How do we keep Brieux happy?'

'I don't know.'

'He's not married, is he?'

'Divorced.'

'Girl-friend?'

Loussier smiled. 'Several. His women's clothes go to the top Paris houses. So he's a very popular man and not just in Provins.'

'What are his strong points in your opinion?'

'He's tough and resourceful. Respected and liked by the men. Car permit. Protection from Paris and lived in Provins all his life. Knows every inch of the countryside.'

'Are there any other contenders?'

'No.'

'I'll talk to them both but I'll give it to Mendes.'

They had gone over the strengths and weaknesses of each of the eight towns and it was dark by the time they finished. The snow was too deep for them to get back to Melun that night. The family had given them an evening meal and beds for the night. The next day the tractor had taken them and their cycles down to the road. The driver told them that a German convoy had gone through in the night and the road back to Melun was passable.

Maclean hesitated for two days before ringing the number of the photographer in Paris but when finally he gave up the struggle it was Anne-Marie herself who answered the phone.

'Anne-Marie, it's Philippe. Is it OK to talk?'

'Yes. But . . .'

'I was thinking of coming to Paris for a couple of days at Christmas. Can we meet?'

'Oh God. I won't be there. There's a problem at home, and I've promised to take *Maman* down to the country for a week.'

'Where?'

'Our house near Provins. You know the one.'

'What's the problem?'

'He's walked out on her. She's on her own now. She's terribly upset. What can we do to see one another?'

'When do you leave for the country?'

'On the twenty-third.'

'OK. I'll see you that evening. Remember the summer-house?'

'Yes.'

'That's where I'll see you. About eight o'clock in the evening. OK?'

'I can't believe it. Are you sure you can make it there?'

'I love you, kid. See you on the twenty-third.'

'I love you too,' she whispered. And he hung up.

For the first time in many months he smiled. As he walked back to the bakery he thought of his mother and wished that she could be there at Christmas too.

As he walked into the bakery the old lady was serving a customer but as she turned towards the till she put her fingers to her lips and looked up at the ceiling.

For a moment he hesitated and then he walked up the stairs. The door to his room was wide open and as he walked inside he saw the two men. He knew instinctively that despite their civilian clothes they were Germans. One man sitting on the bed, smoking. The other had lined up some of his smaller canvases on one of the empty shelves.

The one on the bed said, 'Security, may I see your papers?'

The other man didn't even turn to look at him as he handed over his papers. The man opened out the papers, looking at them carefully before placing them side by side on the bed-cover. Finally he looked up at Maclean.

'Rausch. *Sicherheitsdienst*. Your name?'

'Benoit. Philippe.'

'Occupation?'

'Painter.'

'Have you had clearance from any authority to avoid volunteering for work-service in Germany?'

'There's a medical note there from my doctor explaining that I have a weak heart since having a fever when I was a child.'

The man smiled. 'That has no standing, Monsieur Benoit. Just a piece of French paper.'

'I was told that that was all I needed.'

'Who told you that?'

'Several people. I don't remember who.'

Rausch turned to his companion. 'What do you think, Heinz?'

The man turned, still holding one of the canvases. 'Where is this?' he said, looking at Maclean.

'On the river bank by the bridge.'

'How much do you get for them?'

'In marks or in francs?'

'Any way you like.'

'Say fifteen marks.'

The man nodded. 'Are you ready, Klaus?'

The man on the bed stood up. 'You might be hearing from me again, Monsieur Benoit.' He paused. 'You know where my office is?'

'I'm afraid I don't.'

The man grinned. 'Never mind.' He turned to his colleague. 'Pay him, Heinz. The smell of that bread is making me hungry.'

The German handed over the fifteen marks, Maclean asked if he needed a receipt but the man just smiled and shook his head.

As the door closed behind them Maclean stood quite still, knowing what would happen. The door opened suddenly and Klaus said, smiling, 'I'll probably see you again, my friend. Keep painting.'

Maclean moved to the window and watched them walk away.

He wondered what it was all about. The amateurish trick-question about where their office was and the door opening device to check if he looked scared after their visit or relieved that they had gone. It may be amateurish but it had some significance and he wondered what it was.

Loussier had made enquiries around the town and nobody else had been visited and nobody knew of any SD unit in the town.

When they met in the evening to have a bowl of soup

together Loussier had handed over the sealed package from the last drop.

'Why the delay, Georges?'

'I don't know. Masson said it had been mislaid when they were clearing the snow for the Lysander to take off.'

He frowned but slid the soft leather pouch into his pocket. Then he told Loussier about the girl and her mother coming to Provins. Loussier didn't look pleased.

'What's the matter, Georges? Why the frown?'

'Forget it. It's nothing.'

'Tell me. I insist.'

'I don't think you realise, my friend, how much we all depend on you. You're our rock. The one who organised us and trained us, and stopped us from being fools. The network was your only interest. *We* could all have daily lives. But not you.' He paused. 'To find that you have another interest comes as a shock. That's quite unfair. But that's how it is.' He smiled wryly. 'It's like finding that your priest, your father-confessor, has a mistress.' He shrugged and smiled. 'Even that happens often enough but it's still a shock.'

'Will the others think as you do?'

'One or two might, but most of them will be pleased. You've lived like a monk and they'll be relieved to find that you're human.'

'I've loved her for a long time, Georges. She's part of the reason I'm here and she's *my* stake in the liberation.'

'I understand. I'll get used to it. I'll organise things for them to be safe. Where are they staying?'

'They own a house there. Down by the river. It's called La Roserie.'

'I'll talk to Brieux and Mendes to see what we can do for heating and food.'

It took Maclean a long time to get to sleep that night. The visit from the two SD men had been disturbing but nothing more. But Loussier's attitude about the girl had emphasised how alone he was. And that he was liked and respected for what he had done for them, but nobody had ever wondered if his time with them was all that he expected from life. He resented Loussier's attitude as if they owned him.

In the middle of the night he awoke suddenly. He hadn't checked the London pouch. There was a routine note from the family. And advance warning that a large sum in French francs and some gold Maria Theresa dollars would be in the next Lysander trip. Notification of an increase in Field Allowance and then a short coded message. The message said that he could start a limited sabotage campaign at his discretion, on secondary targets only, as soon as he thought necessary.

He had slept fitfully for a couple of hours, his dreams full of railway points, telegraph poles and bridges.

12

They had loaded the truck with potatoes and Lisa had driven him to Provins. He sensed that she knew about the girl.

Mendes and Brieux were waiting for him with Loussier at the turn-off for Chalautre. And at the village they had followed Maclean down to the river bank past the house where he had lived for so many summers to the house that was still the Duchard house. Mendes had got the keys from the old man who checked the house for the Duchards every two weeks.

As they went into the square entrance hall he looked towards the wide, sweeping stairs that led up to a balustraded gallery. He had looked up those stairs so many times, waiting for her to come down and join him when he was painting in the orchard or the meadow. As he walked through the rooms nothing seemed to have changed. But the house was damp and airless and forlorn.

Loussier and Brieux were checking the outbuildings and Mendes sat at the kitchen table with Maclean.

'I'll get fires going in all the rooms for tomorrow. I'll move in with my girl-friend and get the place in good order. I'll have the electricity switched on and the appliances checked. It looks as if nobody's been down for a long time.'

'I think not since the war started.'

Mendes smiled. 'I understand that it's serious, chief. The girl.'

'Yes. We're going to be married when it's over.'

'Why not now?'

Maclean laughed. 'I've got enough responsibility with you lot.'

'Does she know what you're up to?'

'No. But I'm sure she guesses. Why else would I have come back?'

'Better a dead husband than a dead boy-friend. At least she'd get a pension.'

'I don't intend being a dead anything.'

'Me too.'

'How are the new arrangements going with Brieux?'

'Fine. I never talk to him about how the Red Army are kicking the shit out of the Germans and he doesn't tell me how to clean a Beretta.' He grinned and said softly, 'We get along fine.'

'It'll be different in the New Year.'

'In what way?'

'From January on we'll be taking some action. Nothing big. Just testing out what we can do. Seeing if all this training really works.'

'Tell me more.'

'I'll be calling a meeting of all the group leaders and deputies the first day of the year. 1943 is going to mark the beginning of the end.'

'You really think so?'

'I know so.'

'I can't wait.'

'Enjoy the last few days of waiting. It'll come all too soon.'

'Not for me. It can't come soon enough.'

Maclean smiled. 'Check your *plastique* and detonators if you want something to do.'

And then Loussier and Brieux had come back. It was raining as they walked back together to where they had left the cycles and Maclean and Loussier had walked together to where Lisa was waiting with the small truck. It was loaded now with the jars of rose jelly for which the small town was famous.

As they drove back to Melun Maclean said, 'Mendes and Brieux seem to be getting along together, OK.'

'They respect one another as men but there's been too many things said for them ever to be friends. I mean in the past before you came along.'

'Tell me.'

'Well, in the first months after the Germans came in all communists had a rough time. The Russians and the Germans had signed the non-aggression pact. They were allies and the French commies made excuses for the Boche. Nobody liked that. When the Germans invaded Russia then they all changed round. But people didn't forget. Then London gave the word for the French commies to join the Resistance and they're cashing in on that.'

Maclean shrugged. 'If they do their bit with us that's all that matters.'

'I'm afraid Brieux doesn't see it that way. In his book the commies fight for Moscow not for France.'

Maclean regretted that he'd raised the subject of Mendes and Brieux. It was obvious that Loussier at least partly agreed with Brieux. He liked both men himself, in different ways.

13

Maclean and Loussier met in Janine's room. She had managed to collect wood for the stove and had opened the cast-iron door so that she could use an old-fashioned toasting fork to make them some toast. When they had all eaten the girl left them alone as they sat by the stove.

'Let's talk about our first target, Georges. Any ideas?'

'Depends on what you want to do.'

'Go on.'

'Well. Do we want to let the population see that we can strike if we want to, or do we want to cause trouble for the Germans? Or maybe both.'

'First of all we pick a target that is not in the immediate area of one of our group headquarters. Secondly, I want to do something that doesn't anger the Germans into retaliation against local people. Hostage taking and that sort of thing.'

'You sound as if you've got it all worked out.'

'I went up yesterday to look over Corbeil-Essonnes. It's not really in our area and because it's so near Paris the Germans will think that one of the Paris networks is responsible. There's a nice railway target there. Two in fact. The station itself which backs on to a cemetery and an engine-shed and repair works. There's a switching-line comes off the main line and splits into three at the sheds. If we take out the junction and the locomotives in the sheds that would be a good night's work.'

'There's no other network covering Corbeil?'

'No. The Paris networks are all in the city.'

'So who's going to do it?'

'We'll take a risk for the sake of experience. We'll use all the group leaders except one. We've got to have somebody in reserve in case anything goes wrong.'

'So who in reserve?'

'You, I'm afraid. But I want you to coordinate all the reconnaissance.'

'What's that mean?'

'Checking what we'll need to take out the switch points. Checking when the maximum number of locomotives are going to be in the sheds. Checking the guard arrangements at both places and train times at nights.'

'When do we do it?'

'As soon as possible. It depends on your recommendation. We'll tell them at the group leaders' meeting on New Year's day.'

'Have London OK'd this?'

Maclean smiled. 'It's their orders that we start some small very secure operations.'

'I'll get started straightaway.' He paused. 'When are you going to Provins?'

'On the twenty-third.' He smiled. 'We'll have the group leaders' meeting at Brieux's workplace.'

'Are you staying at La Roserie over Christmas?'

'I'm not sure. I hope so. But it depends on her mother.'

'Mendes is collecting food and various things for their visit.'

'I know. He's a great help.' He smiled. 'So is Brieux.'

'Are you happy?'

Maclean looked surprised. 'What made you ask that?'

'When we went down to the house the other day you looked like you must have looked when you were a kid. Very young and very innocent.'

'Don't worry, Georges. I'm here to do a job. I'll never stop doing it. We're all after the same prize.'

'I wasn't worried. I trust you. We all do.' He smiled. 'Even those who still call you "the English."'

* * *

Lisa had taken him into the courtyard of the Croix d'Or where she was delivering cheese for the hotel. He had no idea how Anne-Marie and her mother would travel down from Paris. He was almost certain that it would be by train. The station was on the outskirts of the town and the only train from Paris that day would arrive at 4.20 p.m. Mendes had arranged for the only taxi-driver to look out for them and stop on his way out of town and telephone Brieux. He would wait with Brieux and Brieux would drive him out to La Roserie. Mendes would be at the house and Maclean would arrive when they had had time to settle in. When he looked at his watch he realised that he had two hours to pass before the train arrived.

Provins had once been the third largest town in France. It was like a small version of Chartres, its town ramparts still encircled beautiful buildings with Mediaeval gables and Renaissance doorways. They had frequently driven into the town in the old days to see the beautiful old cottages with their lush gardens overflowing with roses. It was known as 'the town of roses' and despite the war and the Germans it was still a fairy-tale town. He saw the shop where he had bought Anne-Marie an ice-cream and the café near César's Tower where they laughed together because they had escaped from their families for a quarter of an hour.

But that day there was no sunshine and no roses. The sky was an ominous blue-black, threatening more snow, and as he stood at the ramparts there was still snow lingering on the land as far as the eye could see. He had always remembered those fields as golden acres of corn, dotted with poppies and cornflowers.

Even in the frozen grip of winter there was a calmness about the landscape. A landscape that reminded him of mediaeval German paintings showing skaters and feasting on frozen rivers. He realised that it was a long time since he had looked at his surroundings as a painter rather than as a man looking at woods and hedgerows as protective hiding places for arms and explosives. Even when he painted his canvases for the gallery he painted almost without thinking. Looking and painting but not actually seeing.

As it began to get dark the wind got up and he walked back to Brieux's place. It was warm inside and five women sat at old-fashioned sewing-machines, two of them with treadles, all too intent on their work to notice him as he walked through to Brieux's office and studio. There were pieces of cotton, silk, satin and chiffon hanging from overhead lines and Brieux looked up and nodded before adding a few last strokes to the design on his board. When he straightened up he grinned. 'You want coffee or potato soup?'

'Soup for me.'

'Me too.'

The soup was in a large cast-iron saucepan on the top of an oil stove and he ladled it out carefully and set the plates at the side of his drawing board.

'Are you busy because of Christmas?'

'No. This is all New Year's stuff. Every whore in Paris wants to do her Kraut proud at the Neu Jahrs-ball.' He grinned. 'I was thinking the other day how crazy it is. Three quarters of the tarts who are buying my clothes are going to end up getting their heads shaved when it's all over.'

'People will be too busy getting their lives together to do that.'

Brieux laughed. 'You're crazy. It's the first thing they'll do. And there'll be as big a crowd watching as we got in the old days for the Champagne Fair.' He grinned. 'I've seen the list for Provins. 'All customers of mine except one.'

'And what do they have to do to get their heads shaved?'

'Open their legs for a Kraut.' He smiled. 'I'll start a wig manufacturing business and make a fortune.'

'They're just silly girls, that's all.'

'Sure. And they're pretty and they like chocolates and silk underwear and black market food. But it'll be the plain and ugly old witches who'll shave their heads. Just like the ones who sat knitting around the guillotine.' He laughed. 'They'll be quoting Mirabeau's words – "*Nous sommes ici par la volonté du peuple . . .*" And every man you meet will have been in the Resistance. You wait and see.'

'You're a cynic, Brieux.'

Brieux smiled. 'That train of yours is never on time. It'll be at least an hour late. Sit down. Make yourself comfortable. If you look straight out of the end window you can see the smoke two miles away even in the dark as it starts up the incline to the station.'

'Is there anything I can do to help?'

Brieux grinned. 'Not unless you're any good at putting lace on a dozen pairs of knickers.'

'Were you in fashion before the war?'

'Yes. I had a salon in Paris. Little black dresses and little black suits for all the little *cinq à sept* girls.'

'Weren't they whores too?'

'Good God, no. They were the ones who saved half the marriages in town.'

'How do you make that out?'

'A man gets on in the world. Gets rich and powerful. He's in his fifties. If he's a fool he falls in love with some pretty little cat he wants to screw. He gets a divorce, he ain't rich any more. All his wife's friends and relatives put the word around what a shit he is. His kids are torn apart and everybody gets a bad time. And the cute little cat goes off with some travelling salesman who sells fancy buttons. But the wise guy has his little one, his *cinq à sept*. He pays her well, gives her a good time and nobody minds because he's discreet. He's just one of the boys. Still in the club.'

'And what about the little girl?'

'She opens a nice little hat shop with the money she's made. Makes a pile and marries the accountant who fiddles her tax returns. She's learned all about what men want in bed and keeps her husband happy until they've got three kids. She has an affair with a ribbon salesman and her old

90

man has a girl who sells gloves and scarves at Hermès. Everybody's happy.'

'You know what's going to happen to you, don't you?'
Brieux looked surprised. And interested. 'Tell me.'

'You're going to fall in love with a real beauty. A girl from the country who's never been to Paris. Who wears cotton dresses with roses on the skirt. She still does her hair in braids. And she thinks you're a cross between Maurice Chevalier and Joan of Arc. You'll marry and have three kids and you'll both live happily ever after.'

For long moments Brieux looked at him, and then said quietly, 'You could be right, my friend. You're very perceptive.' He turned away and busied himself with the sketch on his drawing board.

The train was over two hours late and Anne-Marie and her mother were not among the dozen or so passengers who got off at Provins. He had watched from the shadows until the train had continued on its way to Troyes. But Brieux had abandoned his work and they walked to the shed where he kept his old Peugeot.

It was snowing heavily as they left the town. There had been no road repairs for nearly three years and Brieux cursed the pot holes that damaged his tyres and suspension as they drove through the storm. When they turned off the main road the snow had drifted in the wind until it was higher than the hedges and Maclean insisted that Brieux turned back and he would walk the last mile to the river and the house. Even turning the car had been difficult and Maclean stood watching until its lights were hidden by the banks of snow.

Turning up his collar he bent his head and made his way through the snow. There was a narrow strip of the road still visible but when he got to the river bank the path was in deep snow. It was over an hour before he saw the lights of the house. As he got to the stone steps he could hear music. It was Charles Trenet singing *Vous qui passez sans me voir*. He smiled as he got to the door. Mendes was a

Trenet fan. He tried the door handle and the door opened easily. As he stepped inside he felt the warmth of the house. Mendes had done a good job trying to make them comfortable.

He took off his coat and scarf and tossed them on to a chair as he looked around. The music was coming from the big old-fashioned kitchen. It was Tito Rossi now, singing *J'attendrai*.

As he opened the door he saw them. Anne-Marie, her mother, Mendes and a very pretty girl. They were laughing and talking and then Mendes' girl-friend saw him and said something to him. Mendes turned, rising out of his seat, smiling as he reached for his glass, lifting it as he looked around the table.

'Here he is. The one and only English. God bless him.' And the war and the Germans were suddenly a long way away.

They had finished their meal but they sat with him as he had soup, a leg of a capon with a baked potato, a slice of home-made jam tart and fresh cream. And the coffee was real coffee.

As they ate and talked he was aware that Anne-Marie's mother was more than just upset. She was ill, her body and face emaciated, her hands trembling and from time to time her whole body was shaking as if she had an ague. When he had finished he went across the hall and into the small study with Mendes.

As they sat down Maclean said, 'Do you think we need a doctor for her mother?'

'No. Even if we did he'd not get through to us for at least a couple of days. I was intending to leave as soon as you got here but you'll have to put up with us until the snow clears, I'm afraid.' He paused. 'It's just shock. I've seen people like that before. She'll calm down if we all just carry on. She's got some sleeping pills and the change of being here will help her.'

'What about you and your girl and a spoiled Christmas?'

'What's Christmas in times like these? Just another day. Don't worry about us.'

'Thanks. How did they get here?'

'They haven't come for Christmas. They've come to stay. Two hired cars courtesy of the old man and a heap of luggage. The girl wants to join the Resistance.'

'How do you know?'

'She told me.' He paused. 'She's very bright. She'd be very useful.'

Maclean shook his head but said nothing.

It was an hour before he managed to see Anne-Marie alone.

'Tell me about your mother.'

'Tell me about you first.'

'I'm OK. How about you?'

She smiled. 'I'm fine. I couldn't wait to see you again.'

'I thought you'd come by train. That's why I was late getting here.'

'I'm not going back to Paris.'

'What about your job?'

'I've made my father provide money to support us both. And I've made him give *Maman* this house. She owns it now.'

'How did you do that?'

'Got a good lawyer to negotiate on her behalf. He did what I wanted or she wouldn't divorce him.' She smiled. 'He didn't want a scandal; that would lose him his standing with the Germans.'

'Why a scandal?'

'He's moved in with a German girl. A ballad singer. Young and very pretty.'

'I can't believe it. He was such a stuffed shirt. So prim and proper. What made him do it?'

'Like I said. She's young and very pretty. He's besotted by her. And I think she's flattered that an academic has fallen for her. He's much respected by the Germans and he wields a lot of influence in all the arts. He puts her in a different league because the culture bit rubs off on her.'

'Your mother must hate him.'

'It's more shock. Seeing pictures in the papers of him with the girl at concerts or galleries or first-nights at the theatre. And on top of all that she gets the backlash of being thought of as the wife of an open collaborator. Her friends cut her dead. She gets anonymous hate letters and telephone calls. We've even had bricks through the windows at the house.'

'He's a real bastard, isn't he?'

'It's strange but he looks ten years younger. He's genuinely happy. He even has a certain charm now.'

'Charm! I can't believe that.'

'It's true. The girl's changed him a lot.'

'Won't you miss Paris and the job?'

She smiled. 'No. I've got you, my English. That's all I want.'

He sighed. 'Suddenly I wish it was all over. What I'm doing seems such a waste of good time.'

'It's not, Philippe. What Papa and the others like him are doing is living on borrowed time. It's a fantasy world. I've heard Germans talking at the studio. They don't yet believe they've lost the war but they know they haven't won it. The whole world was shocked when the Germans marched into Paris. It didn't seem credible. Even the Germans didn't really believe it. They still don't.'

'And I can't believe you're here. It seems too good to be true.'

'When I put *Maman* to bed just now she said she had always known you would grow up to be something special.'

He smiled. 'What else did she say?'

'She asked when we were getting married.'

'And what did you say?'

She smiled. 'I said – all in good time.'

'It would be irresponsible, my love. I don't want you mixed up in what I'm doing. I couldn't bear having something happening to you. I love you too much for that. Much as I'd like us to be married.'

94

She didn't look convinced but she didn't pursue it.

'How long can you stay?'

'About five days.'

'Do you live in Provins?'

'No. Don't ask me about what I do. It's better if you don't know.'

'Will I see more of you now?'

'Yes. Of course.'

She sighed. 'It's a funny world we live in. But let's enjoy our few days. I like your friend Mendes. He's been very kind.'

'He's a good man. What's his girl-friend like?'

She laughed. 'She's a real sweetie. And they're so different. That great big tough man and the shy, quiet girl. And she's the boss. It's like a lion and a lion-tamer. Just one look from her is enough. Her father's some senior official in Vichy. They're going to get married at Easter. She's a secretary at the brickworks where your friend works.'

He smiled. 'You know more about them in a couple of hours than I do.'

She laughed. 'He said you'd given them all a lecture about sexual relationships and all that. Made you sound like my father. And he thinks you're fantastic. A cross between Renoir and Genghis Khan.'

He smiled. 'It's lovely to see you again.'

'Do you think about me sometimes?'

'I think about you every day before I go to sleep.'

For several moments she was silent as she looked at him before she said softly, 'Speaking of sleep, do you want to sleep with me tonight?'

He woke just on 2 a.m. and eased his way out of the bed to walk to the window. As he pulled aside the curtain he was surprised at the brightness outside. The skies had cleared and the snow had stopped, and somewhere to the west, towards Paris, the long fingers of searchlights probed the sky for intruders. He turned and looked at the girl. She was sleeping soundly, her cheeks flushed, and her lips apart. She was very beautiful, but what moved him most was her trust in him.

The four days of Christmas should have been halcyon days but they weren't. Maclean felt guilty about the girl. Married or not, and largely ignorant of what he was doing, her relationship with him meant that she was involved. The Gestapo and the SD drew no fine distinction between girl-friends, mistresses and wives. They were just pressure points. And he felt guilty about neglecting his duties. Letting himself be deflected by thoughts of marriage and love.

On the day he had to leave they had walked down to the river, crunching through the melting snow, through the orchard and down to the meadow. He was on edge. He wanted to explain that if he seemed pre-occupied it wasn't because he didn't love her and enjoy being with her. But he couldn't find the words. They just talked of when they were children, laughing at things they remembered. Recalling the subterfuges they had used when they were older to be alone with each other. She had seemed happy enough and he clung to the belief that she understood how things were. But there were tears in her eyes when they kissed goodbye and he walked down to Lisa's truck.

14

At the briefing meeting of the group leaders Maclean had
been aware of the flatness of his voice and his routine,
uninspiring words as he outlined the targets and passed
round a large-scale sketch of the target area. But when he
discovered that over the holidays five group leaders had
reconnoitred the sites independently all his old self-
confidence came surging back. All those long months of
training had not been in vain. He had even raised a smile
when Jarry from Troyes had repeated his frequent quote
of the old Army motto – 'Time spent in reconnaissance is
seldom wasted.' They *had* listened. They *had* absorbed it.
He felt a sudden surge of affection and warmth for this
strange, ill-assorted group of men who had thrown in their
lot with him. Cautiously and even reluctantly at first, but
at last they were a network. A team.

He had gone over again the vulnerable spots on a locomotive and the economical use of *plastique*. Shattering one
valve gear box put a locomotive out of action as efficiently
as doing both. He drew diagrams to show where the
explosive should be placed to do maximum damage to
both the main railway line and the feed-line to the engine
sheds. Loussier reported that by midnight on a Saturday
there were always at least three locomotives and a shunting
loco in the sheds. Duras from Fontenay who worked for
SNCF pointed out that repairs would be much more difficult if the crane where the lines split into three to enter
the shed was put out of action. It was Mendes who questioned the wisdom of destroying the station buildings on

the main line. It wouldn't affect the Germans, only the locals who had no other means of transport and many of them worked in Paris. They would lose at least a week's wages. They might well blame the Resistance for adding to their problems instead of harassing the Germans.

Loussier reported on the German troop dispositions in the town. There was an anti-aircraft battery housed in the buildings by the woods called Ambroise Feray, an SS Reconnaissance Unit in a piece of parkland by the church of St Etienne and a Gestapo detachment housed in the police station. There were usually only two soldiers guarding the locomotive shed. The guards went on at 10 p.m. and patrolled through to first light. It seemed that the guard patrol was just a ritual and not taken seriously. There had never been any trouble from the locals. Maclean had never attempted to recruit anyone in the town. It was too near Paris and not part of his area.

In the afternoon they had rehearsed and timed the operation and the plan worked out for dispersing after it was done. Loussier and Maclean would stay behind to watch the Germans' reaction. The plan was to carry out the operation in four days' time, at midnight on the Saturday night. Loussier and Bourdet from Montereau would take care of the two guards. Nobody would be armed. Mendes would be responsible for assembling the explosives and detonators.

They had made their separate ways to the cemetery and were in place at 8 p.m. Loussier and Bourdet had made two silent journeys into the engine sheds with the explosives and detonators for the locomotives. They had reported that there were seven engines there that night. Maclean had allowed for six engines with a charge for a valve gear each and a supplementary charge in the fire-box, hoping that it would destroy the boiler. One of the boiler charges was transferred for the extra locomotive. When Loussier and Bourdet left the third time for the sheds they were to stay there so that they could start laying the charges and

wait for the guard patrol to come on duty at 10 p.m.
Reports said the guards were never punctual.

It was nearly an hour before a *Wehrmacht* truck drew
up at the station and Maclean watched through his night
glasses as the two soldiers stood talking together after the
truck had left. They were armed with old model 98 car-
bines. One of them lit a cigarette and they walked slowly
alongside the track until they disappeared in the darkness.
Maclean saw Estang, Deval and Picard moving toward the
points that controlled the main line and the track to
the sheds. He was tempted to go with them but he had to
stay in case there were problems. He saw the flash of the
torch from the sheds – three Morse dots which meant
that the guards were under control. He ran down the
switch line to where the line split into three before enter-
ing the shed. Estang and Deval were working on the
points and Picard was bending over the control box on
the crane. Maclean ran on to the shed and saw Loussier
working on the second row of locomotives. He couldn't
see Bourdet. He checked the timers on the charges
that had already been set and then hurried back to the
cemetery.

When he checked his watch he was surprised that it was
only an hour since the guards had arrived. Another half
hour and the others could leave. Brieux was taking them
in his car and Brieux had a curfew pass. It would only take
twenty minutes to drop them in Melun. He and Loussier
both had cycles and would go back using only the country
lanes. They needed to stay and see the results of their
efforts. As he settled back behind the tombstone he heard
the air-raid warning sirens in the distance and a few minutes
later there were searchlights from the anti-aircraft batteries
that ringed Paris. The RAF were probably bombing the
Wehrmacht's main arms dump near Villeneuve. It was a
three-quarters moon. A bomber's moon.

Ten minutes later he saw a dim figure crouching as it
came up between the rows of gravestones and seconds
later Loussier huddled down beside him, panting and

breathless. When he had recovered Loussier said softly, 'All the charges are set. The others can clear off now.' He took a deep breath. 'But we've got a problem.'

'What's the problem?'

'The guards.'

'I thought Bourdet was looking after them.'

'He was. I left him guarding them while I set the charges and when I went back they were dead. He'd cut their throats. They're both dead. And I can't find Bourdet. He's done a bunk.'

'Why the hell did he kill them?'

'I'm not sure.'

'Don't play guessing games, Loussier. Why do you think he killed them?'

'His home's in a small village called Sergines. When you made men with families move out of their homes he moved to Montereau.' He paused. 'His wife's been sleeping with a German sergeant who was billeted in the village. He's part of a vehicle servicing unit. Bourdet's very bitter about it.'

'So will the Krauts be when they find those bodies. But it's the locals here in Corbeil who'll suffer the backlash. Any idea where he is?'

'I'm afraid not.'

'It's bad enough if they were killed by the explosives. They could think it wasn't intentional. But with their throats cut they'll go berserk.'

For long moments Maclean was silent and then he reached for his canvas bag. 'There's a small office at the back of the engine shed where the maintenance men fill in their time-sheets. Put the two Krauts in there and use these.' He pulled out the two sticks of *plastique* and their detonators. 'You'd better hurry. Send the others on their way and don't tell them what's happened.'

Loussier took the charges and Maclean said, 'Remind them to wash their hands thoroughly if they've handled any *plastique*.'

It seemed a long time before Loussier came back but it

100

was only twenty minutes. Maclean looked at the luminous figures on his watch. The fuses were set to go off in ten minutes' time. It seemed a long wait.

It was the crane that went first with an orange burst of flame and an explosion whose blast they could feel in the air. It was two minutes before the next explosion. It sounded like two together and then there was a series of explosions that shook the ground. He counted them off but eventually gave up. It wasn't possible to tell whether an explosion was from one or more charges. After five minutes silence they headed off towards the cemetery where they had hidden their cycles. It looked as if the engine sheds were on fire.

In some ways the operation had been more successful than they had expected. It was estimated that the switch line would not be usable for ten days, it would take ten weeks at least for the locomotives to be repaired and the engine sheds had been completely destroyed by fire. The Germans had introduced an indefinite curfew from 7 p.m. to 5 a.m. and had started daily, random checks on identity papers, passes and permits.

Three days after the operation Bourdet's frozen body was found hanging from a tree in the small back-garden of his house. His wife was threatened that if she attempted to attend his funeral she would be beaten up in public. Most of the village attended the funeral. Many of the men wore their 1914–18 war medals pinned to their jackets.

Maclean had spent time visiting every group. Talking not only with leaders but with groups of men, and asked their opinions about his rule that people, particularly group leaders, should move from their houses to protect their families and found the majority supported the rule. But many asked that the rule should be relaxed when a man felt that moving out could put at risk some domestic relationship. He agreed and it was accepted that this meant not only relationships with wives but other relationships too. There was no opposition to his plans for further operations. In fact, the caution was mainly his.

By the time the winter gave way reluctantly to spring they had carried out a series of operations that were intended to extend their practical experience of a wide variety of targets. Telephone exchanges, bridges, a small German arms dump, small German convoys where the network had its first experience of ambushes involving small arms fire. And finally a raid on a Wehrmacht officers' mess during a Saturday night dance. The network had suffered no serious casualties and Maclean's only worry was that they were beginning to fancy their chances in *Maquis* style adventures. They had proved that they had tremendous courage and discipline but their role as defined by London was sabotage and harassment, not taking on the SS and the Wehrmacht.

The Lysander came in over the woods, flying low. Masson loved Lysanders. The Spitfires and ME109s were the race-horses but Lysanders with their exaggerated dihedral were the shire-horses, the work-horses, real planes, their wings spread wide like a sea-bird's wings.

He knew exactly where it would come to a stop. They had a maximum of two minutes to make the changeover and he'd made them rehearse it a dozen times. The incomer scrambling down the short ladder, the pilot handing out the canvas bag and taking on board the return one as the two men returning to England clambered up the ladder. A wave from the pilot and they were on their way. The slow lift, beautifully judged, over the silhouetted trees and they were gone. He waited until the new arrival had been taken over by the reception committee and he and Delors made their way through the damp grass of the meadow towards where their cycles were hidden in the overgrown ditch.

There had been a letter for him in the mail-bag, the

envelope sealed with red sealing-wax with an impression of a triangle in each blob of wax. He touched his jacket and felt its stiffness inside his pocket. He and Delors would have to wait another hour before they rode to the station.

He took off his jacket and draped it like a tent over his head, tearing open the envelope, pulling out the single sheet and switching on his small torch. Palmer wanted him to go to London as soon as possible. But not on a flight that included any SOE personnel. He should use an SIS Z section flight. The usual meeting procedure. He put his jacket on, stuffing the envelope and the letter into his pocket. He'd burn it in the toilet at the railway station. He was always relieved when he had anything from Palmer. Palmer was a professional and the people at Baker Street were amateurs. And there was no place for amateurs when you were playing with the Gestapo and the SD. His contact with Palmer and Westphal was the best life-insurance he could get. Whoever won the war he had a friend at court. He glanced at Delors who was already asleep and then lay back himself against the slope of the ditch and closed his eyes. He wondered what Toto was doing. He was lucky to have her as a wife. A few moments later he was asleep.

15

Masson had found Maclean and Loussier sitting together on one of the benches on the walk-way beside the river. It was the middle of March but it was as sunny and warm as many a June day.

'Mind if I join you, my friends?' He was smiling, his usual aura of self-confidence all-pervading. Maclean smiled back and made room for him on the bench, his eyes taking in the well-cut suit, the real leather shoes and the gold ring.

'You look like you've just come into money, Henri.'

Masson laughed. 'The suit's from Brieux's place. Special order. The shoes are from an old friend. What else is there?' He paused and leaned forward to look at Loussier. 'No word of welcome, Georges?' Loussier didn't respond and Masson turned to Maclean. 'I got your wants lists. Have London agreed this?'

'They haven't answered yet. Why do you ask?'

'I've got a single passenger incoming flight coming in next week. Lysander. For another network. I could do with a load if you can shake them up.'

'I'll see what I can do.'

'I won't be around for the next two weeks. I'm taking a break.'

'Where are you going?'

Masson grinned. 'The sea if I can make it.'

Maclean laughed. 'Knowing you, you'll make it.'

'Can I be serious for a moment?'

'I'm serious right now, Henri. What is it?'

'Are you satisfied with my work. The reception arrangements and all that?'

'You know I am. It's a great relief to have you around.'

'No complaints?'

'Not one, Henri. I wish every other part of the network worked as smoothly.' He looked at Masson. 'Are you getting trouble from one of your other networks?'

'No. They're pretty happy. Have you let London know you're satisfied?'

'No. But London already know that you're doing a good job. What's worrying you?'

Masson smiled and shrugged. 'Nothing. It's OK.'

Masson waved jauntily as he walked off and Maclean waved back before he turned to Loussier.

'What have you got against Masson, Georges?'

'I just don't like him. He's not my type.'

'He does a good job and he never complains.'

'He's got nothing to complain about.' He paused and looked at Maclean. 'How do you think he pays for the fancy clothes?'

'I expect Brieux gives him a special price.'

'Still costs plenty.'

'What are you trying to tell me?'

'He's deep in black market deals.'

'So?'

'That means contacts with the Germans.'

'But Brieux has contact with the Germans. Most of his things are bought by Germans in Paris. He's quite open about it.'

'Brieux's a different sort of man. That's his living. What does Masson trade with?'

'Cheese, meat, butter, fresh eggs – food and wine.'

'Do you know that?'

'Of course not. But they are the usual things.'

'Masson isn't the kind of man to fiddle around with food.'

'So what does he trade?'

'I don't know either. I wish I did.'

'We'd be in deep trouble without him.' He smiled. 'Anyway, we were talking new targets.'

'What has London's reaction been to what we've been doing?'

'They're satisfied. Surprised that we haven't had more harassment from the Germans.'

'That's because you've always insisted on tight security and careful planning.'

'That's what London ordered me to do.' He paused. 'There's a suggestion in the last batch of messages I got that they might want us to report on all German troop movements by road and rail. With details of the troops. Units. Divisions. Functions, and so on.'

'That's no problem.'

'Anything from Mendes?'

Loussier smiled. 'I wondered how long you'd wait. She's fine. But she's pining for you.'

'How's her mother?'

'Much the same. They got the doctor to check her over. Says she's physically OK but suffering from trauma, whatever that means.'

'She was such a delightful woman. It's a shame.'

'Seems there was a piece in one of the papers about him. The Krauts had given him some medal for services to Franco-German understanding.'

'Did she see it?'

'No, Anne-Marie kept it away from her.'

'I'll try and get down at the weekend.'

'I'll warn Lisa and Mendes. He wants to talk to you about marrying his girl-friend.'

'You tell him it's up to him. He's a sensible chap and can decide for himself. He doesn't need my approval.' He shrugged. 'Life has to go on.'

16

Masson walked slowly up the Avenue du Roule and turned off into the tree-lined street where the flat was located. It was a typical Neuilly house that had been converted into flats before the war. The Germans had *beschlagnahmt* the whole house and the top flat was used by Kurt Westphal as a meeting place with agents. His base and living quarters were on the far side of the Bois de Boulogne not far from the race-track. On occasions Masson had been driven there in an unmarked staff car but when their meetings had to be recorded this was always at the flat.

He went through the usual ritual of walking to the end of the street then turning back to the flat. There was no bell beside the heavy door in the porch with its stained-glass window but the door was opened immediately by an elderly woman who silently waved him towards the flight of stairs.

Dr Schmidt was waiting for him at the top of the stairs chatting amiably as he led Masson to the main room in the flat. It was luxuriously furnished and the walls were rich with the works of modern artists.

Westphal, as always, in a formal blue suit, shook hands with Masson and waved him to one of the leather armchairs before sitting down himself. Dr Schmidt sat separately with a clip-board and pencil laid out on a small table. It was he who made notes of the meetings.

Westphal pointed to an envelope on the low table between the two of them.

'The permits and the papers you asked for. And a piece of paper to show to any Gestapo or SD officer if you need help.' He smiled and waved his hand dismissively. 'The rest is there of course. Two months' in advance and the same for expenses.' He paused and leaned forward. 'Tell me about the trip.'

'I just got a message saying I was to go over to see him. No mention to SOE.'

'No indication of what he wants?'

'No.'

'When do you go?'

'Next Sunday night.'

Westphal smiled. 'Where from?'

'Just outside Tours. By Lysander.'

'Have you brought the usual stuff?'

Masson reached in his pocket and as Westphal reached out his hand Masson said, 'Can it be copied now?'

Westphal turned and nodded to Schmidt who took the folded envelope and left the room. Westphal settled back in his chair.

'When do they pick up that stuff?'

'Tonight. It's my last reception until I come back.'

'You think you will come back?'

'You mean they might keep me there?'

'No. But you might decide to cash-in on your good work and stay there.'

'That's not possible. I have obligations here.'

Westphal smiled. 'We all have obligations but sometimes we decide to ignore them.' He shrugged. 'We can all be tempted if people read us right.'

Masson smiled. 'How would you tempt me?'

'A combination of the chance of adventure – taking risks. And of course, excellent rewards.'

'No pretty girls?'

Westphal smiled. 'All my information tells me that I couldn't compete in that area with your own natural talents.' He looked at Masson. 'How is the war in your part of the world?'

Masson smiled. 'I don't think the Wehrmacht or the SS have too much to worry about.'

'I don't want the cost of our arrangement to be too high, my friend. We have to balance the account.'

Masson shrugged. 'You're buying the future. An insurance policy.'

At that moment Dr Schmidt came back and handed the envelope back to Masson.

Westphal stood up and Masson recognised that the interview was over. Westphal walked with him to the door and Schmidt took him down to the street door, opened it and nodded to him before closing it again.

When Schmidt came back he sat down with Westphal who said, 'Was it useful – the stuff he brought?'

'Not now, but for the future it's beyond price.'

'What do you make of him?'

'I was going to ask you that. I don't understand him. I don't understand his motives. What's his reward?'

'You have to look at his background. He has a talent as a pilot which he can no longer use. He came from a poor environment so being a pilot made him a minor hero. But that's gone. So what does he do? He still likes the risk and the adventure so he wants to be an invisible hero until the war is over. He also is not a gambler. When he bets he bets on every horse in the race. So he becomes an informer. He would call himself a spy. And he informs for both sides. For us and for London. And his own countrymen pay the price in the end.'

'Do you trust him, Karl?'

'Good God, no. I wouldn't trust any Frenchman. They were our enemies. They still are. The women are whores and the men are born thieves. They'd sell their souls for a place at the German table.' He waved his hand dismissively. 'One doesn't have to trust people like him – you just use them and let them think they're using you.'

'Do you think London know about his contacts with you?'

'They're fools if they don't. But who it is who knows is another question. If it isn't SOE who is it? Palmer is an old hand but I don't see his connection with Baker Street.'

'Doesn't Masson know?'

'No. He doesn't know one from the other.'

Masson stood alone in the long, wide clearing in the woods, his eyes closed and his head down as he listened for the familiar drone of a Lysander. It wasn't an SOE flight and the incoming passenger was one of Palmer's men, who was to be left to his own devices after he had landed.

It was bitterly cold but there was no wind and the ground was as hard as an airfield runway would have been. It wouldn't even be necessary to turn the plane for take-off and the sky was clear of clouds. The birds stirred first. Rustling in the bushes under the trees. An owl hooted and far away he heard the call of a vixen. Then he heard the plane.

When the Lysander rolled to a stop he ran forward and waited as the passenger climbed down the short metal ladder. He shook his hand hurriedly and then clambered up behind the pilot. The whole exchange had taken less than two minutes and then they were airborne, lifting over the tops of the trees in a wide arc.

They landed at Tangmere and in the squadron office there was a packet for him and the duty officer told him that there was an RAF staff car and driver waiting for him. He opened the packet in the toilet. There was a Canadian passport in his own name. Two hundred pounds in used sterling notes, a bundle of clothing coupons and a book of emergency ration coupons. A typewritten note said that he was booked in at the Dorchester Hotel, Room 504. There was no signature.

It was a pretty WRAF driver and when he went to get in the passenger seat beside her she grinned and said that that wasn't allowed. He had to sit in the back of the car.

He chatted to her as they went through Chichester towards Midhurst and although she responded politely he knew that he was on a loser. She was engaged to be married to a Squadron Leader, a fighter pilot, and she wasn't interested in scruffy civilians even if they did have an accent like Maurice Chevalier.

For most of the journey he slept, but woke as they circled the island at Hyde Park Corner and headed up Park Lane. The hotel was blacked-out but a commissionaire with a small torch took his canvas bag and guided him to the hotel entrance.

Palmer was sitting in an armchair in the foyer, looking over the top of the evening paper he was holding. Palmer nodded towards the reception desk and Masson walked over, showed his passport, signed in and was handed his key. The clerk told him that there was no porter service in wartime as he handed over the room key.

An air raid warning sounded as he let himself into a small but neat room. There was a single bed with the sheet turned down at one corner. A built-in wardrobe and a dressing table with a mirror and stool. In the corner was one small armchair and beside the bed was a reading lamp and a telephone.

He heard a knock on the door and when he opened it cautiously he saw Palmer, who held out his hand, smiling.

'Welcome to war-time London again. Have you eaten?'

Palmer walked in and looked around, seemingly paying no attention as Masson said that he had eaten at the airfield.

'Do sit down,' Palmer said, as if it were his room, pointing at the bed as he settled himself into the armchair. For several minutes Palmer just looked at Masson and Masson looked back. He was never sure about Palmer. Round faced, ruddy complexion, straggling moustache and glasses with narrow gold rims that slightly distorted Palmer's large blue eyes. He looked like an overgrown schoolboy but Masson had learned quickly that the English were very deceptive. They looked so calm and boyish, laughing at childish jokes, never seeming serious. But all the time they were weighing you up. You only had to make one false step, say the wrong thing and they were as stiff and cold as a block of ice. All the talk of cricket and rugby was just a cover as they looked you over.

'So, my friend,' Palmer said, 'How are things in *la belle France*?'

'Much as usual, Colonel. Food's scarce. So is fuel. And the Krauts are everywhere. Living off the fat of the land of course.'

'And your friends in Melun?'

Masson smiled. 'I'm sure you know about them already.'

'Maybe I do. But I want to hear it from you.'

'Benoit's *réseau* is the best run of all the networks I deal with.'

'Remind me. Which ones do you cover?'

'Benoit – the Ile de France area. The Paris network and the two networks in Normandy.'

'Why is Benoit good in your opinion?'

'He's very professional. Didn't rush into things before he had sorted out the men. Organised them, then trained them.' He paused. 'I've mentioned all this in my reports to you, Colonel.'

'Tell me what they've been doing.'

They talked until past midnight and for most of the next day. With Palmer probing into every detail. Wanting names and backgrounds and details of operations that had been carried out. He asked questions about the other networks but he always came back to the Melun *réseau*. Masson couldn't understand why.

He was told that he would be flying back on the evening of the second day and when Palmer had talked with him in the morning the subject had changed.

'Tell me about your German contact.'

Masson smiled. 'I've got several German contacts. Different people want different things.'

Palmer smiled. 'I'm thinking about Sturmbannführer Westphal. What do you trade with him?'

'It's mainly food from the countryside. Cheese, fresh eggs, meat and chickens. He entertains a lot.'

'And what do you get?'

'Cash. Permits and passes.'

'How did you get to know him?'

'I told you, way back, when you first interviewed me. I used to carry post and packages for him when I was flying with Air Bleu.'

'When did you start doing this?'

'Before the war and then after the occupation. I did the same for the Deuxième Bureau. I needed the money.'

'How's your wife, Henri?'

Masson looked surprised. 'She's OK.'

'Where does she live?'

'In Paris.'

'D'you spend a lot of time in Paris?'

'I'm there about once or twice a month.' He shook his head. 'I don't understand why you're asking me these questions.'

Palmer smiled. 'Maybe you will understand one day. I suggest you remember the questions and the answers.' He paused. 'Do you think that your friend Westphal realises what you're doing for SOE?'

'I'm sure he doesn't.'

'What makes you think that?'

'Because if he thought that he'd have me arrested.'

Palmer smiled. 'Don't go anywhere near Baker Street, Henri. That's an order. Understood?'

'Yes, Colonel.'

Palmer nodded. 'Have a good trip back. Let's hope it's all over soon.'

'Do you think it will be?'

'These things take time. But it will happen, believe me. Don't believe what your Germans tell you. Their fate is being sealed around Stalingrad. When we put in our two pennyworth that will be the end for all of them.' He smiled again. 'Just make sure that when the music stops you're sitting on the right chair, Henri.'

Masson had spent the afternoon buying soap, razor blades, aspirin, chocolate bars and sugar. A Humber staff car collected him mid-afternoon and drove him up to the Lysander base at Tempsford in Bedfordshire.

The flight back had been bumpy from the strong winds that were sweeping across Europe from Scandinavia and they had to make three attempts before they could land. It was not an SOE flight and he didn't know any of the reception committee. The landing place was just north of Orleans and that meant a long journey the following day.

Masson, with nothing to fear from the Germans, stayed at a hotel that night and took a train to Paris early the next morning.

Two days later he was in Melun arranging a landing with Loussier near Coutençon. It was Loussier who told him that Maclean wanted to see him urgently. He would be in his room over the bakery all day, painting.

Masson stood looking at the unfinished painting on the easel as Maclean wiped his fingers and brushes on a rag soaked in turpentine. Masson seemed surprised as he turned to look at Maclean.

'I had no idea you were so accomplished. I thought it was no more than a cover.' He turned back to look at the painting of the château at Vaux-le-Pénie. 'You can feel the weather and the time of day.'

Maclean laughed softly, 'What time of day?'

'It's early summer and it's late afternoon on a beautiful day. But tomorrow there will be some rain.'

'Not bad, Henri. Must be your instincts as a pilot for weather conditions.'

'The light is fantastic. I've seen it like that so many times.'

'This area was always famous for its light. A whole group of artists came here because of that light. They were called the Barbizon School – Corot, Rousseau, Cézanne, Renoir, Monet and poor van Gogh, of course.'

'I knew about van Gogh but not the others.' He smiled. 'Loussier said you want to see me.'

'Yes. By the way, did you have a good vacation? You're back earlier than I expected.'

'It wasn't bad but I got bored so I came back.'

'Do you fancy a trip to London?'

'What?'

Maclean smiled at the shock on Masson's face.

'I had a signal two days ago. They want you to go over as soon as possible. They suggest a Lysander next week when they send a new weapons officer over for me.' He paused. 'Can you lay out a reception in that time?'

'Yes. Of course. What do they want?'

'No idea.'

'Can you ask them what it's all about?'

Maclean looked at Masson. 'Henri, you'd better remember that you're here to carry out London's orders. You're a very valuable officer but don't let that go to your head. So let me know when conditions will be suitable – next week.'

'OK. I'll contact you tomorrow when I've checked the weather forecasts. Who's the new weapons chap?'

'His name's Tom Price. He's very young but they tell me he's very competent.'

'Will Georges look after him as I won't be on the ground?'

'I expect so.'

Ten days later Masson was back from London. It had been something of a nightmare the first two days with three of them asking question after question. The same questions again and again with different emphasis and in different contexts. But all of them always polite and calm. They said it wasn't an interrogation, just a routine check on how things were going on his part of the SOE operations in France.

His old friend Roger Carlton had been one of them, his questions as penetrating as the others for those first few days. A whole day on his black market dealings and his relationships with any Germans.

Then in the evening of the second day they seemed to be more relaxed as if they had decided that any doubts they had were unfounded. But all through the second day he realised that Clive Palmer had been preparing him for the questions on Westphal and the other Germans. It was that second evening when, in front of the others, Roger Carlton had offered to take him for a night on the town, with the implication that he would be going back to France the next day.

Carlton had taken him to a club in Soho and had told him that all expenses were being paid by SOE as a friendly gesture to him.

As they sat with their drinks, double whiskies for Carlton and tomato juice for Masson, he had said, 'Can I ask what all this was about, Roger?'

Carlton grinned. 'They do it to everybody, Henri, once in a while. The security chaps find they've got nothing better to do, so they say – "I'm a bit worried about old sunshine. I think we'd better have him in and talk to him." And some poor sod is dragged back from Madrid or Lisbon or Stockholm. They ask a few loaded questions and the poor blighter answers as best he can and in the end everybody's happy. If you're army you probably get a promotion at the end of it for being a good boy.' He laughed. 'If you're a civilian like you you get a night on the town and smiles all round.'

'Who decided that it was my turn?'

'God knows. It's generally some hint from SIS.'

'What's SIS?'

'SIS? They're the so-called professionals. Career intelligence officers. Most of them old hands from Middle East or Far East posts. Charming old boys, but quite useless. They have a rush of blood to the head now and again and hint that some poor wretch in SOE or some other private army is having it off with some floozie whose father is a commie or a member of the Peace Pledge Union. Nobody takes any notice of them. If it's one of ours we go through the motions and everybody's happy.'

'Who suggested me?'

'Honestly, I've no idea.' He laughed. 'Probably picked your name out of a hat. They think it keeps us war-time chappies on our toes.'

'How much longer do you think we've got to go on playing these games?'

'The war, you mean?'

'Yes.'

'Well, with the Americans in with us now it's going to shorten the time, provided the Russians can go on holding out. But it's a fantastic operation organising a landing in France and keeping it supplied and serviced.'

'What do you think? Another year?'

'I've no idea, Henri. I'm not a military man as you know.' He paused. 'Anyway let's go and eat and then we'll go to another little club I know.' He grinned. 'Rather special, Henri. Some really fabulous girls. The best in town.'

As he thought about the two days he felt that he'd come out of it pretty well. Right from the start, when they recruited him, he'd told them about his black market connections with the Germans. They didn't know which Germans. Only Palmer seemed to know that. And from what he had understood Palmer wasn't likely to tell SOE. Westphal had often told him that one of his problems was that in Berlin it was the same, where the three German intelligence services, the *Abwehr*, the *Sicherheitsdienst* and the Gestapo were bitter rivals who never exchanged what they knew.

He wondered if Benoit knew about the interrogation. He was almost sure that he didn't.

17

In the third month in April the network sustained its first casualties. Pierre Jarry, the group leader based in Troyes, had led a forty-strong attack on a German convoy taking supplies to an SS division further east. Jarry's men were well-armed with Sten guns and were well trained, but unexpectedly the convoy had been given extra protection by a detachment of SS from the divisional support group.

The ambush had been set in a steep-sided valley with the main force hidden in dense woods on the northern side of the road and only ten men on the grassy south slopes. It seemed an ideal place for an ambush and in the evaluation later Maclean felt that that was probably the major mistake.

To the trained and experienced fighting men of the SS it would have been equally obvious that it was an ideal place for an ambush. They had fought their way across the whole of Europe and like true professionals they took no unnecessary risks. Surprise had been the main element in the group's plan and their knowledge of the terrain had been the other plus. They knew every inch of the woods and had a plan for drawing the Germans deeper and deeper into the woods to make heavy machine gun fire lose its power because of the density of trees and undergrowth.

The surprise had lasted for about fifteen seconds and then the fire from Stens and rifles had been returned by heavy machine guns and mortars on both sides of the road. The open grassy slopes of the southern side had made the men there hopelessly exposed. Firing hose-pipe the machine guns had fanned across the hillside remorselessly.

Only two men on the hill had been left alive. And the SS group were too canny to leave the cover of the convoy vehicles and take on the main group in the woods.

Eight men had been killed outright. Six had been wounded, one of whom died later that night. The Germans had made no attempt to check the results of their fire-power. They had orders to protect a convoy and when there was no longer any firing from the woods the convoy moved on. So far as they knew there had been no German casualties but a canvas-hooded truck was on fire as the convoy moved off.

The men who had died had shared a joint funeral service and burial at the church of St Urbain in defiance of the local German commander. Germans in civilian clothes had mingled with the large crowd who assembled for the burial service. Maclean and Pierre Jarry were the only members of the network who attended but a priest carried out a small service in a private house that evening for the survivors.

It was a salutary experience and brought home to Maclean what had previously been only an underlying thought. The very basis of his organisation and training of the network made them unsuitable for those military-style forays. Open battle against the occupying forces had its role in the Resistance. It called for great courage and complete commitment, because it had no reward. Against professional soldiers they were inevitably going to suffer many casualties. They could harass Germans, even kill some of them, but the cost was too high. When the time came for supporting the invasion his network could do far more to help the Allies by carefully planning the destruction of strategic targets. And with his insistence on security they would suffer far fewer casualties. It wasn't heroic, but it was effective, and it was his responsibility to stop any further para-military games-playing.

The last weekend in April he spent at La Roserie. Three beautiful, sunny days with Anne-Marie and her mother.

Marie Duchard was much improved. She no longer trembled or sighed so heavily. Her memory was failing and sometimes she burst into tears but she soon recovered. She could remember quite well things from her childhood and when Anne-Marie was a little girl. She could recognise Maclean's face but she had no idea who he was. She never spoke about her ex-husband. The divorce had gone through and Duchard had married his German girl.

On the Sunday the two of them had walked hand-in-hand along the river bank to the place where they had picnicked all those years ago. There were the same pale-red field poppies and white marguerites. He showed her where a reed warbler had built its nest above the water.

'It's going to be a dry summer this year.'

'How do you know that?'

'Reed warblers always build their nest about forty centimetres above the highest point that the water will rise to. Its nest is quite low.'

'How does it know?'

'I've no idea but it always knows. Just like the birds who hoard berries in the autumn against a hard winter. Squirrels do the same with acorns.' He smiled at her. 'When they're wrong it really doesn't matter they just leave what they don't need. After a soft winter you can find their dreys in the roots of trees and under piles of leaves.'

'Do you still paint?'

'Only pot-boilers to earn some money.'

'Why didn't you come to Mendes' wedding?'

'I was too busy.'

'But he's a friend of yours.'

'He's a senior man in my network but there are many others. I don't have time to have friends.'

'But you obviously like him.'

'Of course. I like the others too.'

'How are your parents?'

'I don't really know. I get a letter every couple of months but they can't say much.'

'Do you miss them?'

'No. Not really.'

'They must miss you. Especially your mother.'

'If I were not here I'd be in the army in Africa or flying a plane.'

'What's Tom doing?'

'He's dead. He was in the Royal Naval Reserve. His ship was sunk.'

'Why didn't you tell me before?'

'I didn't think about it.'

She looked up at his face, frowning because the sun was in her eyes. 'I wish I could do something to make you happy. Really happy.'

He smiled. 'Just being here with you makes me happy.'

'But you're always thinking about the other part of your life.'

'I can't help it. A lot of people depend on me thinking.'

'Is it all worth it?'

'You think France should be left for the Germans?'

'No. But if there is an invasion will all this make a difference?'

'The people in London seem to think so.'

'Do you?'

'I don't think about it. I'm neither a politician nor a philosopher.'

'Are you cross with me for asking about it?'

'No. I just don't have the answers.' He paused. 'Is there anything you need that Mendes can't get for you?'

'You mean black market things?'

'No. I mean things I could get sent over from London.'

'Yes, there is something.'

'What?'

'There was a photo of you and me sitting on the steps by the carp pond at Fontainebleau. Your mother had it in a silver frame. Could you get a copy of it for me?'

He smiled. 'I'll try, honey.'

Maclean had taken Tom Price down to the walk alongside the river. They stopped at the boat-house and old Jean-

Paul the boatman gave them coffee and chatted with them. He never acknowledged that he knew what Maclean was doing. He and Loussier had taken several loads of ammunition down the river in one of the boats that Jean-Paul hired out for a few francs. Jean-Paul listened to the French service on the BBC and he told them that London had said that the Afrika Korps had surrendered at Tunis the previous day, and thousands of prisoners had been taken. Maclean had smiled but said nothing, waiting for Price to finish his coffee before they walked on.

'They gave a very good report on you from London, Tom. Seems you did well on your course.'

'I'm surprised. I got the impression they were glad to see the back of me.'

'I gather you know this area quite well. How was that?'

'My mother came from Chartres. We spent a lot of time there when I was a kid. My father was a stone-mason and he spent a lot of time working in Chartres.'

'Do you know Chartres well?'

'I did. It's probably changed since then.'

Maclean smiled. 'Not even the Germans have managed to change it much.' He paused. 'I was thinking of sending you there with one of my men.'

'To do what?'

'There's a safe-house there and a good Frenchman who runs a night-club who would give you cover. There was a network based there that was badly run. It was largely wiped out. I want to build up a new network. Do you think you could do that?'

'I'd like to try. If you think I'm good enough.'

'Spend another week here with Georges Loussier. Ask any questions you like and then we'll get you over. You'll have full local authority and your own supplies. In fact it's easier building up a new network than taking control of an existing one with bad habits.'

Janine was waiting for him when he got back to the bakery. They went upstairs and when he'd closed the door she said, 'An urgent radio message came through for you on the emergency schedule.' She handed him a sheet of paper. He read it carefully. London wanted him back as soon as possible.

'Have you acknowledged it yet?'

'No. I waited for you to confirm.'

'OK. You ack it and confirm for me. I'll let them know when I can go. Do you know where I can find Masson?'

'He's with Brieux at Provins.'

There was a Lysander reception already scheduled for two days' time and he got Janine to inform London that he would be on it.

It had been a Tangmere landing and Mathews was already there with a car.

'Good flight?'

'A bit of flak as we came over the coast otherwise it was quiet all the way.'

'I've booked us in at "The Ship" in Chichester for the night. You've got a busy day tomorrow and I thought you'd better get a good night's sleep. And I want a chat with you anyway.'

They had drunk a lot of coffee and eaten beef sandwiches from the RAF mess and in the empty lounge Mathews said, 'You're going to meet someone very important tomorrow.'

'Who is it?'

'I can't tell you. I don't even know what it's all about. All I was told was to get you over here as soon as possible.' He paused. 'You'll be seeing this person tomorrow after-noon.'

'Have I done something wrong?'

'Quite the opposite. He wants to see you because you've earned a reputation for being a good leader.' He paused. 'The man's office told us he wanted to talk with one of our best men in France. We submitted your name with a report on what you've been doing. Then we got the order to bring you over. This man takes a special interest in SOE. He's on our side. He likes talking to our people when they're back here for a few days.'

'I think I know who you mean, except I can't believe it.'

'I don't want to play guessing games, Phil. Let's just leave it for now.' He stood up and smiled. 'Let's get some sleep, soldier.'

They hadn't gone to Baker Street and Mathews turned the car on to Horse Guards Parade and switched off the engine.

'Somebody else will be taking you to the meeting. Here he is now. He knows your name. When you've finished somebody will bring you to the Travellers' Club. I'll be waiting for you there.' He smiled. 'Best of luck.'

The man was in his fifties and he shook Maclean's hand warmly as he got out of the car. As they walked towards the concrete block-house by the Admiralty Arch the man said, 'When you've had your chat with the PM one of our drivers will take you back to our friend Mathews. But I want you to understand that you are to tell nobody about this meeting or what is said to you. And I mean nobody. Not even your seniors at Baker Street. They won't ask so you'll not be embarrassed in any way. For the rest of the world this meeting never took place. Understand?'

'Yes, sir.'

There was a Royal Marine guard at the main entrance who saluted with his rifle as they went in and then there was an identity check with the civilian vouching for him before he signed the book. A Royal Navy officer led them down two flights of concrete steps, along a short corridor and into a small waiting room. The officer said that the Prime Minister would see Captain Maclean in five minutes' time.

It was nearly fifteen minutes later when a pretty WREN officer opened the door and nodded at the civilian then turned to Maclean.

'The PM's ready to see you now, Captain.'

It was an hour later when Maclean came out of the block, squinting because the sunshine was so bright and unexpected. For a few moments he stood there until he was aware of the driver standing holding the car door open for him.

It was only five minutes' drive to Mathews' club and the club servant escorted him to the Members' lounge where Mathews was reading the evening paper.

Mathews asked no questions and when they went by taxi to Baker Street he was warmly welcomed but the only questions he was asked were about his network. He answered as best he could but his mind was in a whirl trying to grasp the full import of what he had been told.

That night in his hotel room he wrote down a long list of what he needed and the next day he handed it over to Mathews who read it without looking at him before he excused himself and went into another office.

When Mathews came back he said quietly, 'It will take about three Hudson drops. Say ten days altogether. Is that OK?'

'That's fine. Can I get a message to Loussier on tonight's schedule?'

'Yes. Our stuff can wait until tomorrow.' He paused. 'What about you?'

'I can drop from the first Hudson.'

Mathews shook his head. 'We'll lay on a Lysander for you tomorrow night. Let's take no avoidable risks. Is there anything you'd like to do while you're over here?'

'No. I just want to get back.'

18

Masson had organised a landing area for the Lysander that
was well outside Maclean's network area but Loussier had
insisted on being there. Masson was worried that Maclean's
recall to London might be the outcome of his interrogation
by SOE.

Maclean had been surprised when he was told that Roger
Carlton would accompany him on the flight. When he
had asked Mathews what Carlton was doing he had been
unusually evasive.

'Somebody wondered if Masson's contacts with the Germans and the black market were a security problem.'

'If you're dealing in the black market you're bound to
be dealing with the Germans. They're the customers.
They've got the money.'

'What about your chap Brieux. Would you suspect him?'

'Never.'

'Perhaps you should, Phil. Suspicion is insurance.'

'Brieux isn't in the black market. The clothes go to
couture houses in Paris, not to the Germans direct.'

'Well, the powers that be want Roger to give a report
on Masson's operations. He won't be with you. He'll be
based with one of the other networks.'

'Let me know what he reports, will you?'

'Of course.'

The landing, as always, had been uneventful and there had
been no return passenger. Maclean had been aware of the
surprise on Masson's face as he saw Carlton clamber down

the ladder. He watched Masson take Carlton to one side, talking urgently, leaving it to the others to watch the Lysander take off. Carlton put his arm around Masson's shoulders, and turned to wave to Maclean before the two of them disappeared into the darkness.

Then Loussier was walking towards him and as they gripped hands Loussier said, 'We'll have to sleep in the woods tonight. Friend Masson didn't offer us a safe billet.'

'That's OK. Where the hell are we?'

'Just south of Le Mans. Didn't they tell you?'

'No. It was some security problem concerning the other chap.'

'Who is he?'

'None of our business, Georges. He's only here for a week. And nothing to do with us.'

'I did a recce while it was still light, there's a decent place not far away. Good shelter and pine needles. I've brought some coffee and bread and cheese.'

When they had eaten Maclean lay on his back looking up through the trees. There were birds stirring in the trees and bushes and he heard a clock chime the half-hour in the distance.

'What time is it, Georges?'

'Three-thirty. First light at four-thirty.'

'What day is it?'

'Sunday.'

'Remember this day, Georges. It's very special.'

'In what way?'

'In every way. Everything's different after today.'

'What are you on about?'

'Let's go to La Roserie, not to Melun. We've got a lot to talk about.'

'If I didn't know you I'd say you were drunk.'

Maclean laughed softly. 'I am, Georges. I am. Let's go to sleep.'

They took a train to Chartres early the next morning and Picquet drove them to Provins. Brieux took them to

La Roserie. Anne-Marie came running from the orchard, long hair streaming, laughing as she flung her arms around him.

'Why didn't you let me know you were coming?'

'I couldn't. Are you OK?'

'I'm fine.' She leaned back to look at his face. 'Something's changed. You look different.'

'In what way?'

'I don't know.' She laughed. 'Maybe it's just the sunshine.'

He smiled. 'Georges and I are going to talk for a bit in the study. Is that OK?'

She smiled and shrugged. 'Help yourself. You're the boss.'

They sat at the old mahogany table in the study. Maclean not sure how to start and Loussier waiting expectantly. Finally Maclean said quietly, 'Everything's changed, Georges.'

Loussier nodded. 'Tell me.'

'It's going to be much sooner than we all expected. And we've got a key role. We're really in business now. The real thing will start in September or October and we've got to prepare the way for them. All the waiting and all the caution are over. We've been given a free hand. Just one instruction – harass the Germans.'

'You're sure they really mean it?'

'Mean what?'

'That the invasion is September or October.'

Maclean smiled. 'It came from the very top, Georges.' He looked towards the window and then shook his head impatiently. 'We'd better get started.'

'Can this be passed on to the others about the new situation?'

'We'll have a meeting, Georges. With all the group leaders. But you and I have got to have a general plan worked out before we do that.' He looked at Loussier. 'Has the new man Price gone to Chartres yet?'

'He went two days ago.'

'We may need to use Chartres as our base from now on.'

'Tell me more.'

'We've got huge supplies coming over in the next couple of weeks. *Plastique* and detonators, grenades and launchers, automatic weapons and ammo and field radio sets. And a lot of bits and pieces.' He paused. 'They want us to raise hell all through the summer. Bridges, railways, roads, telecommunications, arms dumps, factories working for the Germans and isolated military units that are not too big. They want us to cover our present area and spread the network from Chartres towards the coast as far as we can go.'

'How long have we got to prepare in?'

'It's up to us. They want it as soon as we can get going. Say, the end of this month. Last week in June. OK?'

Loussier smiled. 'Doesn't sound like you, rushing in like this.'

Maclean grinned. 'This is our pay-off, Georges, for being patient. We are the start of it all.' He stood up. 'We need all the maps we can lay our hands on. Where can we get them and then get them copied?'

'Leave it to me.'

'When?'

'Tomorrow maybe. Wednesday for certain.'

Maclean laughed. 'I still can't believe it. And I can't wait to get started.'

Loussier smiled back. 'Looks like I'm going to be the one who has to steady *you* down.' He laughed. 'It'll make a nice change.'

They had made love that night and afterwards she had looked at his face as he lay beside her.

'Something *is* different Philippe. What is it?'

'I'd love to tell you but I can't.'

'Why not?'

'If I told you you'd be a target for the Germans if anything happened to me.'

'But surely they'd assume that I knew anyway. Like they'd assume that Mendes' wife knows that he's in the Resistance.'

'I couldn't bear to think of you being beaten up by those bastards.'

'What about Denise Mendes being beaten up? Doesn't that worry you?'

'She is an active member of the Resistance. She knows the risks they both take.'

She said quietly, 'I think I take the same risks without ever knowing what is happening. And that's unfair.'

'In six months' time I can tell you a lot more. Maybe sooner.'

'Why is it you accept Denise Mendes into the network but not me? Aren't I patriotic enough or brave enough to be a member of the Resistance?'

'Is that what you want?'

'Yes. I want to be on the inside, not outside as if I were a child or a coward.'

For long moments he was silent and then he turned his head to look at her face. 'Do you really understand what the risks are?'

'Of course. I was in Paris. I heard what they did to Resistance people they caught.'

'Like what?'

'Torture, electric-shock treatment, beatings, brutal interrogations.'

'And you'd risk all that happening to you?'

'Of course. Just the same as the others risk it.'

'Why?'

'The same reasons you said you came back.'

'When did I give any reasons?'

'In the café that first time we met after you came back. I asked you why you came back. You said you came back for me and . . .' she shrugged '. . . *la belle France*. I love you just as much as you love me and I care about France. But not as much as I care about you.'

He looked away from her for a moment and then back

at her face, as he said quietly. 'I think maybe I've been very very stupid. Maybe selfish too.'

She smiled. 'What's that mean?'

'It means I'll do a deal.'

'Tell me.'

'If you join the network I want you to marry me as soon as we can arrange it.'

She smiled. 'Mendes can arrange it.'

'How do you know?'

'We talked about it. He knows a priest in Provins who will do it. After we've been to the *mairie*.'

He laughed softly. 'I'll shoot that man.'

'Don't say things like that. Not even as a joke.'

'When can we do it?'

'He needs three days' notice.' She grinned. 'Saturday would be a nice day.'

Brieux had made her a wedding dress and Mendes and Brieux had worked their magic at the *mairie*. Anne-Marie had a genuine birth-certificate but Maclean's in the name of Philippe Benoit had been the work of one of Mendes' ex-girl-friends who was an official at the *mairie*.

They all ate afterwards at the Croix d'Or in the courtyard at the back. Long tables and benches under vines already heavy with unripe grapes. Maclean ate very little but was aware of a tremendous wave of affection and pleasure from their guests.

For almost the first time he was looking at them as friends. Just men; not members of a Resistance network. There was Duras from Fontenay. Tall and thin in his pre-war suit. Talking in those slow measured tones he used as a lawyer in court. The plump Roussel with his round, apple face. Smiling as always, as if the world was a good place to be in. Nobody would have been able to tell from his appearance the chronic sadness that lay behind it. Sadness for an epileptic son and a grief-stricken wife. He had once heard Loussier ask him how he managed to be so cheerful and he remembered Roussel's reply. 'If you want to save someone who is drowning you reach down from the bank. You don't get in the river with them.'

Bazin had come over from Sens. Bazin was a silversmith whose work had been in demand all over Europe before the war. And now it went to Germans and the more successful black-marketeers. He was a quiet, reserved man with a passion for music. A gifted guitarist, embarrassed by his fondness for Wagner. He sat listening to Mendes holding forth on the similarity between Christianity and communism. Smiling from time to time at some extravagance of the pro-Russian young man who had never heard of Tchaikovsky and Rachmaninov.

Jarry was there from Troyes. Jarry with the deep voice and the melting brown eyes that caused such havoc among the women. Quite unaware of the reason for his attraction and fondly believing that it was his skill at bridge that produced so many invitations to an evening meal. He ran an antiquarian bookshop that earned him a bare living.

Picard had a broken ankle and Mercier had come in his place, representing the group at Nogent-sur-Seine. Mercier and Picard were partners doing house repairs and decorating. They had married twin sisters and rumour had it that both were fonder of their sisters-in-law than their wives. Rumour also had it that they had re-arranged their households accordingly. Both men had served in the army and had escaped from a prisoner-of-war convoy in the confusion of the first days after the surrender. Picard looked vaguely Italian and was much in demand by the Troyes amateur dramatic society.

And sitting next to Anne-Marie was Loussier. Fifty years old and stronger and fitter than most men half his age. Both wise and shrewd. A rock. A shaft of sunlight on his lined, tanned face made him look like a painting by Rembrandt as he listened to something that Anne-Marie was saying.

There were toasts to the bride and groom and Alwyn Williams had composed several verses in French which he read with a lovely Welsh lilt.

Maclean sensed that Loussier didn't share his enthusiasm for the new instructions from London. He seemed unconvinced. Even sceptical of Maclean's judgement. Two days after the wedding he decided that maybe he hadn't put the new thinking over well enough and he gathered them together in the study at La Roserie. Anne-Marie, Loussier and Tom Price.

He looked at each one of them as they sat around the small table.

'I want to talk about the change of emphasis in our instructions from London. I may be wrong but I feel that I've not convinced you all.' He smiled. 'Especially my old friend Loussier. I've included Tom Price because he knows the people in London. He can be devil's advocate if you want. And I've included Anne-Marie because she's my wife now and that makes her a prime target for the Germans to get at me. So – Loussier. Any questions?'

Loussier looked at him for several moments before he spoke.

'I'm not doubting your good faith, my friend. But the change worries me. Why so sudden? You heard the words with your own ears, we haven't. Are you sure you interpreted them accurately?'

'Let me tell you, then, what I was told. The Russians have been pressing for a second front, and now the Americans are doing the same. They agree that Britain alone needed a long build-up of men and material before we could invade Europe. But the Americans say that all that is changed. There are the men and the material coming over day after day. They want to get on with it and get it over. They say we are dragging our feet. They want action this year, 1943, not next year.'

'Who was it told you this, skipper?' Tom Price said quietly. 'Was it Gubbins or Buckmaster?'

Maclean shook his head. 'I can't say, Tom. It was much higher than them.'

'You mean somebody higher than them actually told you to your face?'

'Yes. I wasn't allowed to discuss it even with either of them. They obviously knew something but not as much as I had been told.'

Loussier said, 'And you believe this man, whoever he was?'

'Absolutely. Why should he lie to me? I'm not important enough to be lied to.'

Price said, 'How many other networks are involved in the changed plan?'

'As far as I know, none.'

'Why us?'

'Two reasons. First we're in the right place. Second they think we're competent to do it. I suspect that if we succeeded then all the networks will be involved.'

'Are we really so special?' Price said.

'I think that it's partly because we have been so careful, so security minded that they feel that with this support with what we need, we can prove the case for a more aggressive attitude.'

'Have you told us everything they told you?' Price asked.

'No.'

'So tell us the rest.'

'I swore I wouldn't, for security reasons.'

'Did the extra information convince you about the rest?' It was Anne-Marie who spoke, for the first time.

'Yes.'

'That means you feel more obligated to men behind desks than to the network.'

'It doesn't.'

'My God, it does, my friend,' said Loussier angrily. And Tom Price backed him up.

'It does, skipper.'

Maclean stood up and walked over to the window. Looking out over the orchard, but seeing nothing. They were right. But he'd given his word. But they were entitled to know. Their lives were going to be at risk. And the lives of at least two hundred others. He turned slowly and looked at them.

'The invasion will start in the autumn. We've got two months to harass the Germans. It's part of a deception plan so that they miscalculate where the landings will be.'

Loussier said, 'Was it de Gaulle who talked to you?'

'No. It was an Englishman.'

Loussier nodded. 'OK. I'm convinced. You can rely on me not to talk.'

'Me too,' Price said, smiling because he felt that Maclean had justified it all.

19

A week later Tom Price and Picquet had identified a dozen prime targets covering a hundred kilometres to the north-west of Chartres. There were over thirty secondary targets. They all matched London's instructions and covered all forms of communication: telephone exchanges, railways and bridges, transport depots and petrol and oil storage.

In the Scorpio network area Maclean and Loussier had even more potential targets because they knew the area. The set-up in Chartres was operating in virtually unknown territory.

There had been a dozen Hudson drops in just over two weeks and Masson had asked him to tell London to lay off further drops as it was becoming too dangerous.

Another week went by as Maclean informed London that the operation west of Chartres was risky. There weren't enough trained and experienced men left from the old network. He could get far better results concentrating on his own area. But London were adamant. They accepted that it meant taking risks but that was what the top brass wanted.

When he talked it over with Loussier and Price there was only one solution. He would spend alternate weeks in Chartres and Melun. Price would be second-in-command in Chartres and Loussier in charge of Scorpio when Maclean was away. There was mounting pressure from London for them to get started. It seemed a strange reversal of London's previous emphasis on good security and caution.

Three days later they had heard it as the BBC's French service gave out the *messages personnels* – '*Les fleurs du mal et le vin de souvenir*.' Maclean smiled to himself despite the surge of excitement as he heard the chopped up sentences of Baudelaire. The half sentence from Anne-Marie's favourite poem – 'La Chevelure'. Baudelaire, the dandy she thought must have been a bit like Brieux. And tomorrow was the day. The plans were all made, the communications were worked out and the time-table allowed for a cautious start and then, with that experience behind them they would make up for all the waiting, all the caution and all the frustration of watching the Germans humiliate and plunder the nation they envied, the civilisation they could never aspire to.

The next morning they sat in the sunshine on the stone steps under the walls of the Tour de César. Anne-Marie, Loussier, Mendes and Brieux. Courtesy of Mendes they had *baguettes* with brie and strawberries and it was almost a holiday mood. Brieux regaled them with the gossip of *le tout le monde* in Paris and Vichy and nobody uttered a word about what they were about to do. It was as if they were all holding their breath, waiting for something to happen.

Maclean intended to spend four days at La Roserie, waiting to see how the operation went before he moved to Chartres.

The telephone rang just before midnight and when the voice at the other end said, 'Yes' and then hung up Maclean knew that the central telephone exchange at Troyes was now out of action. Half an hour later the telephone rang again and the same word told him that the *Wehrmacht* petrol dump on the outskirts of Montereau had gone up in flames. He stayed up until 3 a.m. for the third call that never came.

Anne-Marie stayed up with him and was aware that the holiday mood had gone. And she knew instinctively that there was going to be no more sitting in the sun and no more laughing until the whole thing was done. It was her first experience of seeing Maclean under pressure and she realised why the men admired him so much. He was calm but his mind was totally involved with what was going on in the darkness of the night. When they finally went to bed he was asleep before she was. But when she awoke he had already gone.

He was back at mid-day but had told her nothing of the night's happenings.

Two days later they had blown the bridge across the Seine at Bray-sur-Seine. Unfortunately only one of the arches had collapsed but lessons had been learned. Not only about the correct place in old stone structures to place explosives but also about checking the timing if it was going to take more than one charge to destroy the target. It was a group under Deval's command who had carried out the operation and they had foolishly ignored the advice of a local stone-mason who had helped build similar bridges in Normandy.

Lisa had picked up Maclean from La Roserie and driven him to Melun where he had walked to the bus station. A grim-faced Loussier was waiting for him. Deval and two of his men had been killed in an attack on a German convoy on its way to Paris.

Maclean frowned. 'I don't understand. There were to be no attacks on German troops for at least five weeks. What happened?'

'It seems they had had warning a few hours earlier that this convoy was going through. Deval got his men together and they ambushed the convoy in the Bois de Valence. They had been told that there was only a handful of riflemen guarding it. It turned out that there were two armoured cars in the convoy. Both with heavy machine guns.'

'And what happened?'

'They let the first armoured car go through and fired on a petrol tanker. And got it. The armoured car went round behind them and they were sitting ducks taking it from both directions.'

'Go on.'

'Two more tankers went up in flames and then the woods were alight and Deval had the choice. He either took his men through the flames or across the fire-breaks which were covered in both directions by the Germans.'

Maclean slowly shook his head. 'My God, how stupid. No planning. Incorrect information and out-weaponed. What's happened to Deval's body?'

'The Germans have got it. And the other two bodies as well.'

'The rest got away?'

'Yes.'

'Anyone injured?'

'One man seriously and two just leg wounds. All three are in the big house near Contençon.'

For long moments Maclean closed his eyes, thinking. Then he said, 'Right, my friend. Make sure one of your doctor friends looks after the three of them. Congratulate them, and send the word round the others that they did a great job.' He paused. 'Where are the bodies?'

'In the prison hospital.'

'OK. Get hold of Mendes. Take him over to Montereau and put together a raiding party with Mendes in charge. Get those bodies out and get them buried with a proper service. The Germans won't dare to stop a church service. See that it's well attended.' He paused. 'Then carry on as planned. I'll be back in a week's time.'

'I thought you'd be angry and raise hell about what they'd done.'

'I am angry. Believe me, I'm angry. They were fools but we're going to need fools like them in the next few weeks. I don't want them demoralised. Nor the local population either. Who can you put in charge of them now?'

'A man named Posso. Half-French, half-Spanish.' He smiled. 'From Corsica.'

Maclean half-smiled. 'Sounds just what they need.'

*   *   *

Maclean stood leaning on his broom in the small kitchen, watching the chef and the *sous-chef* preparing the orders for the night-club customers. There were lavish supplies of everything. Beef, chicken, fresh vegetables, milk, cream, butter and cheese. And all the summer fruits. It was free admission for females but a man had to be a member and membership cards were hard to get and were scrutinised carefully by the coloured man on the door.

Most of the men were officers of the Wehrmacht and the SS, and even officers had to have at least the rank of captain before they were accepted as members. The discrimination had been at the insistence of the local commander, a general. He never patronised the club himself but Picquet supplied a stream of young men to the château that had been taken over as the general's residence.

But the officers who patronised the club went because of the girls. There was a trio playing jazz. Drummer, saxophone and guitar. And they were good. Not that the patrons could tell good jazz from bad. They wouldn't be able to recognise even the old classics like *Mood Indigo* and *Tiger Rag*.

That night there was a girl singer from Paris. A pretty girl from Saigon. Tall and slim, and virtually naked, her honey-coloured skin glistening, her eyes flirting with the men as they moved slowly by clutching their partners. They all said that she was the image of 'La Josephine'. And she was. Even her thin, little-girl voice was the same, and most nights she had to sing *La petite Tonkinoise* and *J'ai deux amours* a dozen times.

Picquet wore a dress suit and bow-tie and was every inch *le patron*. Chatting and laughing with his guests, snapping his fingers to summon a waiter. Escorting the pretty 'companion' to her escort's table having already checked whether he wanted to dine before or after the visit to one of the small but elegant rooms upstairs.

As the late night became early morning it grew a little more raucous. And finally, at 3 a.m., the official closing

140

time, it became a little more *bierkeller* than night-club. But Picquet knew how to deal with it. A nod to the trio and *Wabash Blues* slid away into accompanying voices and clinking beer glasses as rank was forgotten in several choruses of *Wir fahren gegen England*, trailing off into a rather tearful rendering of *Lili Marlene*.

Half an hour later Maclean was sitting alone with Picquet in his flat, drinking black coffee. Real coffee.

Picquet grinned. 'Well, what did you think of our masters?'

'I'm amazed. How did they do it?' He paused. 'It's unbelievable. Those men or men like them conquered the whole of Europe and a chunk of Scandinavia. And they've got nothing the rest of us haven't got. How did they do it? And so easily.'

Picquet laughed harshly. '*They* didn't do it. *We* did it. The French. We knew it was coming. We saw it all the way. We saw them putting tanks against cavalry in Poland. Then Holland, Belgium, Denmark. We had plenty of warnings. But we looked the other way. Pretending it wasn't happening. OK, the Germans had taken Holland and Belgium. They'd won the football game and they'd be going back home in a couple of days. The thought of Germans marching into Paris was just a joke. The subject for some crazy modern film.

'But they came, my friend, and they're still here. And we never put up a fight. OK, we'd lost a war but now we could all go back to where we started as if it hadn't happened.

'You've just seen those men. Colonels, majors and the rest. Like you said. They're just ordinary men. But what did we put up against them? Corrupt politicians, a high society that didn't give a damn about France. Titled whores and crystal-ball gazers who spread the word that all this talk of defence and honour was just so much crap. Why fight? What difference will it make? Maybe the Nazis have got the right ideas. A new Europe.' Picquet leaned forward towards Maclean. 'We had leaders like sheep and nobody knew how to change things.' He paused. 'But we do now, my friend. We are paying those bastards four million francs a day for the pleasure of their company. We're paying our debts to history. We're going to wipe the slate clean again.' He said softly, 'And we won't ever forget the foreigners like you who helped us do it.'

Maclean was slightly embarrassed by the Frenchman's vehemence and he said quickly, 'What plans have you made?'

Picquet stood up and walked over to the far end of the room, moving aside a painting and turning the knob on a new-looking combination lock. He stood blocking out the view of what was inside and took out a folder before closing and locking the safe again and putting back the painting.

He walked back to where Maclean was sitting and put the folder down on the low coffee table before turning to look at Maclean.

'What you asked me to think about doesn't make sense. I don't have enough men, not even with your Englishman.'

'Where is he?'

'He's reconnoitring targets in Evreux and Lisieux. I've already decided the targets in Chartres.' He unfolded a well-worn Michelin map and pointed at the three cities. 'We can't go further towards the coast than Lisieux and only Evreux is worth the risk apart from here in Chartres.' He sighed. 'I have only nine men I can trust. And I mean trust. Nothing more. They are not properly trained in weapons or sabotage. Only four of them are physically fit. But they *are* loyal and they are patriots. And I trust them.'

'What if I bring some of my trained men over here?'

'Unless they know the area it would be useless. The Germans know every inch of the ground. They had training and familiarisation exercises from the day they moved in.'

For a long time Maclean didn't reply and then he said, 'I think we'll just have to take the risk.'

'That's what your predecessor here always said. I'm surprised to hear you saying it.'

'We'll try a couple of targets. If it doesn't go well we'll call it a day and go back to my network area.'

'It's up to you, my friend. I'll do it any way you want.'

'Let's talk again when we've had some sleep.'

'OK. D'you want a girl to sleep with?'

'I got married since I saw you last.'

Picquet smiled. 'Don't be so bloody English.'

Maclean smiled back. 'I'm not English. I'm a Scot.'

Tom Price was shaving in the bathroom when Maclean woke the next morning. He put on his shirt and the two of them sat drinking coffee in the small kitchen.

'How's it going, Tom?'

'Not as bad as I expected. I've got two targets. One in Evreux and one in Lisieux. But I'm going to need a couple of experienced chaps to help my lot here.'

'What are the locals like?'

Price laughed. 'An ex-wrestler, a schoolteacher, an accountant and a real prize – a sergeant-armourer from the Chasseurs Alpins. Wounded in the defence of Paris but escaped and works here in Chartres as a tool-maker for a small machine-shop.' He shrugged. 'There are five others, enthusiasts but that's about all you can say.'

'Tell me about the targets.'

'The one in Evreux is a double target. A main bridge on the northern outskirts with a *Wehrmacht* ammunition and petrol dump on one side. I've recced it and done sketches. But I'd need seven men for that.

'The other is the main telephone exchange in Lisieux. It's French operated but with German control. It's used for most *Wehrmacht* communications between the Normandy coast and Paris.'

'How many men?'

'Two for explosives and some protective fire-power. Say three more men.'

'How long to go?'

'Three days for showing them the ground and briefing them, and we can go.'

'Where will you house them?'

'Picquet has got me a barn near the target at Evreux and the stables at the back of a hotel in Lisieux. I've seen them both and the people are strong supporters. They'll be OK.'

'Which is the easier target?'

'Both about the same but Lisieux is going to be difficult to get away from.'

'OK. You do Evreux and I'll take Lisieux. Let's go downstairs and talk to Picquet.'

20

Early in the evening Maclean had a few guarded words with Loussier on the telephone. From what he could gather from the oblique references it seemed that the Scorpio network would be carrying out two operations that same night. The Germans would take the point. Four attacks over a wide area in one night would really worry them. It meant an organised resistance.

Picquet had paid his contact to supply Maclean's group with food. Good potato soup and a beef sandwich each, with a hunk of cheese from Melun.

They spoke very little as they waited and Maclean knew that they were lacking in self-confidence. But there was no point in haranguing them about patriotism. They were patriotic enough, but they were inexperienced and only a success or two would change them.

They were in place just after midnight. The charge that would blow out the big doors at the rear of the building would be the signal to move in. They had been shown photographs of the interior and a plan of the building and they would be using grenades on the main equipment and pipe bombs with delayed action timers for the generators.

He watched the night shift arrive in a small coach and the day shift take their places in the coach. Two left on cycles and one in a car with a *Wehrmacht* number plate.

Ten minutes later all was quiet and he waved the two men over and watched as they went through the open gates and across to the big double doors. He counted the minutes before they were back. He'd given them three minutes and they were back in four, panting and white-faced.

He assembled the whole group behind him and checked his watch. The timers were set for seven minutes. He took them across the road and set them against the brick wall as he watched the building himself. The two blasts went off together with a sheet of orange flame and as the doors disintegrated, the debris seemed to hang in slow-motion in the air, dust swirling across the forecourt. Then he waved his team into action running ahead of them, kicking debris out of the way as he hurtled into the building.

The man with the Sten gun opened up but kept his line high enough just to get the four operators down on the floor. He stayed on guard as the others swerved past him. Maclean stayed in the main room where the switchboards lined three walls. There were lights flickering on some of them but the operators had been herded into a small store-room. He heard a series of explosions as the control panels in the next room were taken out with grenades and then they were all back. The operators were released and led over to the repair shed and locked in.

Maclean checked that the pipe bombs had been placed and decided that grenades were too dangerous to use on the switchboards and they used the fire-axes to destroy them.

Five minutes later they were climbing over the railings into the park and heading for the small copse of chestnut trees with its undergrowth of briar. As they lay in the darkness they heard the first explosions of the pipe bombs. A few minutes later they heard the fire-engines go past and then the siren of a police car followed by the rasp of *Wehrmacht* motorcycles. They heard shots and Maclean wondered what they could be shooting at. Twice they heard the boots of a German patrol running past the park and the last time one of them had swept the beam of a powerful torch across the park.

* * *

They had watched the park gates being unlocked at 9 a.m. but they had stayed under cover until midday when people were coming into the park to eat their lunch-time food or just sit in the sun. They left in pairs at intervals and made their way to where Picquet was waiting with the van that he used for his supplies. He drove them two at a time as far as the cross-roads on the road to Orbec where they walked to the farmhouse that was owned by the lawyer who was a silent member of the old network and who cooperated with the new team because of his faith in Picquet. It was two days before they were back in Chartres.

Picquet knew more about what had happened than Maclean did. It wasn't all good news. The main telephone exchange had been completely put out of action and had been abandoned by the Germans who had had to call in four mobile field exchanges from Paris, and even with those, *Wehrmacht* communications were on an emergency-only basis. But in a first flush of anger the Germans had shot the three senior telephone exchange staff on the grounds that they had made no effort to resist the raid.

Tom Price's operation had gone smoothly but one man had been killed by debris when the bridge was blown-up. And it looked as though only the petrol dump had gone up and the ammunition dump had been better protected than the reconnaissance had indicated. But the teams were elated with their successes.

Picquet told him that the Germans in the night-club the previous night had talked of nothing but the raids. They had heard of other raids to the east but seemed to have no details. They were obviously both angry and worried and several had wondered if it wasn't a sign that there really was going to be an Allied invasion.

Brieux had picked up Maclean from the farmhouse and driven him back to Provins where Loussier was waiting for him. Brieux had refused to talk about the network operations on Loussier's orders but had hinted that they had been successful.

Loussier was waiting for him in a café on Rue Couverte and when the waitress had brought them each a bowl of soup Maclean looked at Loussier.

'How did it go this end?'

'Everything went more or less to plan. Four good targets spread right across our area.'

'So what's the problem?'

'Who said there was a problem?'

'You told Brieux not to talk to me about the operations. And your face says there's a problem.'

'OK. There's two problems. The first one is that Jarry was killed when we went after an electricity sub-station at Nemours.'

'How did that happen?'

'A *Wehrmacht* motor patrol must have heard the first explosion and Jarry was waiting to check that the other charges went off OK. He heard them coming and was half-way across the *place* when they opened up on him with a machine gun.'

'Why didn't we know about the patrol?'

'We did. I timed the operation to miss it by an hour. They came early.'

'Up to then it had been the same time every day?'

'For ten consecutive days anyway. They should have been on the other side of the town checking the railway sheds.'

'I don't like the sound of that.'

'Neither do I.'

'How long had you planned it?'

'I scheduled it two weeks ahead.'

'Time enough for a tip-off.'

'Yes.'

'Any ideas?'

'None at all.'

'You said you'd got two problems. What's the other?'

'It's here in Provins. Brieux and Mendes.'

'Go on.'

'They're at daggers drawn. Not speaking to each other and neither will work with the other.'

'Why, for God's sake?'

'Politics. Mendes accused Brieux of being a collaborator.'

'On what grounds?'

'That most of his output goes to top Germans.'

'But nothing's changed, has it?'

'No. It's politics. And clashing personalities as well.'

'No wonder Brieux didn't want to talk on the journey.'

'What do you want me to do?'

'I'll go and talk with Brieux now, then I'll get him to take me back to La Roserie. And you tell Mendes to come and see me there tonight at about six.'

'OK.' Loussier smiled. 'I heard rumours that your jobs in Chartres had been successful.'

Maclean shrugged. 'They worked, but only just. My little exercise was pretty amateurish. It was more a training run than the real thing. They've got a lot to learn.' Maclean stood up. 'I'd better go and talk to Brieux. Don't forget about Mendes for tonight.'

'He's the troublemaker, not Brieux.'

Maclean nodded. 'Forget it, Georges. Leave it to me.'

Brieux sat on one of the work-benches eating a *croissant* and cheese. He looked faintly amused as Maclean perched on the cutting table.

'Have you come to read me the Code Napoléon on treason, boss?'

'No. Just tell me what's biting Mendes.'

Brieux shrugged, *croissant* waving in the air. 'Nothing. It's the same old rubbish. Trading with the enemy and a touch of class-warfare.'

'How does class-warfare come into it?'

'My stuff is expensive so only rich people or important officials can afford it. So I'm a traitor to my country and a traitor to the working class. The fact that I never was working class seems to escape him. He's a bigot. A left-wing bigot. And I'm not married so to him that means I must be a homosexual.'

Maclean laughed. 'Does he really think that?'

'He hasn't decided yet.'

'What about all your girl-friends?'

'Ah. That's all a front to cover up my real sexual inclinations.'

'Why has this arisen all of a sudden?'

'It hasn't. It's been there all the time. But the feeling's going around the network that maybe it won't be too long before the Krauts are on their way home.' Brieux smiled. 'They're just practising for when it's all over. People like Mendes are looking for post-war victims. Heads to shave, throats to cut and reputations to ruin.'

'Does it worry you?'

'Not yet. It will when it gets nearer the time.' He grinned. 'But I'll survive. Mendes is like an angry bull, pawing the ground and wondering where to charge.'

'I'm going to talk to him tonight.'

'And then what?'

'I'll get him away from you.' Maclean paused. 'Can you look after the group here in Provins?'

'Of course. No problem.'

'OK. Take care.'

'You too.'

He had found her in the orchard, by the river, where they had always gone when they were young. She was obviously pleased to see him but equally obviously she was lonely.

'Why didn't you phone me just to say hello?'

'There were no phones where I was.'

'Why not?'

He smiled. 'Some idiots had put them out of action to annoy the Germans.'

She smiled. 'So, my idiot, how long can you stay this time?'

'I think maybe as long as a week.'

'Can you take me into town – to Provins?'

'I should think so. Is there something you want?'

'I just want to see people. See that the world still exists.'

'I'm sorry. You must get very bored being here all the time.'

'Not bored – just lonely.'

'It won't be for long, sweetheart. We'll make up for all the wasted time.'

She nodded and smiled. But it was a smile that spoke of cooperation, not of hope or agreement. And he was touched by her loyalty.

Mendes came early and Maclean took him into the small study and poured him a drink of local wine. As he sat looking at the Frenchman he was suddenly aware that Mendes was at least ten years older than he was and yet he was there to be disciplined.

'Georges Loussier has told me about your bad relationship with Brieux. I'd like you to tell me your side of the problem.'

'What if I don't choose to discuss it?'

Maclean shrugged. 'Then I shall have to assume that your quarrel is with me as well.'

'I don't understand?'

'In normal life I'm an artist. I don't think you would class that as being a working-man, would you?'

Mendes saw the half-smile on Maclean's face but he went on. 'And you don't work the black market with Germans either.'

'Brieux's business in Paris is not black market. It's just trade like any shopkeeper does. It just happens that it's the Germans who have that kind of money. And we all benefit from Brieux's position. His van, his car, his *laisser passer*, his comparative freedom to move about.'

'His customers are colonels and generals, not private soldiers or NCOs.'

'And Frenchmen who really are on the black market.

Not just a sack of potatoes or a kilo of beef but men with factories making things for the enemy. Pimps and brothel-keepers. But French.'

'Am I supposed to like him?'

'Do you like Loussier?'

'He's OK.'

'You're really rather a snob, my friend, aren't you? Working-men are OK but everyone else is an enemy. Especially if they speak with a Paris accent or don't get their hands dirty at their work.'

'That's how it is.' Mendes shrugged. 'It's a fact of life.'

'That's rubbish and you know it. The reason you dislike Brieux is because he is sophisticated. He knows his way around in Paris. He knows important people. And he went to the Sorbonne. You're jealous, my friend. Nothing more than that.'

'So what next?'

'It's time you grew up, my friend, and behaved like a man, not a boy. You've got things to learn.'

'And who's going to teach me?'

'I am.'

'How?'

'I want you to be my personal liaison officer with all the group leaders.'

'Why me?'

'You're brave, you're tough, you know what it's all about and I want you to keep me in the picture about everything that's happening. Not the operational stuff but about morale, what they're thinking, who needs a break and who needs a kick up the backside.' Maclean paused. 'Do you think you can do it?'

'If you think I can – then I can. When do I start?'

'As soon as you can hand over your group in Provins to Brieux.'

'They won't like that.'

'So that's your first job. Make them like it.' Maclean smiled. 'Let's go and see Anne-Marie. She gets lonely when I'm not around.'

'How about my wife moves in here to keep her company. She gets lonely too.'

Maclean smiled. '*Touché*. A good idea.'

21

Loussier had already identified a dozen potential targets in the Scorpio area and Maclean, Loussier and Mendes were due to get together to discuss them and to decide who should tackle them and a time-table.

Maclean had sent for Alwyn Williams who set up his radio in the attic of La Roserie. Maclean had sent a detailed report to London of all the completed operations but they had to go by Lysander as they were far too long for radio. London had responded quickly with congratulations and a request for as much action in the next two or three weeks as he could mount.

They sat around the table in the study with the two relevant sheets of Michelin 1/200,000 spread out in front of them. Loussier, as always, was the pessimist.

'If we're going to cover more targets we've got to dilute the group leadership everywhere. Counting you and me in we've got ten really capable leaders and if London want us to increase targets significantly it means ten leaders spread over twenty operations. That's too much.'

'A concentrated effort for three weeks, Georges, and then a month's break.'

Loussier shrugged and pursed his lips in disapproval. 'If that's what you want, chief. So be it.'

'What do you think?' Maclean said as he looked at Mendes.

Mendes smiled. 'They can't wait, chief. They want to get on with it.'

'London have asked us to look at the possibility of taking

out the Radio Paris transmitter at Allouis.' He paused. 'It would not only be a real propaganda victory but it would give the RAF some relief because they're using the transmitter to jam RAF signals.'

Mendes smiled broadly. 'That would be really something. They couldn't hide that. The whole of France – no, the whole of the world – would know we had to be reckoned with.'

'It would take at least a dozen men and that would mean taking them from the other operations. We can't have it both ways.' Loussier shook his head.

Maclean smiled. 'But you agree it would be striking a real blow at the Germans.'

'Yes. There's no doubt about that.'

'OK,' said Maclean. 'Let me have one really good explosives guy and Alwyn Williams and five men who aren't particularly vital to the other operations and I'll take charge of the Radio Paris job.' Maclean looked at Loussier and waited. For long moments Loussier looked back at Maclean and then he said quietly, 'You pick any men you need. You'll need all the help you can get.'

'Can you two organise the other operations and give me time to train my group?'

'When do you want us to start?'

'It'll take me two weeks. The recce and the training. Can you start a continuous programme against them in ten days from now?'

'On the agreed targets?'

'Yes.'

'We've done all the preliminary work. Ten days is ample.'

'OK. I'll leave it to you two.'

22

Maclean had moved back to his room in Melun and travelled up to Paris on the early train. He spent the whole
day in libraries and newspaper offices reading everything
he could find on Radio Paris. It was in a hobby magazine
for amateur radio fans that he found what he wanted. It
was a whole issue devoted to the layout and technical
facilities at Allouis, written by an enthusiast and complete
with photographs of the studios and equipment and technical information beyond Maclean's understanding. And
best of all there was a diagrammatic layout of the whole
site, an aerial photograph and a page of photographs of
many of the technical facilities.

He moved from the table where he was sitting to the tall
racks of books and after checking that he wasn't observed
he slid the magazine inside his jacket. Five minutes later
he left the building and he was back in Melun two hours
later. He sent Lisa down to La Roserie to bring back
Alwyn Williams and his radio.

Williams read the article twice and while he was reading
it Maclean drew out an enlarged sketch of the site layout
from the article. Much of the technical information in
French he couldn't understand, not even when Alwyn
Williams translated it for him.

When Williams put the page aside he said, 'OK. What
is it you want to do?'

'I want to put the whole thing out of action.'

'For how long?'

156

'Permanently, if possible.'

'Forget permanently. If you razed the whole bag of tricks to the ground they could be transmitting again inside three months. I can't talk sense unless you tell me the object of the exercise. I can see that even having Radio Paris off-air for twenty-four hours is great propaganda. Is there anything else you want to do?'

'Yes, the Germans are using the Radio Paris installation to jam RAF signals.'

'They don't operate on anywhere near the same frequencies. It must be a separate transmitter. London could tell us a lot more. Shall I contact them?'

'How long would it take?'

'They've gone on to permanent stand-by watch since you got back from London so I can transmit any time. It's going to be a long transmission but I could go out to one of Lisa's farm people and operate in a field if necessary using the battery pack or maybe a long lead to a tractor. London can check with the Free French and with the BBC's chaps at Daventry, which is a similar layout.'

'OK, Alwyn. As quick as you can.'

It was thirty-six hours later when Williams came back full of quiet confidence.

'I've got all we need to know, skipper. And – I've got the perfect place for when we need long transmissions. It's in a shepherd's hut on top of a hill on one of the farms. A couple of miles from any building and accessible for a tractor but not for normal vehicles.'

'Tell me what you've got from London.'

'Have you got the layout plan?'

Maclean laid out his own enlarged sketch of the site and the buildings. Williams looked at it for a moment and then pointed.

'London said don't waste time destroying studio equipment because it can be replaced in days. Just concentrate on the transmitters and the transformers.'

'That means four targets. Two of each.'

'Yes. But the transformers will need heavy charges to destroy them.'

'And how long could the station be off the air?'

'London says two weeks but it means they'll have to rob German radio stations for replacements to get it back on air that quickly.'

'Which farm were you at?'

'The one at Aubigny. *Les Trois Corbeaux*.'

'Is that the elderly brothers' place?'

'Yes. That's the one.'

'Is there enough room there for seven of us?'

'There are three stone-built barns that are dry and could be quite safe and comfortable.'

'OK. Find old Pierre and get him down to Loussier at Provins and tell him to send my chaps direct to the farm. I've got a call to make and I'll join you at the farm in a couple of hours.'

Maclean used the phone by the Town Hall to call Picquet in Chartres. Tom Price was actually at the club and Maclean told him to come over on the bus and contact Lisa who would tell him what to do.

Two days later they were all together at the farm. Price, Williams and Maclean and five men sent by Loussier who had been generous in his selection. He had included Duras who was not only the experienced leader of the group at Fontenay Trésigny but with many years of experience as a blaster at a local stone quarry, whose knowledge would be invaluable.

While he was waiting for the five men and Price to arrive Maclean had cycled to the radio site and covered the whole of the perimeter. He circled it twice but waited until he was back at the barn before he made his sketches and notes. He sent Williams the next morning to check whether the perimeter fence was just barbed-wire or whether there was an alarm wire as well.

Surprisingly there was no alarm wire and the only armed

guards were on the entrance gates. The guards were *Wehrmacht* infantry supported by uniformed Milice. It seemed neither the Germans nor the French authorities anticipated any sort of attack on the station. There was a German ack-ack unit on the far side of the installation but outside the perimeter wire. Some gossiping locals had told Williams that the searchlights were part of the outer air-defence ring protecting Paris but were only used if there was an actual raid in progress.

Maclean had made a rough scale model of the site with sand, and with sticks marking out the perimeter, in a corner of the barn, and had carefully placed appropriately sized stones to show the placement of the buildings with the three places they were concerned with marked with white chalk.

The nearest target building was no more than a hundred metres from the perimeter fence but it was within sight of the guard-room and over totally exposed ground. There would be a three-quarter moon when they were due to go in but there was an alternative route that was almost twice the distance but far away from the guard-room and providing the cover of a small copse at the side of the road. It was bad practice to use the same route coming out as you used going in, but in this case it seemed the simplest solution.

There had only been one Tommy-gun available, the others had to be Stens. Neither Maclean nor Tom Price liked using mixed weapons but the reliability of the Thompson sub-machine gun and the frequent stoppages on Stens made the mixed weapons a necessity. There was a Bren available but it was too bulky and heavy for a quick in and out operation. Maclean always saw it as an infantry weapon not a raid weapon despite its undoubted fire-power.

They had erected a set of posts at the far side of the field and laced them with barbed-wire from the farm store and two men had practised again and again cutting an entrance through the wire, and Maclean had made them go through the process again at night, not only cutting the wire but crawling through and making good so that the entrance was not clearly visible to a patrolling guard.

Two of them unloaded the ancient bicycles from Lisa's van and they were passed quickly from hand to hand and shoved into the bushes. The rest of them jumped down and disappeared into the trees one by one, and then Lisa turned the van and headed back to Melun. It was an hour before the 9 p.m. curfew.

Rain had been threatening all day but the wind had kept the clouds moving across the sky and the almost full moon was low on the horizon. It wasn't autumn but the summer was beginning to turn. The darkness was filled with the stirring of birds and small animals disturbed by the presence of strangers.

Maclean gathered the group together with one of them acting as look-out in the bushes at the edge of the road, a few yards from the woods.

Most of the staff at the radio station went home just after 10 p.m. when the broadcasts finished, and from then on there were only maintenance engineers on duty. They knew almost nothing about the auxiliary transmitter that was used for jamming RAF signals traffic, but it was assumed that it was not only in operation twenty-four hours a day but that it was operated by German staff, probably Luftwaffe controlled. Fortunately the two transmitters were in the same building. There was no guard or staff in the building housing the transformers.

The clicks of the wire-cutters seemed to echo in the stillness of the night but they rolled back the wire easily enough so that everyone went through barely having to crouch. Tom Price took the two men to the transformer building and Maclean took the others to the side door of the transmitter area. A crow-bar levered the locked door open and they headed for the transmitter room. Down a corridor to where a red lamp shone over a door marked 'No Entry'. As the door swung open Maclean saw that apart from a man in

Luftwaffe uniform and a civilian drinking coffee there were no other people on duty. The uniformed man was sitting at a control panel watching a needle swinging in a glass-faced meter. He was smiling as he turned to see who had come into the room. The smile froze as he saw the gun pointing at him.

The civilian reached for a red telephone and screamed as the barrel of the Sten smashed down on his hand. Maclean told them that they wouldn't be hurt if they did what they were told. They were tied up and gagged and dragged into a small adjoining office as Maclean and one of his men placed the explosives on the equipment and set the timers for fifteen minutes.

They ran back down the corridor and out of the building, and Maclean heard the first of four explosions from the transformer area and guessed that their timers had been faulty and hoped that Price's party had got away before the first explosion. They were going through the wire when the first explosion came from the transmitter room. Then three or four together and the tiles from the roof flying in all directions and flames against the night sky. There were distant shouts and then the wail of an alarm as they ran across the road. Maclean helped his men cache the guns in a hole they had already dug and when it was covered with dry leaves and a fallen branch he sent them on their way.

For a few moments he stood with his cycle watching the lights and car headlights inside the radio station perimeter and then he wheeled his cycle to the path along the edge of the field, and twenty minutes later he was back at the farm. All his men were already back.

He stayed up until dawn broke but Tom Price and his men didn't come back. The others had talked about them having to scatter in some other direction for some reason. But Maclean had known in his heart that he wouldn't see them again when he had heard the premature explosions from the transformer booth. There had been too many faulty timers on detonators. When it was a matter of hours, that didn't matter, but when it was only minutes involved it was dangerous.

Radio Paris had been off the air for two weeks and during that time Loussier and Maclean had organised and led raids that had destroyed vital locks on a canal, the stores of machined parts at a factory making tank engine parts, the precision equipment of an optical instrument manufacturer making rifle sights and camera lenses for the German Navy, and had destroyed by fire three thousand truck tyres at a German transport depot.

But these successes gave Maclean no satisfaction. The day after the attack the word had come back that Tom Price, Duras and the other man had all died in the premature explosion. There had been virtually nothing left of their bodies. Throwing himself into the intensive programme of sabotage should have had some anodyne effect but his depression was increased by the ruthless German reaction to the series of raids. Hostages were shot, harsh curfews were imposed across the whole area and the civil population were being systematically harassed.

Loussier seemed to be less affected by what was happening. He was more realistic. They had done great damage to German morale and despite the harassment the civil population had taken heart from the wide-spread offensive against the Germans. London were full of praise and encouragement to continue the campaign. But for Maclean he was suddenly beset by doubts. Not rational doubts, but the same kind of doubts that he had had the first day he landed in France. Doubts about his own capabilities and his judgement. Doubts about the worth of what he was doing. Doubts about whether it all really mattered. But he was alone with his doubts. Loussier, Mendes and the others were thirsting for more action.

He walked down to the church and risked a telephone call to La Roserie. It had been a stilted, banal conversation and as he lay in bed that night he wondered if it wouldn't be sensible to take a few weeks off and spend the last few weeks of sunshine with Anne-Marie.

As he lay back on the bed he saw the flicker of summer lightning across the night sky and a distant rumble of thunder.

There had been no noise, no shouts, they just stood there, one shining a torch in his face as he leaned up on one elbow and another grabbing at his hair. And then the lights came on and he saw that the room was full of men. Seven or eight of them. Two in SS uniform. When he opened his mouth to speak a fist crashed into his face and he was being dragged off the bed. Something struck his head from behind and a red curtain covered his eyes as his body sagged to the floor.

23

He could hear a man groaning as he came to, and then he realised that it was himself. One eye was closed and the back of his head was throbbing. For a few moments he was aware that he was in a moving car and then it all faded away.

He was still unconscious when they turned into the double gates of the house on Avenue Foch, and five minutes later he was lying on the concrete floor of one of the cells that had once been the servants' quarters that lined the long corridor.

When he eventually came to he dragged himself up on to the ramshackle bed and looked around the cell. There were bars from top to bottom on the side facing the corridor, the other walls were concrete with a light covered by a metal grille in the ceiling. There was a heavy lock on the cell door. He had no clear recollection of what had happened and no idea where he was.

It was an hour before he had a visitor. A middle-aged man in the uniform of an SS *Hauptsturmführer*. A *Wehrmacht* corporal unlocked the cell door and swung it open and the SS captain walked inside.

For long moments he looked at Maclean, his eyes taking in the dried blood on his face and around his mouth. With his blond hair and blue eyes he could have been a German.

'So,' he said. 'Not a good day for network Scorpio.'

Maclean said nothing, partly because he wasn't sure that he had the strength to speak. The man spoke in French.

'I'm going to take you to talk with one of our officers.

I'd advise you sincerely to cooperate. It will make a difference as to how you are dealt with.'

He reached forward and tugged at Maclean's torn jacket, steadying him as he got to his feet. His head swam as he stood up, and the walk down the corridor seemed interminable. He was aware of a door opening and bright lights in a room, and a well-dressed man in civilian clothing. There was a wooden chair in front of the desk and the man behind the desk pointed to it.

When Maclean sat down the SS captain left the room. The man behind the desk was tall and good-looking, smiling as he offered Maclean a cigarette. When he spoke it was in English.

'Do you prefer to speak French or English?'

Maclean shrugged and felt a stab of pain at the back of his head.

'OK. Let's talk English.' He paused. 'When you had your training at Wanborough you were told about how to behave when you were arrested and interrogated.' He smiled. 'Name, rank and number, and all that. What they probably didn't mention was that that was what you were required to supply under the Geneva Convention as a soldier or an airman. However, we do not recognise you as a soldier. You are a civilian who has engaged in sabotage and murder against the lawful Occupying Power in France. So . . . my friend . . . that is the basis on which we act. The penalties for your actions are severe. Tried by a military court you will be treated as a spy. And the penalty for espionage is death.' He paused. 'You understand that?'

Maclean said nothing, but his interrogator did not seem put out by his silence.

'At the same time that you were arrested your fellow conspirators were arrested too.' He glanced at a paper on his desk. 'Loussier, Mendes, Williams, Picquet, Brieux . . . and many others.

'We have a very detailed picture of your activities but there are some things that we still want to know or confirm. Those are the things I want to discuss with you.' He held up his hand. 'Not today. I'll have a doctor check you over and we'll talk again in a few days' time.'

He reached over and pressed a button on a panel on his desk and the guard came back in and took Maclean back to his cell.

A medical orderly had come to the cell that evening with a trolley, a bowl of warm water and an array of medical things. Plaster, bandages, several bottles and a few inches of a roll of cotton wool.

He had cleaned up Maclean's bloody face and applied some sort of disinfectant to the cuts and bruises, clipping off the hair at the back of his head and laying on a pad of cottonwool before bandaging it. He had checked Maclean's pulse and taken his temperature, and after making notes on a pad he had left and the cell door had been locked again.

An hour later he was given a bowl of soup and a piece of acorn bread. He wasn't hungry but he ate them to keep up his strength. And to take his mind off the wild, mad thoughts and the sickening, hammering pain.

They had left him alone for a week but they'd gone through all that in his training. It was part of the system to break down his morale. He had been given one meal a day and they had taken off the head bandage on the seventh day. He had marked the days on the wall but he didn't know how long he had been unconscious. But he knew now where he was. He was in the *Sicherheitsdienst* HQ in the Avenue Foch.

He knew now that their method worked. Day after day his small store of resolve melted away. The network had had its fling and the professionals had decided that it was enough. And in one night all the courage and the patriotism went for nought, brushed aside like a troublesome fly with one wave of the hand. But what drained him most was his lack of information. What had happened to Anne-Marie, had Janine been able to inform London, and were the Germans bluffing when they told him the names and claimed that they were prisoners too?

There were hours when he said out loud the multiplication tables, recited nursery rhymes and bits from the Bible to keep his mind free of his real thoughts. But when, in the middle of the night the thoughts came unbidden, they were never clear. A feeling of guilt and failure. The failure was real and actual, he could understand that. But the guilt. Guilt for what? Was it guilt for involving all the others, guilt for abandoning his long demanded security, or guilt for naively accepting London's orders to abandon all he had been taught and go for the Germans? And behind it all was the doubt that any of it was really worth the candle. The whole of the so-called Resistance wouldn't shorten the war by a single day.

On the day when he put the eighth marker on his cell wall he was taken back to the man who had talked to him.

He was greeted amiably and again shown to the chair.

'Now, Monsieur Benoit . . .' he paused, smiling, '. . . or perhaps we can agree that your actual name is Maclean. Philip Maclean. A good Scottish name.'

When Maclean didn't respond the man went on. 'Perhaps before we talk you might like to look at these.' He picked up a dozen or more sheets of paper and handed them to Maclean.

The top sheet was a photo-copy of a letter he had written to his mother six months earlier. It was brief and banal and gave nothing away. But the next five pages were photocopies of his situation reports to Baker Street, which gave names and locations and were totally damning evidence. Two of the pages were of request lists of ammunition and supplies for two Hudson drops. And the last page was part of a revised radio schedule with new warning codewords.

He put the papers back on the desk and the man looked back at him.

'You must have wondered if we were bluffing when I told you that your network was in our hands. As you'll see – we were not bluffing.' He paused and looked at Maclean.

'All I ask is that you tell me where your arms caches are located. In return for that I can offer you certain benefits. The main benefit being that you and your people will be treated as prisoners-of-war, not as saboteurs or spies.'

'Can I see a list of those people who you have arrested?'

The man smiled but shook his head. 'I'm afraid not.' He shrugged. 'The control and rounding-up of your network was on Berlin's orders. They take a very tough attitude to your operations.'

'You say control. What does that mean?'

For a few moments the man was silent. Then he said, 'We've been puzzled by certain aspects. You changed from carefully controlled operations to what seemed to us to be throwing all caution to the winds. As if you were deliberately drawing attention to yourselves. We wondered why. We thought that Baker Street must be playing some elaborate game with us.'

'How did you get hold of that?' Maclean pointed at the papers on the desk.

'Let me say that you've been under surveillance ever since you arrived. More than that I can't say.'

'Who was the traitor?'

The man smiled. 'Maybe you should look in London for that.' He paused. 'Now. The arms caches.'

Maclean shook his head. 'I claim I am an officer in the British Army with the rank of captain and as you know, my name is Maclean, and my army number is 10350556. I ask for the protection of the Geneva Convention and that the Swiss Red Cross be notified of my arrest.'

'You're quite, quite sure? Would you like a couple of days to think about it. Not just for yourself but for your men?'

'I won't change my mind.'

'I used to know one of your chaps before the war. A chap named Palmer. Clive Palmer. Met him several times in Berlin.' The man smiled. 'Tried to recruit me. Pretending to be a journalist. Do you know him?'

'No.'

The man stood up, smiling. 'And if you did you wouldn't tell me, eh.' He stretched his arms. 'Well, I'm sorry we couldn't cooperate.' He shrugged. 'So on your head be it, I'm afraid.'

He never knew whether they did it deliberately but as he passed the other cells on the way to his own he caught sight of Mendes and Brieux in separate cells.

A week later he was driven in a van to Fresnes prison and ten days later his legs were shackled and he shuffled on to a cattle wagon on a siding near the Gare de l'Est.

It had taken ten days to get to the final destination. Ten days with a mug of greasy soup and a tin cup of water as the daily ration. Ten days of clanking wheels, curses and shouting in German at the daily stop, and the cries and curses, stench and screams of thirty-five men in the same wagon.

They arrived late at night and were ordered out on to a siding that faced a wide archway with a banner that read '*Arbeit macht Frei*' – 'Work makes you free'. A Germanic jest that a few would remember for the rest of their lives even though they prayed to forget. But it would be very few who survived the welcoming banner to Auschwitz.

Part Two

1

Harry Chapman stopped the taxi by the Imperial War Museum and walked the rest of the way to Century House. It seemed strange being back in London after the months in Germany with the *Grenzpolizei*. They kept a very low profile but they were incredibly efficient. They knew every metre of that grim border between the two Germanies. Every tree, every mine, every auto-alarm and every inch of barbed-wire. There was a detailed dossier on every guard on the other side, details of rotas and the chain of command. And in the safe in its steel reinforced concrete block were the details of the five safe-crossing points and two plans for emergency crossings where there was only a fifty-fifty chance that the right man would be on duty on the other side. It had taken years of patient, assiduous probing of hundreds of men. Details of their family histories, their own life-styles, strengths and weaknesses, vices and virtues. Surprisingly enough even virtue could provide a subtle pressure point. The *Grenzpolizei* of the Federal German Republic knew more about what was going on on the other side of that ominous frontier than the Soviets and the East Germans themselves.

It had taken six weeks for them to plan how to get his man over, and another six weeks to put the plan into action. But it had been smooth, efficient and as uneventful as if there were no dogs, no mines, no guards and no barbed-wire. SIS were sharing the results of the interrogation with the BND at Pullach and both parties were well satisfied with the deal.

As he checked in at the security desk there was a message for him to see Travers as soon as possible.

Travers was talking on the phone when Chapman walked in and he smiled and pointed at the chair. When he hung up he leaned back in his chair.

'I haven't seen you since you got back from Germany.' He paused. 'I gather that everybody's happy with the results.' He paused again and then said, 'Anyway that's not why I wanted to see you.' He shifted in his chair as if it were going to be a long session. 'Have you ever heard of an SOE chap called Masson?'

'No.' Chapman smiled. 'SOE was a bit before my time.'

'That's why I picked you for this job. We want you to look into the wartime activities of this man. There was a question about him in the House.' Travers pointed at a slim buff file. 'There's a copy of the extract from Hansard in the file. An MP alleges that Masson was working for SOE and SIS at the same time and also working for the Germans.'

Chapman smiled. 'Sounds highly unlikely. Was he?'

Travers pursed his lips. 'That's the problem. It's all a long time ago. Nobody knows. I understand SOE thought he was working solely for them. They had no idea he was also working with SIS. If he was. And I'm sure they wouldn't have agreed to it. The Germans knew he was SOE, that's why they used him of course.' Travers paused. 'I say all that but I can't substantiate any of it. Sir Martin wants us to find out the truth.'

'Where can I find Masson?'

'You can't. He's dead. Died in a plane crash in Vientiane.' He paused and smiled wryly. 'At least he's supposed to have died in that crash, but with a man like him, who knows?'

'Any idea where I should start?'

'Read the file, such as it is and we'll talk again.'

As Chapman was leaving Travers said, 'Keep it low-key. We don't want to make a song and dance about it.'

Chapman opened his mouth to speak and then changed his mind, acknowledging the comment with just a brief nod.

Chapman had had to complete his de-briefing from the German operation and it was late afternoon before he opened the Masson file. After what Travers had said he hadn't expected much but it was even less than he had expected. But he read the dozen or so items slowly and carefully.

He made careful notes of names and places and then listed them against the relevant documents from the file.

At the top of the list was a photostat of a Reuters press cable to their Paris office. The cable said,

FUNERAL OF FRENCH PILOT HENRI MASSON VIENTIANE, 23 NOVEMBER (REUTER) — THIS MORNING AT THE CHRISTIAN CEMETERY AT VIENTIANE THE FUNERAL TOOK PLACE OF HENRI MASSON FRENCH PILOT DISTINGUISHED BY HIS HEROISM IN WORLD WAR TWO.

His pencilled note alongside said,
(*a*) Where the hell is Vientiane?
(*b*) Check Reuters.
(*c*) Survivors? Who identified body?
(*d*) Exhumation?
(*e*) Purpose of flight?

A separate page listed other points.

1. Who can I talk to who was in SOE in those days? (Sir Martin?)
2. Who can I talk to in SIS? (Sir Martin?)
3. Surviving members of Scorpio network.
4. Relevant documents in Public Record Office.
5. What was Masson supposed to have done?

* * *

As he slid the file and his notes into the drawer of his desk he leaned back in his chair and closed his eyes. He wondered if this assignment was some sort of down-grading, some indication that he was out of favour. Nothing about it caught his imagination. There was none of the tension and sense of urgency that usually came with a new assignment. This job was just a piecing together of old history. Obviously no more than an insurance policy against further questions in the House or in the media. Whatever he uncovered didn't really matter. It was all a long time ago. All sorts of rumours had their day in war-time. And from his brief look at the file it looked as if half the people concerned were dead or their present whereabouts unknown.

He opened his eyes, stood up and walked over to the window. It was the first day of spring but the wind was blowing sudden gusts of rain against the window.

She stood watching him from the open kitchen door. He had found a second-hand LP of Korngold's Violin Concerto and was listening to it intently, head to one side, his eyes closed. Despite the strong jaw and the muscles of determination by his mouth it was still a boy's face and rather deceptive because of that. It was deceptive in other ways too. The red hair didn't go with a short temper and the freckles were not a badge of open innocence. Even that genuine love of schmaltzy music was slightly deceptive. It bespoke a heart that could be easily moved but it was the other side of the coin that had a cynical mind, a disbelieving mind as its obverse. Harry Chapman was a strange mixture of vices and virtues that she loved but had never completely worked out. A strange mixture of old-fashioned morality and a ruthlessness that she attri-buted to his job.

Like most SIS wives she knew more about what he did than he had ever told her. SIS wives, once you were accepted in the closed circle, compared notes just as other wives did. SIS didn't mind, it helped without being openly approved. Merely tolerated. Marriage was highly desirable in SIS thinking. The fact that it was a spurious stability in some cases didn't destroy the general theory. When a man left for Century House in the morning and friends were due for dinner that evening and the next time she heard from him was a phone call ten days later from Ankara or Rio it could be more stoically borne by a wife than a lover.

When the record finished she said, 'What would you like for your birthday?'

He turned, surprised and frowning. 'My birthday's two months away.'

She smiled. 'Three actually. Judy asked me. She wants to start saving up.'

He looked relieved, and pleased. 'That was decent of her. She seems to be growing up fast these days.'

'She *is* seventeen, Harry. So what can I tell her?'

He laughed. 'What sort of expenditure did she have in mind?'

'I think a tenner would be about right.'

'Well,' he said slowly, 'there's a very nice fiddle concerto by Vieuxtemps with Perelman and Barenboim.'

She laughed softly and walked over to him, putting her hands on his shoulders. 'And what do you want from me?'

'Nothing. Honestly. Just you.'

'You look a bit down. Are you?'

'Just a bit.'

'Why?'

'They've given me a rather routine assignment. It seems a bit of a come-down after the last thing in Germany.'

'Perhaps they think that it might be a good thing if you free-wheeled for a bit. You can't have tension all the while or you'd go crazy.'

'You're probably right but it's a bit routine, too low-key.'

'In what way?'

'I've got to check on something that happened in the war. A possible traitor. He's dead anyway. It's just a police job really. More MI5 than us. But it was in France not here, so it's the old firm.'

'Does that mean you'll be away again?'

'Yes. But only for a few days at a time. I'll be back here regularly.'

'Any chance of taking me with you?'

He shook his head. 'I'm afraid not, honey.'

'Ah well. Don't forget it's speech-day for Judy tomorrow at three.'

'Have I got to go?'

'Of course you have.'

'I've just remembered. I've got to see Sir Martin tomorrow. I may not be able to make it.'

'Well, try. She'll be disappointed if you're not there.'

'What are we doing tonight?'

'Taking your dad to see *The Phantom*.'

He laughed. 'Why did he choose that?'

'Because he likes Sarah Brightman, thinks she's the spitting image of Jessie Matthews.'

He laughed. 'It was always Jessie Matthews. And Al Bowley of course. And for Ma it was Anne Ziegler and Webster Booth.'

2

Sir Martin had been Director-General of SIS for over seven years. Brought in as a stop-gap when both MI5 and MI6 were under pressure from Whitehall, the media, and any politician who needed a headline in his constituency's weekly. He had been seen as both a calming influence on internal feuding and politically sure-footed enough to deal with outsiders. The fact that he was an insider, rather than some senior policeman brought in to tame the wild men, had paid good dividends.

When Travers had arranged for Chapman to speak to him Sir Martin had suggested that they had lunch together at his Chelsea Home.

It had been a buffet lunch with sandwiches laid out on a low table with a row of bottles and a thermos of coffee and they talked as they ate.

'Which were you, sir, at that time? SIS or SOE?'

'I was SOE. I started in Field Security as an officer in the Intelligence Corps and when SOE were in a hurry to recruit people I was transferred.'

'The MP said that the man concerned worked for both SOE and SIS. Was that possible?'

'Oh, no. Quite out of the question. The two organisations were rivals. Competing for staff, money, resources, planes and areas of influence. It's fair to say that the antipathy was quite one-sided – in the early stages at least – SIS looked on SOE as a bunch of amateurs ruining SIS's enterprises in France and elsewhere. As far as SOE goes only the top brass had any idea what SIS did for a living.

'You've got to remember that in those early days after the fall of France everything had changed. The whole world was shocked, and Churchill created SOE "to set Europe ablaze", to use his own words. But SIS had its own people in Europe with different objectives. They had been there for years before the war, to gather intelligence and get it back to London. With SOE briefed to carry out sabotage and general mayhem, gathering intelligence quietly and efficiently by SIS agents wasn't possible. Or at least it was made a hell of a lot harder.'

'Who recruited Masson?'

'He came down an escape route from Marseilles with a vague recommendation from some American consular official in Vichy. He was passed on to SOE because he was an experienced pilot who said he wanted to assist any way he could. We were having a lot of problems at that time with landings of Lysanders and even with parachute drops because of inexperienced chaps on the other side. I'm not sure who offered him to us but I guess he was snapped up. He became the despatch and reception controller for several SOE networks in France. The RAF at Tempsford said at the time that he was doing an excellent job.'

'Mr Travers said that the MP who raised the question in the House had a brother in SOE. Did you know him?'

'I didn't know him. I'd heard of him. He was with a network south of Paris. A first-class man who was caught by the Gestapo and died in a concentration camp.'

'What happened to SOE's official records?'

Sir Martin hesitated and then said, 'They were handed over to SIS about September 1945.'

'Why to them if they were rivals?'

'Well, they weren't officially rivals of course, and in the internal struggles when SOE was founded SIS claimed control of SOE's supplies and services, including control of their flights. And they were given those controls as a sop to get SOE up and running.'

'So those records are somewhere in our archives?'

'I'm afraid not. SIS destroyed them as soon as they got their hands on them.'

Chapman looked at Sir Martin's face as he asked his next question.

'Why did nobody from SOE stop them?'

'For a very simple reason – they didn't know it was happening.' He paused. 'I only found out recently myself.' He shrugged. 'There were a lot of other things occupying our minds at the time. They seemed more pressing.'

'Do you think there's any possibility that SIS had something to hide as well as just dislike of SOE?'

Sir Martin frowned. 'I really don't think you should expect an answer from me on that score.'

'I'm sorry, sir. I guess that's answer enough.'

'What does that mean?'

'If you thought SIS had nothing to hide I'm sure you would have said so.'

Sir Martin said quietly, 'I'll have to stop our chat now.' He pointed at a folder on the table. 'I've made some notes for you. A few names and bits of background that might help you.' He stood up. 'Don't hesitate to talk with me again if you need to. Just say the word to Travers and he'll arrange it.' He smiled, but this time it was a diplomat's routine smile. All mouth and no eyes, as he held out his hand. 'Best of luck.'

The notes that Sir Martin had handed to him gave the names and last known addresses of four Frenchmen. There were also the names of three Germans.

Chapman put in the call to the Paris Embassy without much hope. But Patterson was an old friend.

'I want some help, Joe.'

'Official or unofficial?'

'Official but off the record.'

Patterson said drily, 'I don't keep records, Harry, no staff. What is it?'

'I'm trying to trace the widow of an SOE officer named

Maclean. Philip Maclean. That should mean she's a British citizen.'

'What the hell do you want with her?'

'D'you know her?'

'You bet. She's a real pain in the neck.'

'Tell me more.'

'There was some problem way back about her widow's pension. She wrote to one of the newspapers here to say she'd been swindled by the Brits. She tried claiming damages through some lawyer here, claiming the British were responsible for her husband's death. We get frosty letters from her from time to time. All passed to me because I'm SIS and he was SOE.'

'Have you got an address for her?'

'I'll have to look it up. I'll telex it to you. OK?'

'Thanks. Anything else on the woman?'

'She doesn't use her married name. Uses her single name. Duchard. That's part of the protest.'

The plane landed on time at de Gaulle and Chapman took a taxi to the small hotel in the Rue des Capucines. There was no restaurant but it was clean and central. And it was well inside Facilities per diem allowance for routine accommodation.

After he had checked in and taken his bag to his room he sat on the bed and checked the street map. It looked as if it wasn't going to be a very useful interview but it had to be done.

The address was a flat in an old house in one of the side roads off the Rue St Antoine. At street level there was a flower shop and a bakery. He made his way up to the first floor. There was a printed card on the door – Mme A.-M. Duchard. He rang twice before the door was opened by a tall, elegant woman. She spoke softly, with a Parisian accent.

'Can I help you?'

'Are you Madame Maclean?'

She frowned, head tilted to one side. 'Who are you?'

'My name's Chapman. Harry Chapman.' He hesitated. 'I'd be grateful if I could talk with you about your husband. Your late husband.'

'Are you a journalist?'

'No. I'm an intelligence officer.'

She looked surprised. 'British?'

'Yes. I have an identity card if you'd like to see it.'

The steady brown eyes looked back at him. 'You must be mad.' She was closing the door but he put his hand against it to prevent it closing. 'Have you heard of a man named Masson? Henri Masson?'

She looked back at him. 'What about him?'

'I've been ordered to check on Masson's activities during the war. I was told you might be able to help me.'

'Who told you that?'

'Sir Martin McTaggart. He's the Director-General of MI6, but he was in SOE during the war.'

'A lucky man to have survived. He must have sat behind a desk in Baker Street, yes?'

'I don't know.' He paused. 'It's been suggested that Masson betrayed your husband's network to the Germans.'

'Everybody betrayed my husband and his network.'

'Why not tell me about what you think happened.'

For a moment she hesitated and then she said quietly, 'Why not?'

She opened the door and turned away with Chapman following her, stopping to close the outside door. She stood waiting for him at the end of the short hallway, pointing to the open door of a large room.

The room was sparsely furnished with a bergère style settee and three armchairs and a low, glass-topped coffee table. One wall was entirely covered with books and there was a large old-fashioned desk under the tall window with a small typewriter and what looked like a pile of manuscripts beside it. When he looked back at her face she was smiling as she said, 'So what did you learn?'

'I'm sorry. I don't understand.'

'You were looking around. Trying to decide what slot in society I fitted.'

'I apologise.' He smiled too. 'I guess I do it automatically without thinking.'

She shrugged and smiled. 'My husband was the same. Never sit with your back to a window. When you go to somebody's place you check all the exits before you sit down.'

'Tell me about him.'

'Philippe? He was handsome, strong, very self-confident.' She paused and shrugged. 'And of course he was a fool.'

'Why was he a fool?'

She shrugged and spread her arms. 'Because he trusted the people in Baker Street.' She paused. 'I warned him time and time again. He listened, because he loved me. But he couldn't believe they'd sell him down the river.'

'What makes you think they did?'

She waved her hand dismissively. 'I don't think it. I know it.'

'You mean Masson?'

'I mean all of them.'

'Tell me about it.'

She laughed sharply. 'It would take months. You'd better ask them, not me. They know.'

'Do *you* think Masson betrayed the networks?'

'Of course he did. But the people in London knew it at the time. They went on using him. Masson was just the weapon. It was the people in London who pulled the trigger.'

'I was only just born when the war ended. I know almost nothing about those days, so I can't really follow what you mean.'

She shook her head. 'It doesn't matter. It's all a long time ago. You wouldn't understand. It was another time. We were all young then.' She half smiled. 'The last of the innocents.'

'Tell me some more about your husband. How you met

him. Why you loved him. Tell me what it was like in those days.'

She smiled. 'It would take a long, long time. I don't think anybody could understand what it was like unless they'd lived in those times. It was like a long dream.'

'A bad dream?'

'Not all of it.'

'So tell me about it.'

'We spent the summers together when we were children. His family rented a house in the country from my father. We lived in a nearby house. We all lived in Paris during the winter. We fell in love when we were growing up. When the war started his family went back to Scotland but he stayed. He was training at art school and made money from his paintings. He stayed on because of me. He had a room on the Left Bank.

'When the Germans marched into Paris he left and made his way back home. He was recruited into SOE because he spoke French. They parachuted him back.'

She closed her eyes for a moment, thinking. 'He had been back in France for six months and he had been put in command of an SOE network.

'I was getting on very badly with my parents at the time. Mainly with my father. I suppose my mother had to support him out of loyalty. My father was very pro-German and I despised him for it. Which was rather unfair really. He was a lecturer at the Sorbonne on German literature and poetry. He was in love with the language and it must have been easy to be in love with the people. He was much admired by German society both here in Paris and in Berlin, and that meant certain benefits for all of us. Food, clothes, theatre and concert tickets.' She smiled. 'I refused them all. And then one day an envelope was delivered at home for me. When I read the note inside it wasn't signed but I knew from the handwriting it was from Philippe. It asked me to meet him. He was waiting for me in a café nearby.'

She looked radiant just recalling the episode. 'It was

crazy. He was eating in the café, waiting for me, with SS and Wehrmacht officers in uniform strolling up and down the Champs Elysées only a few streets away. But it was wonderful.'

'Was he changed very much?'

'Oh yes. He was twenty-five or six. And an old twenty-five. He no longer looked like a young man. Still very handsome. With his blond hair and blue eyes he could easily have been a German. But he was mature now. Very sure of himself.'

'Did he tell you what he was doing?'

'Not *tell* me. He just hinted, but I knew. I told him I wanted to join him. But he was adamant. Said that being responsible for me would be just another load on his mind. But I could help him in small ways. Carrying messages and so on.'

'But in the end you did work with him.'

'Only the last few months after he came back from a trip to London and he seemed to feel that it would be OK. That the war was going to be won and quite soon.' She looked at Chapman. 'That was the trip when they betrayed him.'

'Who?'

'The people in SOE and Churchill.'

'But why should they do that?'

She shook her head. 'When you've finished your investigations come back and see me.'

'I'd like to come back before I'm finished if you wouldn't mind.'

She shrugged. A very French shrug. 'By all means.'

'Can I ask you one last question?'

'Yes.'

'Did you ever meet Henri Masson?'

'Oh yes. Several times.'

'What did you think of him?'

For several moments she closed her eyes, thinking. Then she said, 'He was very typical of a certain kind of Frenchman. Not well educated. I don't know what his

186

background was.' She smiled. 'What we French call *un fripon, un brasseur d'affaires*, in peace-time he would have probably ended up selling clothes or cheap toys at a market-stall in a country town, or maybe an insurance salesman in a city. He had a kind of charm. A great opportunist. And a survivor. I believe his wife is still alive. His second wife. You should speak to her.'

'Where does she live?'

'The last I heard she was in Nice. But that was a long time ago. They lived there for a time.'

'I'll see if I can trace her.'

She laughed softly. 'I'm sure you will. You remind me very much of Philippe. The determination to do whatever you need to do.'

'I'm flattered.'

She shook her head slowly. 'Not just his good points of course but the bad ones as well.'

'Like what?'

She said slowly, 'I think that like him you trust the top people in your organisation. That's foolish like he was.'

'They're different people now.'

She smiled and shook her head. 'They're never different people or they wouldn't have those jobs.'

'Do you get a pension?'

'Yes. Two in fact. One from the French and one from London. London's is much smaller.' She smiled. 'They said Philippe was only an *acting* captain so I got a pension as if he were a lieutenant.'

'I'm sorry to hear that.'

She smiled and shrugged. 'It's very typical.'

Instinct and experience told Chapman that he'd do better to stop asking more at this stage about her husband and the network. He'd made more progress in establishing a relationship than he had expected. Better call it a day for now and come back for more when he knew more.

'Are you a writer?'

She smiled. 'You saw the manuscripts. No. I read for a publisher and I do some translating.'

'Do you like your work?'

'Yes. I like my ivory tower. It's calm and I know what I'm doing. I can work any hours I please. And . . .' she shrugged, '. . . and it does nobody any harm. No winning and no losing.'

'Have you ever thought about writing your own story?'

'A couple of publishers have offered me advances but, no.'

'Why not?'

For a moment she looked away and when she looked back at his face he saw that there were tears in her eyes as she said softly, 'Because it would make me too sad.' She shrugged. 'Sometimes it comes back. A tune or a film. And I take drugs to make me stop thinking.' She looked at him. 'You can have no idea what it was like going day after day to the place where prisoners were coming back from the camps. Showing his photograph to men who were living skeletons. Desperate for news. Even bad news. I was demented. Mad.' She sighed. 'It was two years after the war before those men in London condescended to tell me that he had been shot in the camp.'

'May I come and see you again? I could tell you what I find out if you would like me to.'

She smiled. 'What about your Official Secrets Act?'

'In my opinion you're as entitled to know as my bosses in London, so don't worry about that.'

He stood up and said, 'Thanks for talking to me.'

As he sat in his hotel room that night making notes of his talk with Anne-Marie Duchard he wondered what Mary's attitude would be if he got himself corpsed. He smiled to himself as he thought of how she would react to Crowther's or Travers' soothing words. She'd probably be a real hell-cat to deal with.

He'd go down to Nice tomorrow and root around a bit. There was an address there for Masson's widow and for Delors who it had said in the file was a close associate of Masson.

He reached for the phone and dialled his home number. But there was only the answering machine. Maybe he should have let her come with him. It was frowned on but not forbidden and on most assignments it would not only be inconvenient but dangerous. But on this thing it wouldn't have mattered. It would have been nice to have someone to come home to but they couldn't afford it and he would have found it irksome to have to do things to suit somebody else.

Then the phone rang. It was Mary.

'Is that you Harry?'

'Yes. I tried to get you five minutes ago but I just got the machine.'

'I've only just got back. How are you?'

'I'm OK. How about you?'

'I've got a problem.'

'What is it?'

'It's Judy. She's playing me up.'

'How?'

'She's rude. I told her off about her untidy bedroom and I got a long diatribe about it was her bedroom and mind my own business. She's mixing with the wrong sort of girls and I think she's getting this attitude from them.'

'How long has this been going on?'

'A few months.'

'Why didn't you tell me before?'

'I thought it was just a passing phase and I didn't want to worry you unnecessarily.'

'I'll be back in a couple of days, can it wait until then?'

'Yes, I suppose so. It's so disappointing. We've always been such a happy family.'

'I guess it's just part of the times we live in.'

'She quoted me some piece from a rubbishy girl's magazine that said that when you're sixteen you don't have to do what your parents tell you to do. They've got no legal rights any longer.'

'That's rubbish.'

'It's not, Harry. It's fact.'

'I'm going to say something I never believed I'd ever say.'

'What's that?'

'While you're living in my house and funded by my money you're going to stick to certain rules.'

'You say that and she'll walk out.'

'She wouldn't survive for a week.'

'That's no consolation to me.'

He sighed. 'Just carry on until I get back, OK?'

'How's it going your end?'

'Just grinding along.'

'I'm sorry if I'm being a pest.'

'You're not. It's Judy who's being a pest. Ignore it until I'm back.'

'OK.'

'See you and don't worry.'

'Bye.'

It took two days in Nice and Grasse to discover that Madame Masson had died the year before. He checked the gravestone and the records in the *mairie* and they confirmed her death. A neighbour said she had died from some virus infection.

When he checked out the address in Nice given for André Delors he found that Delors had been living in Paris for at least ten years. The new occupant had no forwarding address but he gave Chapman a Paris telephone number for Delors.

Back in Paris he telephoned the number and spoke to Delors, who seemed pleased to be able to talk to someone about Henri Masson and their time together.

Delors had one large room in an old house near the Gare de Lyon and two days later he answered Chapman's ring on the bell himself.

André Delors was nearly 72 years old but he sat like a small boy on the edge of his chair, his wispy white hair lifting in the slight breeze from the open window, his pale blue eyes ready to smile, but seemingly uncertain about whether Chapman was friend or foe. It was difficult to imagine him as a competent pilot and even more difficult to imagine him as Masson's closest friend for many years until his death. Chapman thought they must have been an odd couple. The brash, florid Masson and the timid, vulnerable Delors. They must have been rather like girls who go around in pairs. The pretty, flirting one and the shy, plain one who always gets the boy with acne.

'What was his background, Monsieur Delors?'

Delors smiled diffidently. 'André. Please.' He paused and shrugged. 'I'm not absolutely sure. He was rather like the man in the American film – Mitty wasn't it, Walter Mitty. It wasn't lies. Well – not really lies. He just wanted to make it nicer than it really was. More glamorous. More romantic.' He paused and smiled shyly. 'I suppose we all do it. But when Henri was telling you one of his stories you believed it. You really did. Even if it didn't fit in with what he'd previously told you himself.'

'You liked him?'

'Oh yes. He was very good to me. Looked after me. We were a team.' He laughed softly. 'Well. Perhaps not exactly a team, but something like that.'

'What did he say his background was?'

Delors shrugged. 'Favourite nephew of a rich uncle. Brought up in a château. Sometimes a World War One pilot. I saw his birth certificate once. He was born in 1909. So he'd only be nine years old when the first war ended.' He laughed. 'Despite that you still believed him.' He paused and said lamely, 'He meant no harm.'

'He sounds like a con-man.'

'People have said that but he wasn't really. He wasn't after people's money. It was mainly just to survive. To get a job or avoid trouble.'

'Was he a traitor?'

Delors looked shocked. 'Oh no. The people who denounced him were taught a lesson. The Englishman – Carlton – swore in court that Henri saved the lives of very many Resistance people. Including him – Carlton. He was a hero and the court case proved that.'

'Some people still think he was a traitor. He admitted that he had contact with German intelligence in Paris.'

'That's what they wanted him to do. The people in London. It was just black market stuff. He got watches and radios for the Boche. Lots of people did that. It paid to have some German contact who could protect you. Get you a permit or something like that.'

'Did you know his wife?'

'I knew both his wives. The second one I know best of course. He loved her. He really did.' He paused. 'She's still alive. Lives somewhere in Grasse. A nice lady.'

'Were you with him when he persuaded the Americans at the US Consulate in Vichy to help him to contact the Resistance?'

'Yes. It wasn't one-sided, you know. The English were keen to get French pilots at that time, and he was a good pilot. Very experienced.'

'You say you saw his birth certificate. Did you see where he was born?'

Delors nodded slowly. 'Yes.'

'Where was it?'

'Are you going to go there and stir up trouble for him? He should be left in peace.'

'Did *you* check up on him?'

'Yes.' He shrugged as if he were apologising.

'Tell me.'

'His family were very poor. His father was a peasant labourer on a farm and his mother was a domestic servant. He was no good at school and his first job was as a clerk in the post office.'

'How did he become a pilot?'

'His mother's boss paid for him to go to an air-school near Paris that trained pilots for military service. He was one of their best pilots when he finished. Then he joined an air-circus that went all over the country giving displays.'

'Did he ever fly for Air France?'

'No. That was just one of his stories. But we both flew for a company called Air Bleu. He was flying planes all over Europe and the Middle East and I know he carried messages for the Deuxième Bureau. That's when I met up with him. I was often his co-pilot. He was involved in the Spanish Civil War as well. I think that's where he first met the Englishman who testified for him at his trial. Roger Carlton.'

'Did you meet Carlton?'

'Yes. Several times. In Paris.'

'What was he like?'

'He was the son of an international lawyer working at the English Embassy in Paris.' Delors shrugged. 'Carlton was not my type. Although he was like Masson in many ways. A great romancer about himself. Wanted to be a spy. He got on well with Henri. They liked the bright lights, and Carlton told him all the embassy gossip. Henri loved the feeling of being in the know.'

'Tell me about when he was in charge of the air transport for SOE. You were with him then, weren't you?'

'Yes. He worked very hard. They never had a bad landing or a missed drop after he took over. He worked out every detail. It was like a bus service. Nobody ever got caught by the Germans after he was in charge and it had been very different before. Planes had been bogged down. Canisters landing far away from the dropping zone. Long delays on the ground.' Delors smiled. 'The Germans never got one of the SOE people. Coming or going. Nobody will ever convince me that man was a traitor.'

'A lot of people still seem to think that he was a traitor and was working for the Germans.'

'Maybe they were jealous.'

'When I know a bit more, can I come back and talk to you again?'

'Of course.' He smiled. 'I like talking about old times.'

'Did he ever tell you about his relationship with the Germans?'

'Just that he got them things they wanted but were hard to get even for Germans.'

'Like what?'

'Marie Thérèse dollars, English sovereigns, diamonds. Things like that.'

'Where did Masson get those things?'

'I don't know. But people had those things. Hoarding them because times were bad.'

Chapman nodded and stood up. 'Thanks for your help, Monsieur Delors.'

'Any time I can help give me a call.'

On the plane back to London Chapman tried to work out what he would say to his daughter. But he gave up. It was like a too carefully planned interrogation that crumbled apart because the answer to the second question showed that you were way off beam through lack of some basic fact.

Mary had met him with the car at Gatwick and he'd listened to her background information. It seemed to him that part of the problem was a clash of strong female personalities who knew instinctively how to aggravate each other. Most of it was a question of discipline and how to make Judy toe the line. Maybe he could sort it out more effectively just because he wasn't around for much of the time. A court of last resort.

Judy's bedroom door was open and she was lying on her bunk bed listening on headphones to a cassette on her Walkman. When she saw him she switched off the headphones and sat up on the bed.

'Hi, Daddy, I didn't know you were back.'

He kissed her and stepped carefully in the litter on the floor as he looked for somewhere to sit.

'Where can I sit down, sweetie?'

She laughed and patted the bed beside her. When he was seated he looked around the walls of the room where posters of pop groups had been blue-tacked to the wall.

'And how are you?'

She shrugged. 'Same as always.'

'Who are your friends?'

'Which friends?'

He pointed at the posters.

She laughed. 'That's UB40, those by the window are Duran Duran.'

He nodded towards the third poster.

'He looks quite human. Who's he?'

'That's Paul Young. He's a wimp.'

'How can you tell?'

'Everyone thinks so.'

He looked around the room. It was a small museum of her life. A mass of cuddly toys in one corner. The mini hi-fi and a pile of records. Singles and albums. A mouse in a straw basket hung from the lampshade and there were tops, skirts and shoes everywhere. The old loves of a small girl's life ranged against nail-polish, lip-sticks and eye-shadow. As he looked back at her face she said, 'Don't say it. I know it's a mess.'

'That wasn't what I was thinking actually.'

'What was it?'

He pointed at a line of small figurines on the window ledge. 'I can remember when we had that trip down to Chichester and you wouldn't let me get petrol except at garages that sold Smurfs.'

She laughed. 'I like hearing about when I was young.'

He took a deep breath. 'Let's talk about now you're old and grey.'

'What about?'

He looked at her. 'You're too bright not to know what about.'

'You mean Mommy?'

'Yes.'

'She's just being a bitch.'

'Let's talk about you.'

'I want to leave school. I don't want to go on with my "A" levels.'

'I'm sure you've got good reasons for that decision. So what next?'

'I don't understand.'

'What are you going to do instead of school?'

'I can get a job. I want to be independent.'

'I'm sure you can. Where are you going to live?'

'I'll live here.'

He smiled. 'Well, you'll have to ask the landlady if she'll have you.'

'What landlady?'

'Your mother. The bitch.'

'This is my home too.'

'But that wouldn't be being independent, would it?'

'You mean I'd have to leave home?'

'No. You could be grown-up and behave as your Moma would like.'

'Well – at least thanks for not saying "never darken my doors again".'

'And thank you for not saying – "I didn't ask to be born".'

She laughed. 'I'd have got around to it.'

'Moma and I are going out for dinner, would you like to come?'

'I promised to go to the roller-disco tonight with some friends.'

'What time will you be back?'

'I don't know. Not late.'

'Make it not later than eleven, OK?'

There was a slight frown but she said, 'Yes. OK.'

They were sipping coffee when she said, 'Do you think she will get a job?'

'No. I'm sure she won't. She'll be thinking about it and you can bet she hasn't thought about it up to now. It's easy to say what you'll do when somebody says you can't.'

'Would you have let her have a job if she really wanted it?'

'I don't know. Let's jump one fence at a time.'

'I hope you didn't treat her like one of your suspects.'

'I just agreed with everything she said she wanted.' He grinned. 'OK, she modified her wants a little but that was all.'

'Why didn't you persuade her to stay at school?'

'I did. I checked with Legal and that bloody magazine was right. We can't *make* her do what she doesn't want to now she's seventeen. You can give her a hard time but why should we? We love her. When you're shoving against a closed door it can be exciting. When the door just swings open you have to think for real about what you want to do on the other side.'

'You've got a nasty mind, my boy. But I hope it works.'

He smiled. 'Me too.'

3

It was one of those days in late March that deceive birds and primroses into nest-building and blooming as if it were spring rather than the last remnants of winter.

Chapman left the car by the church because the lane to the cottage was too narrow for any vehicles, even farm-carts and tractors had to serve the land from the far end of the bridge across the small stream.

The cottage was typically Sussex with curved wooden window-frames, white-washed stone and a well-thatched roof. As he opened the wooden gate he saw an elderly woman bending over a rockery. She heard his footsteps and stood up, smiling as she wiped the back of her hand across her forehead.

'It really is like spring, isn't it? Fine for crocuses but I fear for the primulas, poor dears.' She paused. 'By the way, I don't know whether you know it but *Primula obconica* can give you an awful rash if you're not careful.' She laughed. 'I'm so sorry. You've come about the books I expect.'

'Are you Mrs Langton?'

'That's right.'

'I came to ask if you could spare me a little time to talk to me about your brother.'

She frowned. 'Which brother? Tommy or Phil?'

'About Philip.'

'What is it you want to talk about? They were my husband's books, you know, not my brother's.' She looked at him for several moments. 'We'd better go inside. It's not really as warm as it looks.'

She turned and he followed her into the house through the open French windows into a living room that was so typical of the cottage in its decor and furnishings that it looked almost like a stage-set. It reminded him of an old film he had seen on TV called *Brief Encounter*. She waved him to one of the big chintz-covered armchairs and sank herself with a sigh and a creak of bones into its companion.

'At my age it's not the walking about but the sitting down and getting up that does it.' She patted her skirt into place and said, 'Now. How can I help you?'

'I'd better explain that I'm an intelligence officer and I've been told to look into what happened with your brother's network in France.'

'Oh, my dear, I don't know anything about all that. They told Father he was very brave. But Ma and Pa were very upset. There was no body to bury, no place to remember him. They never really got over it, you know. Never talked about it but it was always on their minds. Especially Ma. He was her favourite.'

'What kind of man was he?'

She smiled and pointed to a photograph in a silver frame on the sideboard. 'There he is. Smiling as usual.' She turned back to look at Chapman. 'You know, dear, it still seems strange when I hear him referred to as a man. We only saw him a few times after he got back from Paris after the Germans walked in, and he was still only a boy really.' She leaned forward and said conspiratorially, 'You know what's wrong with the people who decide these things. They turn boys into men long before nature intended. Not just in war-time. Even now they do it, but of course it's worse in war-time. They call it "doing your bit for the country". What rubbish. And they all sit in offices while the boys fight the wars those idiots started.' She laughed shakily and there were tears in her eyes. 'You mustn't take any notice of me. I'm an old fool.' Her lips trembled and her voice broke as she said, 'But I do miss him, even after all this time. He was such a nice boy.'

'Tell me about when you were both children.'

For a few moments she closed her eyes, thinking, and then she looked at him.

'I was the middle one. Tom was a year older than me and Phil was four years younger. We were always close, Phil and me. He was a lovely boy. Very strong, very tough. But inside there was that tremendous talent. In his drawings and his paintings you can see the real mind. When he looked at things, flowers, animals, insects, he painted as if he understood what went on inside them.' She threw up her hands. 'But with people it was different. I don't think they deceived him but he went along with what they wanted too easily, as if he didn't want to expose them or hurt their feelings.'

'Why did he like France so much?'

She smiled. 'We lived there in the years that matter to young children and I think that later on, like all young men, he found it romantic. An artist in Paris. In those days what more could a young man want? And of course there was Anne-Marie.'

'What made him agree to go back for SOE?'

'I think it was a mixture of things. His love of France. I think our people made him feel he had an obligation to help liberate them.' She shrugged. 'And of course there was Anne-Marie. He loved her desperately. I think that just to be in France where she was meant a lot to him.' She smiled. 'Always the romantic.'

'Have you met Anne-Marie since the war?'

'No,' she said quietly. 'Not since she became his wife.'

'Why not?'

'Ma and Pa always maintained that it was because of her he went back. They blamed her for his death. So many of them died, but not her.' She sighed. 'I didn't agree, but they were hurt enough for me not to say so. Tom had gone down with the *Royal Oak* and not even knowing what had happened to Phil was the last straw. I didn't want to add to their burden.' She paused. 'He came up to see us once when he was brought back for a few days. He phoned me twice when he was brought back from France on a couple of other occasions. But his mind wasn't here. He was only here for a couple of days both times but I could tell that he was anxious to get back. As if he didn't belong here any more. The last time I got a letter was in August '43 and he wrote that they had been married a few weeks earlier.'

'I think she loved him just as much as he loved her.'

'You know her, do you?'

'I've met her just once.'

'A tough person?'

'No. Quite the opposite, but she blames our people for his and the others' deaths. She thinks they were betrayed. She thinks he was too trusting of the people in London.'

'The French always blame everyone but themselves, don't they?'

'I think you might like her. You're quite like one another.'

'Oh. In what way?'

'You both have an air of being quite independent with fixed views on life. Survivors outside, but inside you're not so sure about everything. The certainties are just a life-belt rather than real convictions.'

She smiled at him. Quite fondly. 'And you're very like my Philip.' She shrugged. 'Who knows what we are? We don't know ourselves.' She stood up awkwardly. 'I'm afraid I can't have been any help to you in your task.'

'You've been a great help. When it's finished I'll come and see you again if I may. And tell you what I found out.'

'By all means.'

She held out her hand and as he took it she leaned forward and kissed his cheek.

Chapman had used Scotland Yard liaison to check if Westphal was still alive and at his last known address and the reply had come through two days later. Westphal had not been at that address for nearly ten years. His present address was not known.

Three days later he came back to his office to write his

situation report and there was an Interpol print-out on his desk.

..
WIESBADEN 25841 050586 1205 GMT
ROUTINE
INTERPOL LONDON
RG 19-09 852 ST
YOUR R/M NR 6096 DD 30.4.86. FILE NR
LUN/3209/86 RE WESTPHAL FNS KARL KLAUS
BORN 17 AUG 1924 AND OUR R/M NR 7747 DD
2 MAY 1986 RE THE SAME MATTER. SUBSEQUENT
CHECK INDICATES SUBJECT NOW RESIDES ALTE GASSE
17 GOETTINGEN NR/SACHSEN FED REP GERMANY.
REGARDS.
INTERPOL WIESBADEN
NNNN
$
33314 GMP
+?+ QP FSB
JJJJ:

Chapman walked down to Neuer Jungfernstieg and looked across the lake. The Hamburg pleasure boats were already loading their early morning passengers, heading for the Outer Alster under the Lombard and Kennedy bridges. For a moment or so he stood enjoying the sunshine and the gentle breeze, then looked at his watch and walked back slowly to the hotel.

The Basler Hospiz was a modest, old-fashioned hotel that was patronised mainly by Germans and still maintained a pre-war air as if Thomas Mann might come in for a leisurely coffee. It was the kind of place that would suit Otto Schlegel, ex-SD officer and now an antiquarian bookseller.

When the desk rang his room to say that his visitor had arrived he asked them to send him up. When he opened the door to the heavy knock he was surprised. Otto

Schlegel didn't look as old as he had expected. They shook hands and Chapman pointed to one of the armchairs.

'A drink, Herr Schlegel? A schnapps?'

Schlegel shook his head. 'I don't drink. Never have.'

Chapman sat down. 'It was good of you to give me some of your time. As I mentioned to you on the telephone I wanted to ask you about the Frenchman, Masson.'

Schlegel nodded. 'And like I told you on the phone – he was Westphal's man, not mine.'

'But you were Westphal's deputy. And you knew about Masson's relationship with Westphal.'

'Some of it anyway.'

'How did they meet?'

Schlegel smiled. 'Westphal and I were among the first SD officers to arrive in Paris. About the third day Westphal interviewed the French Director-General of the Interior Ministry.' He paused and laughed. 'Among the material that we took over was all the records of every criminal, terrorist, foreign agent and so on who the French had ever had under surveillance. In fact we were only looking for suspected Soviet agents.

'Not long after this, Westphal met Masson in a café. It seems it was a coincidence, not a planned meeting, according to Westphal's driver. I understood that they had first met in 1938 when Masson had been a pilot and various people had paid him on the side to carry messages. Apparently Westphal had used him regularly in those days, and found him cooperative. The French criminal records were checked and Masson was down there as a black marketeer amongst other things.

'But as I said, at that time Kurt Westphal was more occupied with Soviet agents. In Germany and France. But about July 1941 Kurt sent a message to Masson that the Vichy government was setting up a special new airline, mainly for official visits and French and German officials. Masson took the hint and was taken on as a pilot flying to towns in the unoccupied zone, to the French colonies in North Africa, and sometimes to Italy.'

'Was he trying to get rid of Masson?'

'I don't think so. Kurt was always looking ahead. I guess he thought Masson might be useful some time in the future.'

'Useful for what?'

Schlegel shrugged. 'Who knows.'

'How long before Masson was in contact with Westphal after he came back from England?'

Schlegel smiled. 'Three days. Near the end of January '42.'

'How did Westphal use him?'

'You'd have to talk with Haller about that. He dealt with most of the Masson stuff.'

'I was told that Haller lives in Hamburg.'

Schlegel looked surprised. 'Does he? This isn't his home town, he's a Berliner. His wife came from Köln.'

'Is she still with him?'

'I've no idea.'

'Can I contact you again if it's necessary?'

'Of course.'

'Shall we have lunch together? There's quite a good restaurant downstairs.'

'Thank you. But I'd better get back to the shop.'

Chapman walked with him down to the hotel entrance and waited until Schlegel had waved down a taxi.

The second time that Chapman met Delors they met by the Orangerie in the Tuileries Gardens. It was a perfect spring day. Warm, clear blue sky and the smell of mown grass. Delors was already there, sitting on a bench in the sun when Chapman arrived.

'I can only stay an hour, Mr Chapman.'

'That's fine.'

'You thought of something else?'

'I wanted to ask you about when you and Masson landed in England.'

'We landed in Scotland. A place called Greenock. Two police officers – I think they were called Special Branch –

took charge of us and kept us away from the others. They took us by train to London and then took us to an interrogation centre. They gave us a medical check. We were interrogated separately for four days and then taken to a hotel in a district called Victoria. Then we were separated and I was sent to a small boarding house.'

'What sort of questions did they ask you?'

'About my flying experience. Types of planes. Routes and so on but they spent most of the time asking me about Henri.'

'What did they ask about him?'

'I think they'd realised he'd been telling lies. They asked me if he had been an Air France pilot. When I said I wasn't sure they got quite tough. They told me they knew he was lying and so did I. If I wasn't ready to tell the truth I'd be interned as an enemy alien. In the end I told them he hadn't flown for Air France and they relaxed a bit and asked me about his background.'

'What did they ask about?'

'Asked if he was involved in black market deals and if he had any contacts with the Germans.'

'What did you tell them?'

He sighed and shrugged. 'I told them the truth. We all had black market deals. Sometimes with Germans. They were the ones with money.'

'Did you see him again?'

'We met by accident in the street and he took me for a drink. He was obviously doing fine. Well dressed and full of his old confidence. I told him I was having a rough time but he said he couldn't help. He said he was sleeping with an old girl-friend but I knew he was lying. He was obviously covering up whatever he was doing. I never saw him again until some weeks later.

'He took me to a luxury flat and there was a man there who was obviously an English intelligence officer. He asked me about France and what it was like under the Germans. We just chatted for a bit and then he asked me if I fancied doing some secret work. I told him all I wanted to do was flying. After that he left. I got the impression that Masson was going back to France before long.'

'And that was the last time you saw him?'

'No. The British sent me back to France with him to work for SOE. Then I saw him after the war. We were both genuine Air France pilots then, but Masson wasn't interested in me any more. Maybe he didn't like that I knew about the old days. He chatted but I knew he was already up to something new.' He paused. 'He never learned, did Masson.'

'Learned what?'

'He couldn't leave well alone. Always had to be up to something. Something secret. Something that made him special.'

'Did you go to his trial?'

'Yes.'

'What did you think?'

'Like everybody else I assumed he was going to be found guilty. The prosecution seemed to have all the evidence they needed. And then the Englishman, Carlton, gave his evidence and the whole thing collapsed.' He shrugged. 'What could they do? Carlton had been an officer of SOE. A senior officer who said that Masson had done a first-class job for the Resistance. Never lost a passenger either coming or leaving. And suddenly Masson was a hero. A war-hero. A French hero not a French traitor.'

'Did you believe the Englishman's evidence?'

'No reason not to. What reason would he have for lying?'

'No doubt in your mind about Masson being a traitor?'

Delors smiled. 'Ah, that's different. A man like Masson could be anything. Traitor or hero. Whichever paid off best. Nothing would surprise me about that man. Nothing.'

It was nearly midnight when he got to the flat, and he let himself in quietly, dropping his bag in the hall and picking up his mail from the hall table before he walked through to the kitchen and poured himself a glass of milk from the refrigerator.

Most of it was junk mail. It always was. There was a bill for repairing the dish-washer and Barclaycard statements for both of them. There was a card from an SIS friend showing the sights of Sydney, Australia and the news that he had married a New Zealand girl.

He heard her slippers before she got to the kitchen and then she came in, tying the belt of her dressing gown.

'I thought you must have missed the plane so I went to bed and took the phone up with me.'

'We were diverted to Frankfurt and it's pouring outside. As usual there wasn't a taxi in sight when I got to Victoria. So I walked.'

'And you're soaking wet. Let me get your bathrobe and you get out of those things.'

Ten minutes later they were sipping coffee and she said, 'There's no need to whisper. Judy was asleep early.'

He smiled. 'It's a bit like we're kids having a midnight feast.'

'How did it go?'

'It's not one of those sort of assignments. It doesn't go. It's just turning over stones and having a look what's underneath.' He paused. 'How are things with Judy?'

'Better. But I'm keeping my fingers crossed. She's decided to stay on and take her "A" levels.'

When he smiled she said, 'Don't look so bloody smug. Smirking doesn't suit you.'

'So why the crossed fingers?'

'She's polite, her room's not quite so bad as it was. But she doesn't tell me much. If I ask her what she did at school she says "nothing".'

'Don't ask then. Then you'd probably get sick of hearing about school.'

'It's all right for you to say that. You've got other things occupying your mind. I've only got this place and her and me.'

He looked at his watch. 'We'd better go to bed, I've got to see Sir Martin tomorrow at ten. Probably wants to kick my backside for getting no place so slowly.'

As he stood up he said, 'Oh, I forgot. I got something for you. It's in my bag. Hold on.'

When he came back with a small package she opened it eagerly, tearing off the fancy wrapping paper like a small girl at Christmas. For a moment she looked at the narrow leather case and then she opened it. She looked up at his face.

'Oh Harry. They must have cost a fortune. They're beautiful.'

She held up the pearl necklace and touched it to her cheek. He laughed and said, 'They're excellent imitations, aren't they?'

She smiled. 'You're a bad liar, Harry Chapman. These are the real thing. And so are you.'

She flung her arms around his neck and kissed him, and wore the pearls in bed until she was ready to sleep.

Chapman's second interview with Sir Martin was in the D-G's office and Chapman guessed that he was being subtly signalled that this time it was to be more formal. Maybe his asking if the D-G thought that SIS had something to hide had gone a bit too far.

But Sir Martin looked amiable enough as he waved Chapman to a chair by his desk.

Smiling he said, 'I've been glancing at your sit-reps – you seem to have a very tangled web to unfold with this one.'

'Yes, sir. It's probably not as tangled as I'm making it. It's just that most of the people concerned are dead so I have to piece it together from the edges and try and get to the centre.'

'So how can I help you?'

'I wanted to ask you about Mr Palmer, sir.'

'*Colonel* Palmer.' He smiled. 'Very much the colonel.'

'What was his actual status?'

'He was Deputy Head of SIS.'

'He seemed to do other things.'

'Like what?'

'There's mention in the files of something called the Z Organisation, some sort of private army that Palmer ran – that he started before the war.'

'No private army, my boy. It was the grounding of all MI6's network in Europe. Men who were all hand-picked by Clive Palmer himself. His boys.' He smiled. 'I was one of them before I transferred to SOE. I was his boy in Brussels.'

'What kind of man was he, sir? Some people I've spoken to say he was a great charmer, others see him as something of a monster.'

'He could certainly lay on the charm, and he was certainly ruthless. Probably a bit paranoid, and certainly with a vitriolic temper, but in his own rather selfish way he was a patriot.'

'Why are there such divergent views about him?'

For a few moments Sir Martin looked towards the window and its array of cactus plants. Then he looked back at Chapman.

'He was a very secretive man. A law unto himself. He would brook no interference, and he contrived his position so that he was virtually accountable to nobody. Not even the D-G. But with his chaps in the field he had a very special relationship. He really cared about you. Not just show, but for real. He was like a very protective uncle, and totally reliable. Totally secretive too. A great believer in what the eye doesn't see the heart doesn't grieve about.'

'You liked him, admired him?'

'Liked – yes. I'm not sure about admiration.'

'Why not?'

'It's all too easy in secret intelligence work to become obsessive. Obsessive about the area that you work in. You can see it today in the obsession with the Soviet Union. In those days it was the Nazis.' He shrugged. 'It's difficult to explain. He wasn't obsessive about the Nazis. Not even about winning the war. He took all that for granted.'

'So what was his obsession?'

'It's probably unfair to criticise with hindsight. But I

sometimes felt that his obsession about secrecy was really a cover for an obsession about power for himself. I've seen him literally foaming at the mouth, beside himself with rage because someone – even the D-G – had criticised very mildly his organisation. Perhaps not even criticised but just asked out of interest about what was going on in Paris or Madrid or wherever?'

'Was he successful?'

'An interesting question. Oddly enough I don't think his success or otherwise was ever called into question or independently evaluated. Probably because nobody really knew what was going on. There was a whole raft of information and reports coming out of the two organisations. But where it came from – who knows?'

'But he was given a knighthood. Somebody must have thought that he was successful.'

Sir Martin gave a wry smile. 'We don't have to take knighthoods too seriously, do we?'

Chapman shrugged, uncertain how he should respond.

Sir Martin laughed. 'Not a fair question. Anyway, what else do you want to know about friend Palmer?'

'Could I ask you a personal question, sir?'

'Go ahead.' He smiled. 'That doesn't necessarily mean I'll answer it.'

'The first time you let me talk to you I asked you if you thought SIS had something to hide and you brought the interview to an end. I had the impression that I was being choked off. Was I?'

Sir Martin leaned back in his chair until it creaked. 'Let me be frank, Mr Chapman. I thought that it was a tactless question. Even an impertinent one. To ask the D-G of SIS if he thought they were dishonest. Whatever my thoughts were on that, you were not entitled to know them.'

'I apologise, sir. I hadn't realised that it could be seen in that light. Can I re-phrase the question?'

'You can try.'

'Ignoring proof – do you think Masson was a traitor?'

There was a long pause with Sir Martin looking up at

the ceiling. When he looked back at Chapman he said, 'It seems a ridiculous answer but it's the best I can do.' He hesitated and then went on. 'Let me say I'm quite sure that Masson committed acts that any sensible man would consider treason. However, I'm not at all sure that he was technically a traitor.' He smiled briefly. 'Sounds a bit Irish but it's my only answer. You'll have to make do with it. And I'm not choking you off as you put it when I say I've got another meeting to attend.'

Chapman's second visit to Anne-Marie Duchard had been arranged by telephone. She had put forward several excuses for avoiding another meeting but in the end his persistence had paid off. He had asked if he could take her out for a meal and she had agreed, provided it could be the small restaurant near her flat.

The patron and his wife obviously knew her well and she was received with genuinely fond greetings. Chapman was introduced as a friend and they were given a secluded table in the far corner of the small restaurant.

After they had given their order Chapman said, 'What was it like when the Germans marched into Paris? It must have been a terrible shock.'

'Shock is the right word. Like when somebody receives a terrible wound. At first there is only shock and no pain. The pain comes afterwards. They had a special phrase for that day – "*La grande peur*".'

She smiled. 'For me, all that mattered that night was that I had a date with Philippe and my father wouldn't let me leave the house. That really *was* all that mattered to me. Official Paris disintegrated that night and headed for Bordeaux but for the rest of us our worries were more personal.'

They talked generalities as they ate but when the coffee came Chapman ventured a question.

'Do you know if there are any survivors from the network?'

'Why do you want to know?'

'I'd like to talk to them.'

'About what?'

'Mainly about Masson.'

'Most of them never met him. Those who had anything to do with him were like everybody else. Some were charmed. Others thought he was a phoney.' She paused. 'Maybe you should talk to Charles Mendes. He was an important man in the network.'

'Where can I find him?'

'He lives in Provins.'

'Have you got his address?'

She smiled. 'You don't need an address. He's the mayor of Provins and everybody knows him. He was awarded the Croix de Guerre. He was very brave. He was in Auschwitz with my husband. Philippe admired him but he was a problem sometimes because he was a rabid communist. Very political, but very patriotic.' She smiled. 'I'd like some fresh air, shall we walk home?'

When Chapman took out his wallet she put her hand on his arm. 'We don't pay here. They would be offended.'

'Why don't we pay?'

'The restaurant is owned by a friend of mine.' She smiled. 'Let's go.'

They walked down to the Quai Henri Quatre and stood watching the boats on the Seine, lights reflecting on the water and the faint sound of music.

She turned and looked at his face. 'Are you married?'

'Yes.'

'Children?'

'A daughter aged seventeen.'

'Are you happy?'

He smiled. 'Most of the time.' He paused. 'Are you happy?'

She looked away from him towards the river, then she looked at her watch. As she turned to look at him again she said, 'Are you in a hurry?'

'No.'

'Let's find a taxi. I want to show you something.'

He laughed. 'OK.'

They got a taxi on Rue Mornay but he didn't hear what she said to the driver. They crossed the river and turned right with the lights of Ile de la Cité on the right. Ten minutes later the taxi stopped just beyond the School of Oriental Languages where she paid the driver.

'It's five minutes' walk from here.'

She walked slowly and he wondered what she wanted to show him. Then she stopped at a large building, looking at it only briefly before she turned her head to look at him.

'Do you know this building?'

'No. What is it?'

'It's a museum now but it used to be called the Gare d'Orsay. Thousands of people pass it every day without even noticing it. But for me it was where I learned what real unhappiness was. Where I realised that at twenty-three I wasn't a girl any more.' She sighed. 'It looks so ordinary, doesn't it?'

'Tell me about it.'

'This was the place that all the people who had been in concentration camps were brought to be registered. They were brought here in lorries and buses. The officials here were the only people who knew who had survived and who had died. Nobody was allowed inside except the officials. So there were always huge crowds of women looking for their sons or husbands. Showing photographs to the men as they came out. Asking if they recognised the man in the picture. They were half mad, those women, with grief and fear, but hoping against hope that their man might have survived. I came here almost every day for four months until the place closed down.'

He saw the tears streaming down her face and he said, 'Let me take you home and we'll talk about it.'

Like an obedient child she nodded and he took her arm. Fifteen minutes later they were back at her flat.

As he sat looking at her he realised that she must have been very pretty, even beautiful.

'Did you know what had happened to him?'

'I knew he'd been arrested by the SD and I'd heard that he'd been sent to Germany. That's all I knew. And then one of the network contacted me. He'd been in Auschwitz with Philippe but he didn't know what had happened to him. They were in different parts of the camp. He'd only seen Philippe, not talked to him.' She looked at him. 'The newspaper published lists of names but one still went there every day. It was nearly two months before the Germans finally surrendered but there was still no news of thousands of men. You can imagine what it was like for the women who still had no news. Looking back I think we really were literally out of our minds. And the bureaucrats in that building behaved like bureaucrats always do. Unfeeling and unhelpful. Too busy and too self-important to care about the distraught women outside.' Her voice quavered and she couldn't go on.

'You don't need to go on. I can imagine what it was like.'

She shook her head. 'I used to pray to a God I didn't believe in. I told myself just to accept that he was dead but I couldn't. And I tried to remember what were the last words we had said to each other. But I couldn't remember anything. It seemed a whole different life and long, long ago.'

'When was he arrested?'

'The middle of August 1943.'

'Nearly two years earlier.'

'Yes. Then Mendes came back and he told me that Philippe had been executed – shot.'

'When were you officially notified?'

'December 1945. A four line letter from the War Ministry in London.'

'What else did Mendes tell you?'

She shook her head. 'I told him I didn't want to know any more.' She shrugged. 'I wanted to know but I knew I couldn't bear to know any more. For a long time I couldn't really believe that he was dead. Every time the phone rang

I thought it might be him. That there'd been a mistake and he was still alive.'

'I'm sorry if I've brought all this back.'

She shook her head. 'You haven't. It's never gone away. It never will. In a way it helps, because you're in the same kind of business so you know what it's like.'

'Shall I keep in touch with you or would you rather not know any more?'

'I'd like to know about Masson.'

'Did you go to his trial?'

'Yes.'

'What did you think?'

'I found it incredible. All that proof that he was working with German intelligence and then all of it swept away by that pathetic Englishman swearing on oath that Masson was a hero. It was crazy.'

'Do you think it was he who betrayed the network?'

'I just don't know. None of it fits. Operating on the black market is one thing. A lot of people did that. But not with the head of German intelligence in Paris. A man in his position didn't need to go to the black market to get what he wanted. But it was true that Masson never lost an SOE man on the flights. If he was hand-in-hand with the Germans they could have picked up anyone they wanted. They could have picked up the radio operators and worked them back to London like they did with SOE in Holland. But if it wasn't Masson who betrayed them who was it?'

'Maybe they didn't take any action so that Masson couldn't be suspected of being a traitor. Maybe nobody betrayed them. Just their luck ran out.'

She shook her head. 'Speak to Mendes. He's quite sure there was a traitor.'

'Who does he think it was?'

'I don't know. I'd guess he thinks it was Masson but he agrees it didn't fit.'

Chapman stood up. 'It's nearly midnight. I'd better get going.' As she walked with him to the door he said, 'Thank you for talking with me.'

'That's OK. I think it did me good.'

She smiled as he leaned forward and kissed her cheek.

Chapman hired a car and drove down to Provins. When he was getting petrol he asked the garage owner where he could find Charles Mendes. The man looked at his watch.

'He'll still be at the Town Hall.'

'How do I get there?'

The man gave him careful directions and ten minutes later he parked his car and walked to the Town Hall. A policeman showed him the way to the administration section where a secretary said that he would have to make an appointment if he wanted to see the Mayor. It would have to be in ten days' time.

He booked himself in for two days at the Croix d'Or and phoned Anne-Marie Duchard to ask if she could intervene on his behalf.

He was having dinner alone when a waiter handed him an envelope. When he opened it it was a handwritten message from Mendes. There was a car and a driver outside the hotel ready to take him to Mendes' home for a drink.

Fifteen minutes later he was dropped at a stone-built cottage on a hillside just outside the city ramparts. When he rang the bell a middle-aged woman opened the door.

She smiled and said, 'You must be the Englishman.'

Chapman smiled back. 'Yes, I am.'

'Come in, my husband's expecting you.'

She showed him into a pleasant living room and he saw a man sitting in a wheel-chair. The man smiled and held out his hand.

'Glad to see any friend of Anne-Marie. What'll you drink?'

'Thanks, could I just have a coffee.'

The man nodded to his wife who left them.

'Make yourself at home. Sorry I can't play the host because of all this.'

Both hands banged on the arm-rests of the wheelchair.

'It's good of you to see me Monsieur Mendes. I had no idea you were disabled.'

'Didn't that silly bitch tell you, for God's sake?' He laughed. 'How is she anyway?'

'I'd say she's OK, but lonely.'

'She should get married again. She's a handsome woman. She's had plenty of offers. She needs a man. Anyway you didn't come to talk about Anne-Marie, did you?'

'I came to ask you about Philip Maclean and Henri Masson.'

'My God, that was a long time ago. Why now?'

'One of our MPs asked a question in Parliament about an SOE network being betrayed deliberately. I've been ordered to investigate it.'

'What do they mean – betrayed deliberately? If it's betrayal at all then it's deliberate.'

'The suggestion seems to be that the network was betrayed by officials in London.'

'Oh, for Christ's sake, we've been through all this sort of crap here in France. Accusations, innuendo, collaboration – the lot. But that was all over years ago.' Mendes laughed sharply. 'Listen to our politicians after the war and every one of them was a Resistance hero.' Mendes shook his head. 'Even if you *were* in the Resistance it wouldn't get you a vote today.'

Mendes' wife came in with the coffee for Chapman and a beer for Mendes, placing them on a wheeled table beside Mendes.

'Denise, our young friend here says people say that somebody betrayed the network. What do you think?'

'I think they're right.'

Mendes looked at Chapman. 'You don't think it was Maclean surely?'

'No. I don't think it was him.'

'You mentioned Masson. Is he your suspect?'

'He's a possible.'

Mendes looked at his wife. 'What did you think about Henri Masson?'

She laughed and shrugged. 'It's hard to say. He was a charmer, always joking. I liked him but I wouldn't trust him as a husband.'

Mendes laughed. 'He was a bloody crook, was Masson. Out for himself. A loner. And I wouldn't trust him an inch.'

'Could he be a traitor?'

'Yes, if it suited him.'

'When the network collapsed can you remember what happened?'

Mendes sighed and looked away and it was several minutes before he looked back at Chapman.

'I'd gone up to Melun and was with Georges Loussier that night. They burst in on us about two in the morning. That's all I remember.'

'And you never saw any of the network until after the Germans surrendered.'

'I saw Loussier and Maclean and Brieux when we were in Auschwitz.'

'Did you talk to them about the collapse of the network?'

'The only one I spoke to was Benoit – Maclean. The others were in different parts of the camp.'

'What about after the camp was liberated?'

Mendes shrugged. 'Loussier and Maclean had been executed by then.'

'And Brieux?'

'You'd better ask Anne-Marie about him.'

'Was Masson in the camp?'

'No.'

'Could he have been in some other prison or camp?'

'He could have been but I'm damn sure he wasn't. Masson wasn't the kind to get arrested.'

'Did you go to Masson's trial?'

'No. I knew he'd get off, one way or another. He'd have done some deal with someone, somewhere.'

'Who would have any interest in protecting him?'

Mendes laughed. 'Who knows? Your people sent that bastard over to testify on his behalf. The Krauts might have helped him. I'd guess there would be a good number of French who'd help him too.' Mendes took a swig of his beer and when he put the glass down he looked at Chapman. 'What does it matter who betrayed us? It was a long time ago and it's all over now. Who cares?'

To his surprise Chapman saw that there were tears in the Frenchman's eyes. He looked too tough a man to be given to tears.

Chapman said quietly. 'A lot of people care, Monsieur Mendes. The fact that I'm here is proof of that.'

But Mendes was too distressed to reply and his wife said quietly, 'Come back tomorrow afternoon and you can talk again. OK?'

He had phoned Anne-Marie to ask her about Mendes and she had apologised for not having warned him that Mendes was disabled.

They had carried out some crazy medical experiment on him in Auschwitz. An experiment which had affected his central nervous system so that the once tough and active man was now a hopeless invalid, paralysed from the waist down and prone to fits of depression that left him dependent on his loyal wife to give him the courage to carry on.

They sat, that afternoon, on a patio behind the cottage. In the shade of an old vine that was heavy with grapes just beginning to change colour. He noticed a phial of tablets on the white table beside Mendes' wheelchair.

'Can I ask you about Philip Maclean?'

'Go ahead.'

'What was he like?'

'He was a very young man to be boss of a network but he was an ideal leader. Most of us loved him and even those who didn't, respected him.'

'Did you have much opportunity to talk to him in the camp?'

'Not at first, because we were in different huts but later on I changed places with another prisoner in his hut.'

'Was that just for mutual support?'

'Not only that. He was a changed man, he needed help.' He looked at Chapman. 'If I tell you about him I don't want you to repeat it to Anne-Marie. She's suffered enough already. Understood?'

'Yes, of course.'

'When the SD interrogated him they showed him photo-copies of various documents. His handwritten reports to London. A letter to his mother. Top secret radio schedules and codes. He knew then that the network had definitely been betrayed. It seemed to tear his mind apart. He didn't believe it but the facts were there, and undeniable. There was no other way the Germans could have got them. The Germans had hinted that it was someone in London who had betrayed us. It seemed possible – and that was more than he could cope with. He seemed to fall apart both physically and mentally. If I hadn't worked with him in the network I would have thought he was mad. Medically insane. He just kept saying the same things over and over again. Talking about the documents they'd shown him.

'He got thinner and thinner. He got dysentery and that was really the end for him. Then the word came through that Resistance people were to be shot. If they'd waited another couple of weeks he'd have died anyway. They shot Loussier the same day.

'I was put in their bloody experimental unit a week before they were executed. And I was still in there when the camp was liberated. They brought me back to Paris and I was in hospital for just over a year. They did their best . . .' He shrugged helplessly, '. . . but it was too late.' His voice quavered but then he grinned and said, 'So I came back home here and the stupid bastards made me Mayor and I've lived happy ever after.'

'Was Brieux executed too?'

'You'd better ask Anne-Marie about him.'

'Can I ask you one last question – no, two last questions?'

'Ask away.'

'Was the network betrayed – in your opinion?'

'No doubt about it. Those bloody documents prove that. We were betrayed all right.'

'Who did it?'

'My money's on Masson but I've got no proof. In fact I don't even have a shred of evidence.' He laughed drily. 'Probably just my prejudices coming out.'

Chapman smiled. 'Anne-Marie said you're a communist. Is it that kind of prejudice?'

Mendes shook his head. 'She's way out of date. I gave up that game when they went into Prague. I wouldn't join any political party if they paid me. No, the prejudice is against two-faced bastards whether they're creeps like Masson, or politicians, tycoons or fraudsters.'

'What happened to Masson after his trial?'

Mendes laughed. 'The politicians gave him a Legion of Honour or some bloody medal. He went on flying for Air France and then I read somewhere that he'd died in an air-crash, somewhere in the Far East.' Mendes grinned. 'He'll be around somewhere. Lying low for some reason.'

'Why do you say that?'

'Bastards like Masson don't die in air-crashes. Too clean for them. He'll die with a bullet or face down in some canal. You mark my words.'

They had talked for another few minutes about the town and Anne-Marie and then Chapman had left.

4

Chapman sent summaries to Travers of his interviews but expressed no opinions on what he had learned. There was no response from London, not even an acknowledgement. He had been annoyed at first at the lack of response, but after a few weeks he was too absorbed in what he was doing to care about London. Meeting people from what seemed a different world, from a long time past. For the first time he realised what it must have been like to be in a real war. None of them seemed to have escaped. Those who hadn't died were walking wounded, still carrying their nightmares with them despite the fronts they put on for the rest of the world.

For the first time in his life he realised that even now there were the same kind of casualties. SIS men who ended up in their middle thirties living alone because their marriages and relationships couldn't survive sudden departures and long absences. Men who lived a life of marital deception, because they could no longer survive lonely nights in hotel bedrooms in strange and hostile cities. Ordinary men who learned how to tell lies glibly and convincingly as part of their work. Who in the end found their fantasy world more real than the truth.

And always that pervasive conflict and division between those who gave orders from behind a desk and those who carried out their orders. A conflict that could end as mutual hate between people who were supposed to be a team.

Men could be trained or persuaded to think and act to suit the requirements of the State, but in the end they reverted to being just human beings, the mixed products of their genes and environment, bearing the cost of finally not fitting some heroic mould. There was no lush film music in the background when you walked down a mean street in Berlin on a rainy night. No tinkling piano and Ingrid Bergman when you got back to your room and cleaned your Walther PPK. And no flags fluttered in the breeze as you checked in at Century House. You went home to the second letter from the bank, a library book reminder and worked out yet again on the back of an envelope whether you really could afford that mortgage any longer.

Anne-Marie seemed genuinely pleased to see him. As they sat talking he remembered the word Mendes had used about her – handsome. She *was* handsome and he realised that she must have been very beautiful when she and Philip Maclean were young. She wore a white silk dress that emphasised her slimness and the natural grace of her body.

'And how about the translations? How have they been going?'

'I'm only reading at the moment. Unsolicited manu-scripts to publishers – budding Prousts and would-be Sagans.'

'How many will be published?'

'I suppose one in a thousand. The French are not great readers, especially if anything is innovative. It doesn't encourage publishers to take many risks. The winner of the Goncourt sells in thousands but that doesn't mean that it's read.' She smiled. 'We like our writers dead.' She paused. 'And how about you? How did you get on with Charles Mendes?'

'I liked him very much.'

'Was he any help?'

'He seemed quite certain that the network had been betrayed, and in his opinion it was Masson who did it.' He smiled. 'But he admitted quite openly that he hadn't got any evidence, he just didn't like the man.'

She laughed. 'They used to call him "*Charles le Rouge*".'

'He told me that he gave up communism a long time ago.'

She shook her head. 'It's like being a Catholic, you never really give it up. Whether it's hearing Fauré's Requiem or the Red Flag it all comes pouring back.' She looked sad as she spoke.

'What are you thinking of?'

'I was thinking of a song that Philippe loved. He only knew a few lines but he used to sing it to me very quietly when we were sitting in the orchard before the war.'

'What was the song?'

'*J'ai ta main dans ma main, je joux avec tes doigts, j'ai mes yeux dans tes yeux et partout l'on ne voit . . .*' She shrugged. 'His hair used to lift in the wind because it was very fine, like a girl's hair.'

'I asked Mendes about Brieux, but he told me to ask you.'

She looked surprised. 'Why me, the idiot? He knows as much about Brieux as I do. Probably more.'

'Did he escape from the camp, or what?'

'I don't know. One doesn't ask those questions of people who were in concentration camps.'

'Why not?'

'Those people just don't want to be reminded of it. It arouses bitter feelings and unhappy memories.'

'What does he do now?'

'Have you heard of Salon d'Or?'

'No.'

'It's a very upmarket fashion house for women. Not quite *haute couture* but very stylish. It covers cosmetics and toiletries for women as well. He owns it all. Apart from that there is a men's equivalent under the name of Coeur de Lion. Not quite as successful, but making a lot of money all the same. He's a dollar millionaire many times over.'

Chapman smiled. 'Would you ask him to see me?'

'OK. But I shall make clear that the questions are all yours and not discussed with me.'

'That's fine. I'll tread very carefully.'

The Salon d'Or was like a small version of the Pompidou – all glass and exposed tubes and shafts, and clothes and tropical plants instead of museum pieces.

A stunningly beautiful girl took him up in the lift to the penthouse floor where he was handed over to another equally beautiful girl. The smooth white door opened from the girl's remote-control pad and gave on to an outer office which was all black glass and soft lights with a whole wall given over to a vast aquarium. An elegant woman smiled, opened the inner office door and waved him inside.

The office was all white and the furniture all white. Even the large blow-ups on the walls were black and white prints by Ansel Adams and Edward Weston. The man smiling at him came forward with his hand outstretched.

'She made you sound like a cross between Robert Redford and Mitterrand himself.' He laughed. 'Anyway, welcome.' He pointed to a soft, white, leather armchair and sat down himself on a couch to match.

'Well, I'm Brieux, what can I do for you?'

'I'd like to ask you about network Scorpio if you're agreeable.'

'Of course.' Brieux shrugged a perfect French shrug. 'Are you writing about it? Anne-Marie didn't say.'

'No. I'm a British intelligence officer. One of our MPs asked a question in Parliament about an SOE network in France being deliberately betrayed and I've been ordered to investigate what happened way back in 1943.'

Brieux leaned forward looking intently at Chapman's face. 'You mean they haven't tried to sweep it under the carpet?'

'No. That's why I'm here.' Chapman suddenly realised that in fact Brieux was the first person he had talked to about Scorpio who was impressed by his orders to investigate.

'Well, now. Where do you want to start?' He laughed and held up his hand. 'There's not going to be any answer, you know.'

'Why not?'

'It's too confused. I've thought about it sometimes but I've always come to the conclusion that I'd never get the right answer because I don't know the right questions.'

'I don't know yet whether they're the right ones or not. But I'd like to ask you a question if I may.'

'Go ahead.'

'Maclean and Loussier were executed, Mendes came back a cripple. How did you get back?'

Brieux looked serious for the first time. 'Not a bad start. Do you really want to know? The truth, not some fancy story of heroism.'

'Whatever it is I'd like to know it.'

'You'll be shocked.'

Chapman smiled. 'I doubt it. But shock me.'

'I ask one promise from you first. What I tell you, you don't ever let Anne-Marie know. Agreed?'

'OK.'

'Did you know that in those days she lived in a nice house just outside Provins?'

'No.'

'Did you know that her father was a collaborator?'

'No. I didn't.'

'Well our friend Mendes and I were in charge of the group based in Provins. In the last weeks Maclean took Mendes on his staff and left me in charge of the group. And he asked me to take care of Anne-Marie. She was no problem because she was way out of town.

'The night the Germans came one of my men warned me and I drove out to Anne-Marie and moved her to another house. I knew they'd come to the house and I stayed there. When they got me they were satisfied that there was nobody else there.

'I had a small fashion business that was almost entirely for important Germans and I asked to be put in contact with a couple of them. They just ignored me. I was put in a cell in Fresnes and I bribed a warder to get a message to a man outside. A Frenchman.

'He came to see me in the jail. I told him how I'd protected his daughter, Anne-Marie. I laid it on pretty thick and told him if it hadn't been for that the Krauts wouldn't have got me. I told him he owed it me to get me out. He said he would.

'But two days later I was on that bloody cattle train to Auschwitz. I was there for two months and then I was called to the Camp Commandant's office. I was being released and shipped back to Paris. When I got back here I contacted him. By then the Allies were across the Rhine and he was shit-scared that they'd string him up as a collaborator.' Brieux grinned. 'I fixed him up with false papers and gave him a paper signed by me that he was part of my group in Provins. Of course I made the bastard pay.' Brieux waved his arm around the room. 'It got me started but it was my talent made all this.'

'Does Anne-Marie know this?'

'Good God, no. She thinks he's dead.'

'Where is he?'

'He's in Diego Suarez.'

'Where's that?'

'Madagascar. The Malagasy Republic. Used to be a French possession.' Brieux laughed. 'Was working as a teacher trying to make the natives speak with a *seizième* accent.'

Chapman took a deep breath. 'Can we talk about the network?'

'Why not?'

'Do you think it was betrayed?'

'I'm sure it was.'

'Why?'

Brieux shrugged. 'They picked up everybody all over the Ile de France that night. It was a carefully planned operation. They knew all the names and they knew where to find us. That means an insider.'

'Who do you think it was?'

'Have you heard of a guy named Masson? Henri Masson?'

'Yes.'

'That's who it was.'

'What makes you think that?'

'I've been dealing with guys like Masson all my life. They're tricky, they're double-dealers, they'd sell anyone down the river to save their own skins. I know what they're like, my friend, because I'm not too different from them myself.

'You get to recognise the signs. Normal people are easily deceived. If you look them straight in the eyes when you're telling them lies, they believe you. Guys like Masson have always got something to offer. They're salesmen. They sell themselves. They know in an instant what you want, from the tycoon who wants little girls to the priest who wants little boys. And whatever it is, Masson can get it for you. You don't even have to pay on the nail. The pay-off comes later.

'Germans are no different from the rest of us. They're greedy and lecherous and Masson could keep them happy. And in return he got whatever he wanted. Permits and privileges. But the SD and the Gestapo didn't need any help from the likes of Masson, they could get anything they wanted themselves. They just took it. They didn't need a Masson, or the black market. So what did they get from Masson?' He smiled and shrugged. 'Your guess is as good as mine.'

'Did you go to his trial?'

'No. I keep well away from all that stuff. But I read about it in the papers.' He grinned. 'It was like a fairy-story where the nasty frog turns into a handsome prince.'

'And he died in an air-crash in the end.'

Brieux laughed. 'You think so?'

'Don't you?'

'Every flier who knew him said he was the best pilot they'd ever met.' He shook his head, still smiling. 'You can bet your life something was catching up with friend Masson. The cops or a woman or some crook he'd tried it on with once too often. Masson will either die an old, old man, peacefully in bed or with a knife or a bullet in his back. Men like Masson don't die in plane crashes.' He laughed. 'Especially when they're piloting the plane themselves.'

Brieux stood up. 'I've got a meeting. Any more?'

'No. Thanks for talking so frankly.'

'And none of this goes back to Anne-Marie. OK?'

'Of course.'

5

The Embassy had phoned him at the hotel to say that there was a letter for him that had come in the diplomatic bag.

When he picked it up it looked very official and he took it back to the hotel. It was a letter sealed with red wax imprinted with the royal cipher and marked 'Secret'. It was from Travers, and despite its contents he had laughed aloud as he read it. It was so like them.

Dear Chapman,
   I have carefully noted your various reports, and found them useful even if they lead to no conclusion. Not that we expected very much. Keep at it.
   Facilities have asked me to raise a small point with you. Is it necessary to keep on the room in the hotel when you are at other locations? Just a point to bear in mind.
                                   Yours aye,
                                      John Travers

Instinctively he crumpled it up and tossed it into the waste-paper basket. And equally instinctively he retrieved it and burned it in the basin, powdered the charred paper into a paste and turned on both taps to swill it away.

He had felt from the start that it would be best to leave any interview with Westphal until he had heard other people's opinions on what had happened so that he had at least a basic knowledge of the facts. But what he had learned, particularly from the French people involved, was much the same. Strong suspicion of Masson or, in the case of Delors who had known Masson well, that he was an innocent victim. Only the Germans who had been his contacts would know the truth.

It was time to see Westphal. But a lot would depend on the German's attitude. He had no right to insist that any of these people should even talk to him let alone tell him the truth. The French people had cooperated because they were interested themselves in finding out what had really happened all those years ago. But Westphal could just send him packing. There was no legal pressure he could apply and Westphal could well feel that talking to him could dredge up facts from the past that he would prefer to keep hidden.

6

The train journey to Göttingen was long and tiring and Chapman had slept until mid-day after he had booked into his hotel. It was late afternoon when he knocked on the door of the address he'd been given by Interpol for Kurt Westphal. It was a substantial pre-war house, well-cared for and in a street of good houses. Göttingen, a university town, had not been a target for Allied bombers.

The man who opened the door was of medium build with broad shoulders and a slight paunch. He was wearing a check shirt and grey trousers and well-polished black shoes.

Chapman said in English, 'Are you Herr Westphal?'

The man looked back at him. 'Who are you?'

'I'm a British intelligence officer and . . .'

'I've been before the State War Crimes Commission twice and I've nothing more to add.'

'. . . and I wanted to ask you about the Scorpio network.'

For a few moments the man was silent. 'On what authority do you come to my house?'

'I've been asked – ordered – to carry out an investigation of how it collapsed. And to find out about a man named Masson. A Frenchman.'

'Which intelligence service do you work for?'

'SIS. MI6.'

'Have you any proof of identity?'

Chapman took out his ID card and opened it, holding it up for the German to see. Westphal looked at it carefully and then looked back at Chapman.

'Anything I say would be off the record and if you tried to use it in a court I should deny it. Is that understood?'

'It's not a judicial case, Herr Westphal. Just a look back at what happened to put the whole thing to rest.'

Westphal smiled. 'Nobody's ever going to put that little episode to rest unless I'm very much mistaken. But come in all the same.'

The room Chapman was taken to could have been a room in almost any traditional pre-war German house. Expensively furnished but in an old-fashioned traditional style. Large oil-paintings on the walls and no signs of any feminine influence.

When they were both seated Westphal said, 'What luck have you had so far in putting the jig-saw puzzle together?'

Chapman smiled. 'Well, I've got a lot of jig-saw pieces but sometimes I wonder if they all belong to the same puzzle.'

'How did this all get started, your investigation? It's all a long, long time ago.'

'A Member of Parliament asked a question in the House which suggested that a network had been betrayed deliberately as part of some war-time deception operation. The MP's brother was a member of Scorpio and was killed. My people felt we should find out a bit more in case the question is followed up when Parliament meets again.'

'Who was the man who was killed?'

'His name was Price. Tom Price.'

'I don't remember his name. Was he killed during the round-up? I don't remember any deaths.'

'I think it was a month or so before the round-up.'

'That would be a local matter. Probably in the hands of the Wehrmacht, not my people.'

'You were SD – *Sicherheitsdienst*.'

'Yes.'

'Do you remember Masson?'

Westphal smiled. 'I remember him very well.'

'Some people say that it was Masson who betrayed the network.' He smiled. 'Are they right?'

'It was much more complex than that. Masson certainly played a part but I was never sure what his role was or what his motives were. Or the motives of the people in London who controlled him.'

'But you had a lot of contact with him?'

'Oh yes, over many years. I knew him some years before the war started.'

'What was he doing then?'

'He was a pilot for a small French airline. I used him from time to time to take letters and packages to my people in various places.'

'Was he paid for doing that?'

'Yes. He had a retainer and was paid for each delivery.'

'That means you trusted him?'

Westphal laughed. 'Good God no. Well – I trusted him to make the deliveries but there were always checks on him. There was no evidence that he tried to tamper with the material. And none of it was more than confidential.'

'What happened when the war started?'

'I met him quite accidentally in the street in Paris. It was obvious that he was having a thin time. Some time later I suggested he applied for a job with a French internal airline that was used by the French government in Vichy. I gave him a few small delivery jobs for us and that was all.'

'Did you have in mind that he could be useful in the future?'

'I don't really remember. He wasn't important to us at that stage. I think I lost track of him and then heard that he'd given up his flying job. I assumed that he was in the black market but I didn't pursue it.' He paused and reached for a pipe that lay on a table beside his chair. 'It must have been a couple of months, maybe more, when he contacted me again.'

'He always maintained that his contacts with you were just black market deals.'

Westphal smiled. 'What rubbish. Anything I wanted I could have. If you're head of SD in an occupied country there's no need to do more than drop a hint and whatever it is will be on your desk the next day.' He paused. 'Anyway London, or somebody in London, knew that he was in contact with me. That was part of my problem.'

'What problem was that?'

'When he came to see me he was offering his services to me. Said he'd been trained in England as a spy and was now a member of SOE, Special Operations Executive, and would be in charge of all landings and drops for several SOE networks in France.'

'And you took him on to turn him?'

'I was very suspicious at first. He'd gone to England quite voluntarily. He said he'd been recruited and trained and was now an official member of SOE. So why should he come straight to me? It seemed highly likely that he was a plant.' For a few moments Westphal loaded his pipe. Then, 'I pretended to go along with his story and asked him why he was doing it. He said he believed in Hitler's plans for Europe. The Thousand Year Reich and all that. Some of my people thought he'd been briefed to say that but I didn't go along with that. If he'd been briefed to say anything it would have been by people who were experts and they would know that telling that tale to a senior German intelligence officer wouldn't hold water.'

'Why not?'

'Because we knew too much about what was going on in Berlin. France, even Europe, wasn't what mattered. It was defeating communism that mattered. The first six months I spent in Paris was mainly tracking down communists and breaking up their organisations.'

'You didn't believe in the Thousand Year Reich?'

'Nobody believed in it.'

'Does that mean you were anti-Nazi?'

'Not at all. I joined the party in 1938. I was anti-communist then, and I still am. But I didn't let it affect my assessment of the facts. With the United States and Britain against us we could never hold down Europe for long. We were both hated and feared, and sooner or later there would be an invasion. Our only hope was to convince the so-called Allies that it was in their interests to let us take on the Russians and settle their threat once and for all. In return Europe could go back to some sort of independence.' Westphal frowned. 'Didn't you read the report of the War Crimes Tribunal on my case?'

'No. Should I?'

'It's up to you. It's there in the records. It was in the newspapers too.'

'What was the result?'

'I served three years in prison but they couldn't pin any war crimes on me because I didn't commit any.' He shrugged. 'But if you're on the losing side in a war you must expect some kind of revenge. It could have been worse.'

'What happened after you were released?'

'Are you really interested?'

'Of course.'

'Why?'

'Just human interest.'

'You won't remember what it was like in Germany immediately after the unconditional surrender?'

'I'm afraid not.'

'Not a pretty sight. Of course I'd seen it all before. In France. The terrible destruction, homeless families, girls and women selling their bodies for a bar of chocolate or a packet of Lucky Strikes. It was chaos. Some people collaborated with the occupying powers, both at top level and on a day-to-day level. People had to learn how to survive. And they learned very quickly.' He paused. 'So. I came out of prison. By then my wife was living with an American sergeant and had taken our two children with her.

'I started divorce proceedings. I just wanted to be free of her but I wanted access to my children. He got her a smart-ass American lawyer and she contested access and counter-claimed that I had left her unsupported for three years.' He smiled wryly. 'The years I was in prison. She also put in her claim that I was a convicted war criminal and therefore a danger, moral and physical, to my children.' He sighed and shrugged. 'There's no point in fighting all the resources of the US Army so I called it a day. I haven't seen her or my kids since then. She went to the United States with him as his wife. They were divorced two years later and the last I heard my son was a welder at General Motors and my daughter Heidi was a secretary and my ex-wife was a short-order cook in a small town in Texas.' He smiled grimly. 'Not a pretty story.'

'And what did you do afterwards?'

'I was recruited from the *Kriminalpolizei* originally so I'm entitled to a half-pension from them. I lived in one room, saved some money and put it into a small electrical business with a friend of mine. It did very well for both of us. Still does, but I'm retired now. I got married again but it didn't work out.'

'Why not?'

'Are you married?'

'No.'

'Well, if you've got my kind of background you can't win. If you have even a minor quarrel it's easy for the other person to throw your past back in your face. You aren't just wrong, or in a bad mood, you're a war criminal. A Nazi. And all the rest of it. At first you ride it but in the end you get sick of it. We got a quick divorce. She's not a bad woman. I see her now and again. Have a meal or a chat. I think she'd like to start over again. But it wouldn't work. The weapon's always there and it's bound to get used. It's human nature.'

'Do you remember an officer named Maclean?'

'Ah yes. A nice chap.'

'Was it you who interrogated him?'

'No. It was one of my juniors. Major Haller.'

'Is Major Haller still alive?'

'I think so. Last I heard of him he was in Berlin. Had a travel agency.'

'Would it be possible for you to ask him to give me an interview?'

'Where are you staying?'

'Gebhardt's Hotel.'

'Very nice. They do you well, your people. I'll give you a call tomorrow if I can do anything. OK?'

'Thank you. And thank you for your help. Can I ask you one last question?'

'Sure.'

'Masson was reported killed in an air-crash in the Far East. Did you know that?'

Westphal smiled. 'I read a paragraph somewhere, in one of the French papers I think. I didn't believe it, of course.'

'Why not?'

'Masson wasn't the kind of chap to get killed piloting a plane. He'll be somewhere around. I'd bet on it.'

'Doing what?'

'God knows. Something crooked or he wouldn't be happy.'

7

Westphal had called an hour after Chapman got back to the hotel. Haller would see him and his business and house were in Marburger Strasse.

He took the train to Frankfurt and a plane to Berlin and a taxi to Hotel Remter which was itself in Marburgerstrasse. He had a meal at the restaurant next door to the hotel and then strolled up the street to the junction with Augsburgerstrasse. Haller's place was between a night-club and a radio and hi-fi dealer. It was small but had the look of a well-run business. There were show-cards offering trips to Turkey and posters of Spain.

Back at the hotel Chapman phoned Haller's home number but got only an answering machine. He tried twice more at hourly intervals but when it was still the machine he put on his jacket and walked up to the Kurfürstendamm.

It was nearly midnight but there were teenagers roller-skating in the area behind the Gedächtniskirche, and cafés and restaurants still busy with diners and drinkers.

Chapman knew Berlin well, many of his assignments over the last few years had been in Germany and most of them had a Berlin connection. He liked the city and its people. The liveliness and energy that came from being a beleaguered city and the tension that made living in Berlin like living life on a theatre stage. It was almost the last place in Europe that still reminded the world of the war every day. The war had never really ended here. The Wall made sure of that.

It was hard to believe that most of this thriving, cheerful city had been razed to the ground. He had seen pictures of the Ku-damm itself, just one pile of bricks and masonry after another with a German tank deep in a shell-hole where the Kaufhaus stood now. And it made him aware that what he had been investigating of what had happened all those years ago wasn't just the vague memories of old people who had once fought in an almost forgotten war. There were people here now who could remember the Russian tanks grinding their way through the mountains of rubble. Coming for their turn of revenge and their share of the loot.

For weeks he had been listening to people who talked only of when Germany dominated Europe but now the giant had been cut in half by its victors and the Wall and the long defensive border were an attempt to ensure that the same giant couldn't recover and do it all over again. But it was hard to believe that these people in the street could even contemplate such a thing. The pretty girls, the elegant women and the obviously successful men were not maniacs or fanatics. They were just people, much the same as the Frenchmen he had been talking to. And these people had had their share of being the vanquished and the individuals who had physically survived had not survived unscathed. There would have been thousands of men like Westphal whose lives had been changed dramatically by small betrayals and heartbreaks.

As Chapman turned and walked back towards the hotel he wondered for a moment if perhaps mankind needed a war sometimes to remind it that there were no winners in a modern war. No nation that was born to be the final victor. When the music of war stopped playing there was always one chair too few.

Haller was tall and painfully thin, elegantly dressed, and his office was tastefully furnished. Real wood not veneers and simple designs that had a touch of the Bauhaus in their structure.

'You obviously made a good impression on Kurt Westphal, Herr Chapman.'

'Did I? We didn't spend all that much time together.'

'You want to talk about Scorpio, yes?'

'You were in charge of the rounding-up, I think.'

'Rather more than that. I was put in charge some six months before that. Just checking on what they were doing. In the end Berlin decided that it was time to finish their activities.'

'And it was you who interrogated Maclean.'

'Yes.'

'What did you get from him?'

'Nothing. Literally nothing. Name, rank and number, of course, but nothing beyond that.'

'Did you put any pressure on him?'

Haller smiled drily, 'If you mean did I beat him up, then – no. But I obviously applied psychological pressure.'

'What kind of pressure was that?'

'I showed him photo-copies of some of his reports to London, letters to his parents, various top-secret documents written in his own hand. Enough for him to realise that we had all the proof we needed of what he and his people had been doing.'

'How did you get hold of the material?'

'It came into our possession before it was despatched to England.'

Chapman smiled. 'That isn't an answer to my question.'

'It was handed to us by a member of the SOE organisation in that part of France.'

'Who was he?'

Haller smiled. 'I think you probably know already.'

'You mean Masson?'

'Of course.'

'How long was he collaborating with you?'

'He contacted Westphal a few days after he first came back from England to take charge of the aircraft drops and landings.'

'What did he provide for you?'

'Virtually everything that was sent to London.'

'How was it done?'

'If there was time it was photographed in Paris, if not it was done locally, in Melun, which was Maclean's headquarters.'

'So you knew all about the network almost as soon as Maclean took over?'

'He'd been there two months before Masson came back. We didn't even know he existed until then.'

'Was Masson paid by the SD?'

'Of course.'

'Why did you wait so long before you rounded up Scorpio?'

'We were puzzled. A lot of things didn't fit. We wondered what your people were up to.' He paused and shrugged. 'And in the beginning, the first year, they were doing no harm and we were learning a lot about how SOE networks were operated.'

'And in the end you were satisfied that they were just careless or fools?'

'You mean SOE?'

'Yes.'

'Oh no. They were certainly not fools. Amateurs maybe but not fools.' He smiled. 'Right to the end we wondered if we were not the fools.'

'Why?'

'There was something wrong with the whole set-up. Twice Masson went back to England and on neither occasion did he fly back on an SOE Lysander. He went on planes run by other English organisations operating in France, and nothing to do with SOE.'

'Who was operating those planes?'

'I don't know. We never found out.'

'Why didn't you ask Masson?'

'We were worried that if we pressured him in any way he might go back to England. If we arrested him then we would lose all contact with the SOE networks.' He shrugged. 'There was a lot that didn't fit.'

'What else didn't fit?'

'The sudden change in the network's operations. It made no sense. They had been moderately successful by being very cautious, never over-reacting, never doing anything that would really arouse the occupying forces. And then, Maclean goes to London, and within weeks of getting back they throw security to the winds. Carrying out aggressive operations all across the Ile de France that were bound to attract the attention of not only the local military commanders but Berlin too.'

'Why were Berlin concerned? They were slogging it out in Russia, surely some small operation in France had no significance.'

'Importance, I agree, but significance, that's different. Berlin knew that sooner or later the Americans and the British would launch an invasion. Any clues as to where they would land were of vital importance. Berlin's view was that one of the first indications of when an invasion would be launched would be an increase in activity on the part of the Resistance. It could also give an indication of the location of initial landings.'

'And what the Scorpio network were doing worried Berlin?'

'No. Actually it didn't. We didn't believe it. It was too limited. But that was just one point of view. Others in Berlin saw it as significant. And their main argument was that if it wasn't significant why had Scorpio been ordered to change its tactics so radically and so suddenly?

'They also argued that if it was a piece of deception by the British it was better to round up the network to make it look as if we had fallen for the deception and see what happened. So Scorpio came to an end.'

'Could I take you out to lunch and ask you a few more questions?'

'You don't need to give me lunch.'

'I'd like to. I thought we might try Kempinski's.'

'Ah, well,' Haller laughed. 'That's different.'

*　*　*

243

Haller smiled as they settled in the back restaurant in Kempinski's.

'I've never been in this part of Kempinski's before. This was where the rich men brought their young mistresses before the war. In the front restaurant they could be seen from the street.'

'Weren't they scared of being recognised by their friends and business acquaintances?'

'No. It was a kind of honour among thieves. They all stuck together. They were very arrogant men most of them.' He smiled. 'Real Prussians. They've all long gone but I prefer the outer room. So does my wife.'

'We should have asked her to join us for lunch. Is it too late to get hold of her?'

'She's at hospital today having treatment.'

'What's the matter with her? Nothing serious, I hope.'

'She suffers from agoraphobia.'

'That's a fear of open spaces, isn't it?'

'That's the common description. Actually it's almost the opposite – a fear of people and crowds. She goes for therapy but it doesn't seem to help. She comes out with me once a month but at the end of a couple of hours we have to go home.'

'Will it ever improve or get cured?'

'The doctors talk of time and patience. And when doctors talk of patience it means they don't know what the hell they're doing. She feels safe with me and that's all that matters.' He paused. 'But it worries me about what will happen to her when I'm no longer around. I've got a heart condition that makes me a bad risk.'

'When did it start?'

'In 1945. In June. She was fifteen then.'

'Did it happen suddenly?'

Haller sighed. 'I suppose you could say that. She was raped. Here in Berlin.'

'Oh, my God! How terrible. I'd heard the Russians were out of control in the first few weeks.'

'It wasn't a Russian, Herr Chapman. They were British soldiers. Five of them.'

Chapman was at a loss for the right words to say, because there were no right words.

Haller said, 'You don't have to apologise, my friend. You are not responsible for what some of your countrymen do or did. It's too easy to blame a whole nation for what some hooligans have done. Most Germans were decent, well-behaved people despite the Nazis, but we were blamed after we had lost the war for everything the Nazis did.'

Haller was silent as the waitress brought their soup and then looked back at Chapman's face.

'It may be hard for you to believe but there were even Nazis who were normal decent people who never did anything wrong. They were patriots. They believed we had been badly treated after the First World War. In the 1930s the only way to show you were a patriot was to join the Party.' Chapman could see the flush of anger spreading on Haller's cheeks. 'They're not Germans or English who do these things – they're men. Rotten men. And where they were born was an accident.'

'I'm still very sorry about what happened. It was cowardly and shameful.'

Haller nodded. 'Let's change the subject. You had some more questions for me.'

'Yes. I expect you know that Masson was tried in a French court as a collaborator. Did you know about the trial?'

'Of course. I made a sworn statement to the *Kriminalpolizei* here in Berlin and a notarised statement for the French prosecutor.'

'What did you tell them?'

'Everything. Exactly what I've told you.'

'Were you surprised when he was found not guilty?'

'No.'

'Why not?'

'For a lot of different reasons. First of all the French

always look after their own. Secondly, and more importantly, because of that Englishman who gave evidence on Masson's behalf.' He stopped eating to look at Chapman. 'Why the hell did the British let him give evidence on Masson's behalf?'

'Carlton was a civilian then. The British authorities couldn't have stopped him if he wanted to give evidence.'

'But they could have sent over half a dozen ex-SOE officers who could have given very different evidence.'

'I suppose they could have done that.'

'So why didn't they?'

'Tell me.'

'Maybe your people in London had something to hide themselves and wanted the trial to be over quickly and quietly.'

'And let a traitor escape?'

'It wouldn't be the first time that's happened. Or . . . or maybe they didn't class Masson as a traitor. Or even better they *knew* he wasn't a traitor. Because everything he'd done was on orders from London.'

Haller was stirring his coffee as Chapman said, 'Then why did they let him get put on trial?'

'It was the French who put him on trial. They're not friends of yours, you know.'

'So why did the court accept such flimsy evidence by Roger Carlton against the statements by you and Westphal?'

Haller shrugged. 'Maybe London were so worried about what might come out in court that they either put heavy pressure on the French or did a deal with them.'

'What kind of deal?'

'God knows.' Haller looked at his watch and then at Chapman. 'I ought to get back to the office, we're short-handed at the moment. Is there anything else?'

'Could I contact you again if I need to?'

'Of course.' He smiled. 'Especially if you let me know what it really is all about.'

8

The Remter Hotel was comfortable and homely but it was not the sort of place that induced inspiration, and Chapman sat on his bed surrounded by papers and plastic bags of returned laundry.

It was time he started drawing some conclusions, even making a decision. He had phoned Travers and given him a summary of his findings and Travers had been amiable but showed no signs of calling it a day. Keep plugging away, was Travers' comment.

At the back of his mind were two things that he knew he was avoiding. The Churchill business was one and the other was the doubt that several people had expressed as to whether Masson really had died in that air-crash. He had mentioned the suggestion to Travers that if the question was pursued in the House the Minister should just state the truth. An investigation had been carried out but because it all happened so long ago it was impossible to reach any firm conclusions. Many of the people concerned were dead, etc. etc. But Travers had been very cagey about that, insisting that it wouldn't wash. The powers that be saw it as a time-bomb ticking away that the Opposition might seize on in a desperate attempt to find something that would ruin the government's smooth passage through its second year in office. One of the tabloids had done a piece on the intelligence services hinting of corruption, inefficiency and political bias. The Augean Stables had been referred to.

But the two unexplored areas both had inherent

problems. Finding out whether a war-time Prime Minister had sacrificed an SOE network would be well-nigh impossible. The doors would not only be closed but locked and barred. And it didn't even sound likely. Why on earth should a PM even know about the network? With a world war to cope with he wouldn't give a moment's thought to the whole of SOE let alone one insignificant network. What would have been the objective?

The second problem was Masson: dead or alive. There was only one way to find out and that was by going to Vientiane. And as he now knew, Vientiane was in Laos, just over the border from Thailand. Not a place where the British government had the kind of clout that could lead to the exhumation of a foreign national's grave. And then, as so often happens when the impossibility of doing something seemed conclusive, he had a sudden thought. The Reuters' people who had sent the cable to Paris might be able to give him a lead. But he didn't think that Travers would go to the expense of letting him go to Bangkok on what could well be a fruitless journey.

And as if to prove the theory that once you gave up thinking there would be a flash of wisdom he wondered if one way of checking on the Churchill business might be to talk with someone from SIS in those days who was no longer in the business and as defensive as Sir Martin had been. Johnny Boyle would be the one to tell him who to contact.

He invited Johnny Boyle out for a drink at the pub in Soho that was much patronised by middle-rank SIS men.

'You said you wanted something, what d'you want?'

'I want to talk to somebody who was in SIS during the war.'

'Why?'

'I want some background for an investigation I'm doing.'

'What about my old man, he was around in those days?'

'Would he talk to me?'

'He would if I said he should.'

'I've talked to the D-G but I want somebody who doesn't feel protective about what went on in those days.'

Boyle grinned. 'Sounds like my old man all right. Said he'd never trust any of 'em, including Sir Martin.'

'When can I see him?'

'I'll phone you tonight.'

'Where does he live?'

'Just outside Croydon, a dump called Sanderstead. What are you investigating, something internal?'

'You know better than to ask me that, Johnny.'

'God, not another mole.'

'What's he like, your old man?'

'Early sixties, retired a couple of years ago. Tough. Much tougher than you and me. Army. Parachute Regiment then SAS. French and Spanish. Field agent in Germany and Argentina. Canadian liaison. Got hammered in an operation in South Africa and was given an office job which he hated.' Boyle smiled. 'You'll like him.'

There was a conservatory built on the back of the house and Jack Boyle was obviously proud of his geraniums and a large *Begonia* 'Lucerna'.

'Are you a gardener, Mr Chapman?'

'I'm afraid not. We live in a flat.'

'Nothing to stop you from having a *Fatshedera* or something like that. They don't need much attention.' He waved to a canvas chair. 'Well, sit down boy. Johnny says you want to talk about the old firm.'

'I've been asked to look into what happened to an SOE network in France. It looks as if they were betrayed to the Germans. There's no doubt now that they were betrayed and I'm trying to find out who was responsible.'

'How do SIS come into it?'

'Do you remember a man named Palmer? Clive Palmer?'

Jack Boyle smiled. 'Of course I remember him. I didn't work for him, thank God, but I saw a lot of him in the old days at Broadway House.'

'Does that "thank God" mean you didn't like him?'

Jack Boyle frowned, looked out towards the garden where a sprinkler was sweeping across the well-kept lawns. Then he looked back at Chapman.

'Nobody *liked* Palmer. He wasn't that kind of man. He had no friends and he didn't want any. All he cared about was his work.'

'Was he a good intelligence officer?'

'No. I don't think he was. But none of them were all that good in those days. They were just ex-coppers, mainly from colonial police forces. India, Malaya, Rhodesia. The intelligence they gathered was quite useless. Some old pal would come back on leave from Kuala Lumpur or somewhere and they'd say, "we'd better take old Charlie to White's and find out what those bloody Chinks are up to". It was a farce. Fortunately nobody in the Foreign Office or the government took the slightest notice of what they produced. They were a joke.

'But there were a few like friend Palmer who saw what was coming and set up chaps in various countries who sent in reports on what was happening. Not much more than gossip and opinion but it was informed opinion.'

'So why don't you rate him?'

'Because most of what he got he kept to himself. He was an empire-builder, energetic, but ambitious to a point that some of us thought was paranoia.' He shrugged. 'I never understood why the top brass put up with him. Probably too dumb or too idle to care about what was happening.' He smiled. 'Maybe that's not fair. They'd got plenty of other things to worry about. But if you wanted promotion it was easy in those days. The Philbys and Blunts and the rest of them found it easy pickings.'

'Did you yourself have anything to do with SOE?'

'I gave lectures on surveillance and avoiding tails at their place, Beaulieu, outside Southampton. That's about all.'

'When people escaped from Occupied France and got

back to England and offered to go back who would check them over?'

'They'd go first to an interrogation centre. If they seemed clean they'd go to another centre like the Royal Victoria Patriotic School. If they had useful potential somebody from SIS would look them over and if they were suitable they'd be used or passed to SOE or some other intelligence outfit.'

'Would it be possible for a man to be working for SIS and SOE at the same time.'

'No way.'

'The D-G implied that there was real deadly rivalry between the two organisations. Did you feel that?'

'Were you talking about Palmer when he said that?'

'Yes.'

'Between the two organisations there were certainly problems. SOE's remit and SIS's job didn't fit together. So there was friction. But after all we were both fighting the same goddam war. But in the case of Palmer the D-G was right. He had a pathological hatred of SOE.

'I was in the same meeting with him and others when the news came through that an SOE network in Norway had been wiped out and Palmer said something like – "serves the bastards right." He didn't even hide the fact that he was delighted that a lot of our chaps had lost their lives. Delighted because they were SOE.'

'Why didn't somebody do something about him?'

'I think in a way they were all half scared of him. Didn't know what he was up to. Weren't even sure that he hadn't got something on them. It was a funny atmosphere in those days. Kind of sick. Great tensions and people under great strain. Maybe nobody wanted to rock the boat at that time.'

'If such a thing *had* happened, so that a man was controlled by SIS, say by Palmer, and he was on active service with SOE, leading a network in France.' He paused. 'What benefits would there have been to Palmer?'

Jack Boyle looked back at Chapman for a long time, and then he said slowly, 'I don't like to think of what the answer could be to that.' He looked away again and then back at Chapman and said softly, 'Do you think that really happened?'

'It's the only thing that fits the facts.'

'You really think that's what happened?'

'It looks like it.'

'My God, if that's true then you'd better be careful, my boy.'

Chapman laughed, surprised. 'Me? Why me?'

'D'you think the folk in Century House are going to pat your head if you drop that little bone at their feet?' He paused. 'I suggest you walk very carefully, boy. If you're going to turn up those sorts of stones you might find more than you bargain for.'

'But I was told to do this. Why should they order me to do something if it's going to cause trouble?'

'They've got to give some sort of answer to that MP who raised the issue. That's number one. Number two is that maybe whoever told you to investigate knew exactly what happened and knows there's no way you can find it out. And number three is that they don't know anything but they ain't gonna like it when you tell them.' Boyle flung up his arms. 'What do they do – tell a flat lie to the House and hope that the MP can't prove anything? Because believe you me they ain't gonna let that kind of cat out of the bag.'

'I don't see how they can keep it in the bag.'

Jack Boyle shook his head in slow despair. 'Maybe we weren't all that bright in the old days but at least we knew what two and two added up to.' He raised his voice. 'There's an easy enough way to keep the cat in the bag, my innocent friend – try wringing the cat's neck.'

'You mean they order me to forget what I've discovered.'

'Oh sure,' he said decisively. 'And they let you wander around with a bomb in your hand so of course they can never deny you anything you want, never be sure you won't decide to make a fortune telling all to one of the newspapers. You turn SIS inside out and probably bring down the government.'

'But they know they can trust me.'

Boyle laughed harshly. 'If you believe that, laddie, you'll believe anything.'

'What are you suggesting – that I just let it go cold and don't pursue it any further?'

'I'm not suggesting anything.'

Boyle sat back in his wicker chair so that it creaked like a ship in a gale.

He sighed as he said, 'Look. Just think of what you would be telling them. A senior man in SIS, who later became Deputy D-G, put a man into SOE – for reasons best known to himself – probably to spy on them – and then orders that man to collaborate with German intelligence and in the end orders him to betray that network and send God knows how many people to their deaths. Not accidentally, but deliberately. And why? Because he wants to destroy SOE, because they're getting in his way.' Boyle leaned forward.

'Can you imagine what the press would make of it? Not only here but in France. Most of the victims were French.'

'I'm afraid it's even more far-fetched than that.'

'Tell me.'

'You read about the question being asked, did you?'

'Yes.'

'What was your reaction?'

'I assumed it was rubbish, some MP trying to get himself some cheap publicity.'

'He also said that the betrayal was done on orders from Winston Churchill.'

'I don't remember that.'

'You'd have remembered it if you thought it was true, wouldn't you?'

'I sure would. But it's probably why none of it stuck in my mind. The guy's crackers.' He looked quickly at Chapman. 'What did this MP say by way of proof or explanation when you tackled him?'

'I was ordered not to talk to him right at the start.'

Boyle shook his head slowly. 'I tell you what, son. I said I wouldn't tell you what to do next – and I won't. But I strongly advise you – whatever you decide to do from now on – don't tell a soul. Not your top brass, not anybody. Not even my boy, Johnny. From now on – play dumb.'

'If I wanted to try and check on the Churchill part where should I go?'

Boyle opened his mouth to speak, then closed it slowly, shaking his head.

'You're on your own, laddie. No more from me.'

They had had Johnny Boyle and his wife round for dinner and when they were clearing up after they had gone she said, 'Does Johnny do the same kind of work that you do?'

'More or less. Why?'

'He's very different from you.'

'In what way?'

'I'd think he was a very ruthless sort of man.'

He laughed. 'What makes you think he's ruthless?'

'Those little piggy eyes and the way he treats Paula. He tells her what to do as if she was an employee.'

'She was in the business herself for a short time. She knows the score. He's a good field agent is Johnny.'

'So are you or you wouldn't have got promotion but you're different from him altogether.'

He grinned. 'We all have our own ways of skinning the cat, sweetheart. Did you pack my bag for tomorrow?'

'I packed my part, the domestic bit, I assume you'll put in your toys.'

'I'd better phone my contact before it's too late.'

As he walked to the phone he knew that her reference to his 'toys' was a kind of protest. The short-wave transceiver, the code pads, the Beretta and the bunch of lock-picking tools.

He dialled Anne-Marie's number in Paris and she answered after a couple of rings.

'It's Chapman, Madame. I just wanted to ask how you are?'

'I'm fine. How're you?'

'I'm over in Paris tomorrow for a few days and I wondered if I could call in and say hello.'

'Is this part of your investigation?'

'Yes.'

'Where are you going to stay?'

'I usually stay at that place in the Rue des Capucines. I'll probably be there.'

'Look. There's two spare bedrooms in my apartment here. Why don't you use one of them?'

'D'you really mean that? Won't I be in your way?'

'Yes, I mean it and no I won't let you get in my way.'

'I was thinking of flying out tomorrow, would that be OK?'

'Of course. Just come on over, I'll be here.'

'Thanks, that's cheered me up a lot.'

'See you.'

And she hung up.

When she opened the door she looked pleased to see him and she laughed when he pointed at the geranium in the clay pot outside her door and said it needed watering.

The room she gave him was sparsely furnished but there were sweet-peas in a vase and a framed Renoir print above the bed. And despite the sparseness the room had a friendly welcoming air. He smiled as he saw the two paperbacks she had put on the bedside table. Montaigne's *Essays* in French and Cyril Connolly's *The Unquiet Grave*.

She had taken him shopping in the local market in the afternoon and in the evening they ate at the restaurant where they had first eaten together. And again he wasn't allowed to pay. As they strolled back to the apartment she said, 'Did I tell you who owns the restaurant?'

'You said it was a friend of yours.'

She laughed. 'Not exactly a friend. Brieux owns it.' She linked her arm in his. 'I shouldn't have said that.'

'Why not?'

'Because you probably wish you could forget all that.'

He stopped and looked at her face. 'You know, it's very odd. But I'm beginning to feel I was part of it all.'

'I know the feeling. Most of the time it all seems so long ago that I'm not sure it really happened. But sometimes I wake up in the morning and I think I'm in the house at Provins waiting for Philippe to come back.' She shrugged. 'Let's not think about it. Any of it.' She smiled. A slightly forced smile. 'How are Mary and Judy?'

'Well, Judy's been a bit of a problem and that worried Mary because she has to cope with it every day.'

'What's the problem?'

'Wants to leave school and get a job. All that teenage independence bit. Thinks she's old enough to do it her way.'

'What did you do about it?'

'Told her to go ahead and leave school and do whatever she wants.' He smiled. 'She decided that she'd finish her "A" levels.'

Anne-Marie smiled. 'That was very wise of you. Or was it just very cunning?'

Chapman laughed softly. 'A bit of both. And oddly enough a bit of you too.'

'Why me?'

'I often think about what you told me about what it was like when you and Philip fell in love, and about your lives before the Germans walked into Paris. I've often wondered how it would have all turned out if your father had been different. More sensitive about your feelings, and Philip's.'

She nodded. 'That's very perceptive of you. No wonder you're so good at your job.'

He smiled. 'I doubt if my bosses would agree.'

'It warms me to think of you wondering about me and Philippe. And to think that he lives on in another person's mind. It's very consoling.'

Back at the apartment they had sat talking until midnight. Talking of a novel she was editing and the people she met at the publisher who employed her. When he was going to his room he turned.

'I hope you don't mind but I left your telephone number at the office in case they needed to contact me.'

She shrugged. 'That's OK. Sleep well.'

'Thanks for having me here.'

'I'm glad to see you, glad to have your company.'

On the Thursday he went out for a bottle of wine and when he got back she turned from her work and pointed at the table.

'A man named Boyle phoned. He left a telephone number and asked you to ring him.'

He wondered what Johnny Boyle wanted as he dialled the number. But it wasn't Johnny Boyle who answered, it was Jack Boyle.

'Is it OK to talk?'

'Yes.'

'The Churchill business. Have a look at an operation code-named Cockade, C-O-C-K-A-D-E. OK?'

'Yes. Anything else?'

But Jack Boyle had already hung up.

As the Air France plane banked he could see the lights of Paris twinkling below and for some reason he felt sad. Sad, but not unhappy. He would miss Paris and he would miss Anne-Marie. She was about the same age as his mother had been when she died but she looked much younger. She was obviously not well off but she was elegant and calm. Once she had been very pretty, even beautiful, and now she was handsome. She knew important people but wasn't impressed by them, preferring her own company and the routine of her secluded life. She lived her life day by day without speculating on the future. The only emotion she had ever shown was her anger and disgust at how her husband had been treated by the British. Not that she was much less scathing about the French. Her avoidance of any kind of intimacy with people seemed to be some kind of defence from a world that she no longer trusted. He was beginning to share her distrust of the same mirror-world in which he worked. Jack Boyle's words had made him feel, for the first time in his life, that maybe he was naive. He closed his eyes and wondered what the hell Operation Cockade might be.

9

Chapman phoned the Imperial War Museum and was passed from one official to another. They were not being obstructive, they just didn't know what he was talking about. But finally he spoke to a specialist on British Army operations in World War Two.

'What is it you want to know, Mr Chapman?'

'Like I said, I want to know about an operation named Cockade.' He paused. 'Was there such an operation?'

There was a long silence, then. 'Original documents on that subject are not available to the public.'

'I'm not a member of the public. I'm an intelligence officer.'

'Where do you work?'

'At Century House.'

'Perhaps we could have a chat. Can you come here?'

'Of course. When would it be convenient?'

'Right now if you want. Ask for me – my name's Hawkins, Roger Hawkins.'

'I'll be right over.'

Hawkins was tall and slim and expensively dressed. Chapman guessed that he must be in his late forties. He had the charm and amiability that so often went with what Chapman felt was an affected upper-class accent. He chatted about the Museum as they made their way up the stairs to the administrative floor and into a small office.

Hawkins pointed to a chair and sat on the edge of his desk, one long leg swinging as he looked at Chapman.

'It's a long time since anyone enquired about Cockade. I thought maybe people preferred to forget it.' He smiled. 'Are you researching that period?'

'I suppose I am in a way. A question was asked in the House about an SOE network being deliberately sacrificed. Somebody suggested that I look at Cockade.'

'That, if I might say so, is a very shrewd piece of thinking. Or perhaps some first-hand knowledge.'

'Can you fill me in about Cockade?'

'Tell me, was any date suggested for this SOE theory? The betrayal.'

'As far as I can tell it was May or June of 1943.'

'That fits very neatly. That was when Cockade was on the go.'

'What was Cockade?'

'Is your investigation desperately urgent?'

'Not really.'

'Well I suggest you read our material first. It's a bit of a mixed bag. Some Cabinet papers, bits and pieces from the Public Record Office. Some RAF records. Quite a collection from the MMR – Modern Military Records from the US National Archives. A book or two. And several box-files of odds and sods. There's a reading list too. You'll find the books in our library.' He paused and smiled. 'When you've looked through it we could talk more use-fully. I'll be interested to hear what you think.' He stood up. 'I've put all the available material in one of the small rooms we keep for researchers. It's at the end of the corridor. Don't hesitate to come and see me if you need any help.' He smiled. 'Despite your status I have to ask you not to make notes because it's restricted material.'

'Who decides what's restricted?'

'Various authorities. In this case I think it was a Cabinet decision.'

Hawkins had looked in to tell him that the Museum was closing for the night.

'What did you make of it?'

Chapman smiled. 'Not much, I'm afraid. I'm obviously not a historian.'

'Well it was, of course, a classic cock-up. Half the people concerned with it didn't really understand what it was all about.' He paused. 'If you'd like me to give you my version how about we go for a drink at my club?'

'Are you sure you can spare the time?'

'Of course. I've always been fascinated by the deviousness of it all. Too many cooks spoiling the broth and all that.'

Hawkins took him to the Garrick and they sat in the lounge by the bar, Hawkins with a Bloody Mary and Chapman with a glass of red wine.

'Of course it all started at Casablanca, you know, with Stalin in the background raising absolute hell about the lack of a second front to relieve the terrible pressures on the Red Army. And Roosevelt was scared that the Russians might decide to do a deal with the Nazis. They'd done it once with the Ribbentrop–Molotov pact, and they could do it again. Churchill knew that we weren't anywhere near ready for an invasion of Europe despite the Americans being in it. But he knew he'd got to do something to appease the Soviets. Something to keep the Germans from sending their divisions in Europe to the Russian front. And that was the birth of Cockade.'

'So it was never meant to be a real invasion? Not even a probe?'

'No. It was deception from start to finish. It's only object was to make the Germans feel that it was the real thing so that Churchill could claim that we were pinning down German divisions in Europe.'

'So why didn't it work?'

Hawkins laughed. 'It got out of hand, out of control. It wasn't only the Germans who had to be deceived but people on our side too. Most of the staff who worked on the operation believed it was for real. Only a small handful knew it was a bluff. They had a silly code. Those who knew the truth were designated as Cockaded. So if some staff member raised some tricky point you needed to ask if he had been Cockaded.' Hawkins smiled. 'That must have led to a few puzzled faces.'

'That means that all our government departments and the armed services were also being deceived?'

'Yes. Just think what that meant in some cases. The BBC, for instance, who prided themselves on the truth of their broadcasts. They were being fed information that was totally spurious and broadcasting it as fact.'

'And the troops and boats that were being assembled didn't have any idea that the whole thing was never going to happen.'

'Exactly. It was a perfect example of the old adage – "Oh what a tangled web we weave when first we practise to deceive".'

'But the task force actually started out across the Channel.'

'Oh yes.' He laughed. 'But when they were half-way across and they hadn't even seen one German reconnaissance plane it was obvious that the Germans not only knew all about Cockade but were laughing at us. And the order went out for the task force to turn round and come back.'

'The question asked in the House suggested that Churchill himself had sacrificed the SOE network. And both the network collapse and Cockade were at exactly the same time. It could have been part of the deception.'

'What was the code-name of the network?'

'Scorpio.'

'Well, I've seen in the records that Churchill did from time to time ask to meet SOE chaps who were over here to talk with them about their operations.'

'But is it credible that Churchill, the man who instigated SOE, would deliberately sacrifice a whole network?'

'Well, putting aside the personality, it would have fitted in very well with the Cockade deception. Maybe he wanted a lot of Resistance activity on the ground to lend credence to the scenario of an approaching invasion.'

'Would a man like Churchill really sacrifice men so cold-bloodedly?'

'You could ask the same question about any general. If I remember rightly Montgomery estimated that he would lose thirty thousand dead in the first few days of Alamein. The chaps who ran SOE must have known that many of the men and women they were sending out were being sent to their deaths.'

'That's not quite the same. The allegation is that Churchill personally told Maclean, the network leader, that there would be an invasion in September '43 and to start a big campaign to harass the Germans in his area. They were all in the bag inside a few weeks. Looking a brave man in the eyes and telling him a pack of lies that will certainly end in his death and the deaths of his men is a very different thing from accepting casualties in a battle.'

'What was this chap's name? The SOE chap?'

'Maclean.'

'And he's supposed to have been seen by Churchill in May or June '43?'

'Yes.'

'D'you know where the meeting took place?'

'No. I'm afraid not.'

'Leave it with me. I'll see what I can find out.'

'It's not likely to be recorded anywhere.'

Hawkins smiled. 'I'm an historian and used to ferreting around. Anyway I'll see what I can find.' He looked at his watch. 'I'm sorry but I must fly, I'm taking my wife to see *Cats* tonight. I'll phone you in a couple of days' time even if it's just a nil report.'

It was three days later when Hawkins rang and suggested that he went over to the Museum. When Chapman asked him if he'd found out anything Hawkins said that he didn't want to talk on the phone. He would meet him at the main gates.

Hawkins was waiting for him at the gates, his hair blowing in the gusty wind.

263

'There's a café round the corner, let's go there.'

With two coffees in front of them Hawkins seemed reluctant to start, even though he was aware of the look of expectancy on Chapman's face. Then he sighed deeply as he started to speak.

'I don't know whether to call it good news or bad news.' He took a sip of his coffee before looking at Chapman again. 'I've got a dear old aunt. Aunt Rosa. She was in the Royal Navy in the war. She was a Wren. In '43 she was a clerk at the bunker at Admiralty Arch. Churchill's HQ. She can remember an SOE officer being brought to see Churchill about the last week in May. She had been Cockaded and she had been told that the SOE man was being briefed about Cockade.' He paused and looked away. 'And she was told that he had not been Cockaded. That's about all she remembers.' He shrugged. 'But I guess that's enough.'

'There must be an official diary of Churchill's appointments.'

'There is. The entries for the whole of that week are missing. There are several other missing pages from the diary. I suspect they have been deliberately removed and probably destroyed.' He paused. 'She remembers that there was another man, an older man who acted as escort to the SOE chap but she doesn't remember who it was. Quite frankly, I don't think you'll find out any more. It was just chance that my old aunt happened to be there.' He smiled. 'And I happened to remember her.'

'It sounds as if the MP was right.'

'Why don't you ask him?'

'I've been ordered not to contact him.'

'Sounds pretty ominous, as if someone already knew he was right.'

'I think they suspect he was right but they know he can't prove anything because there is no proof.'

'But they give you the job of investigating and then they can say it was all a lie.'

'It's more complicated than that. There's the possibility

that a senior officer in SIS put his own man inside SOE and let him sell them down the river to the Germans.'

'My God. All round, not a pretty story. What are you going to do about it?'

'I don't know. There's still a lot more to find out.'

10

Chapman caught the evening plane to Paris. He had phoned Anne-Marie to ask if he could stay at her flat again and she had not only agreed but had told him that she had some news for him. She wouldn't discuss it on the phone but she sounded excited.

When she had made coffee for them and they were sitting comfortably she said, 'I think I've got something useful for you. A contact.'

'Tell me.' He smiled at her excitement.

'I had an article to translate for a journalist. A freelance. When he came to collect it we got chatting. He used to be Reuters' bureau head in Hanoi. I asked him if he knew the name Masson. He laughed and said he'd reported the funeral when it happened. I tried to probe but he wouldn't play. He needs work and I think you should meet him. I think he knows something.

'He's a Greek. His name's Synodinos. Panayotis Synodinos. Like I told you, he was bureau head of Reuters' in Hanoi at the time of Masson's death. Apparently he flew up to Laos to file the report on the funeral. I'm sure he knows something. But whatever it is he wouldn't tell me.'

'What was the piece you were translating for him?'

She shook her head. 'Nothing significant. It was about the effect of the Vietnam war on the politics of the United States.' She smiled. 'A so-called "think piece".' She laughed. 'Crystal-ball gazing.'

'Will he talk to me, do you think?'

'I've got a hunch he would. Maybe you could offer him some research work, I know he's living from hand to mouth.'

'When can I see him?'

'I spoke to him after we spoke on the telephone. He was a bit cagey but he agreed to come here tomorrow evening. I've arranged to visit a friend of mine so after I've introduced you, he's all yours.'

'I'm very grateful.'

'It's getting a bit like the old days. Standing on the side-lines and trying to help but not get in the way.'

Chapman smiled at her. 'I'm sure you never did that.'

She laughed. 'It wasn't through lack of trying to get in the way of some of the more reckless things that they got up to.'

'Have you got a lot of work at the moment?'

'A rather boring and badly-written historical romance and a very good straight novel set in South Africa. Reading both for the same publisher. And proof-reading a translation of a German political biography.' She grinned. 'Rather heavy going.'

Synodinos looked like a casting director's idea of what a foreign correspondent should look like. Deeply tanned, with a mane of greying hair, large features and heavy-lidded brown eyes that advertised a permanent disbelief in what he was seeing and hearing. He wore a washed-out blue denim shirt with press-studs instead of buttons, blue cotton trousers and worn Nike trainers.

When Anne-Marie left she had put out a large thermos of coffee and two plates of sandwiches. Chapman noticed that the Greek reached for a beef sandwich even before he sat down. It looked as if Anne-Marie was probably right. He was not only broke but hungry.

As he ate, Synodinos looked at Chapman.

'She said you want to talk about Masson.'

'I understand that you filed the report of his funeral. Did you actually attend the ceremony?'

Synodinos nodded. 'Of course.'

'Some people have suggested that Masson is still alive.'

The Greek smiled. 'Maybe they're right.'

'Did you know him – Masson?'

'I'd met him quite a few times over the years after the war.'

'What did you think of him?'

Synodinos shrugged. 'I didn't spend much thought on him. He was a con-artist. He could have lived OK being straight but he liked deceiving people. Under all that charm he was a very sick man who lived in a fantasy world of his own making.'

'What were his fantasies?'

'He was Maurice Chevalier, François Mitterrand, de Gaulle, Cary Grant, Jean-Paul Sartre, Kim Philby, James Bond – you name it. And underneath all that was a small-time crook who was always scared he might fall off the high-wire, so he wanted safety. He was a guy who bet on every horse in the race.'

'You seem to know him very well.'

'What is it you want to find out about Masson?'

'I want to find out if Masson betrayed a Resistance network during the war.'

'Read the transcript of his trial. The Germans who he worked with signed statements that he worked for them.' He shrugged, spreading his hands. 'What more do you want?'

'But he was found not guilty.'

'So what. You asked me if he did it. He did and it was there for everyone to see. OK, some Englishman is pulled out of a closet to say he was a good boy. That wraps it up. What else is there?'

'Why should a French court change from a tough prosecution of a suspected traitor – almost overnight – and on the testimony of one man the accused is not only found innocent but becomes a war-hero and is awarded a medal for bravery?'

'That's pretty obvious. The French would rather have a

hero than a traitor. What's more interesting is why that Englishman came over and got Masson off the hook. It was Englishmen he betrayed, not just Frenchmen.'

'He was a friend of Masson before the war.'

'Any man who's a friend of Masson is suspect in my book.' He paused. 'Why don't you ask him why he gave that evidence?'

'He's dead.' He paused. 'Was Masson flying the plane when it crashed?'

Synodinos laughed. 'Of course he wasn't.'

'So how did he die?'

'Who says he died?'

'Your report to Paris.'

'I just reported the facts as I was given them.'

'And now you think they were wrong?'

'I know they were wrong. I knew six months later.'

'How?'

'I saw him. And I talked to him.'

'Where was he?'

'In Bangkok.'

'What was he doing there, and what about the plane crash?'

'Are you writing a piece about Masson?'

'No. I'm not a journalist.'

'So why are you interested in Masson?'

'Didn't Anne-Marie tell you?'

'No. She just said you were a friend.'

'I'm a British intelligence officer and I'm trying to find out who betrayed an SOE network in France during the war.'

'SOE, was that the Resistance?'

'Yes.'

'What's that got to do with Masson?'

'He was in charge of parachute drops and secret landings.'

'He never said anything about that to me.'

'Could you put me in touch with Masson?'

'Is there anything in it for me?'

'You mean money?'

'Yeah.'

'I'm afraid not.'

'Is there a story in it for me?'

'No.'

Synodinos laughed. 'You're a cheeky bastard, aren't you?'

'Do you pay people when you cover news events?'

'No. But I get paid for what I write.' He smiled. 'And sometimes I get paid for what I don't write.'

'I could pay you for some research.'

'Research about what?'

'Masson was put on trial for working with the Germans. I'd like to know what went on at the trial. Newspaper reports or the court records. Would you be interested in that?'

'How much do you pay?'

'Do a day's checking and come back and tell me how long it will take you. OK?'

'How much for the day?'

'A thousand francs.'

'Make it fifteen hundred.'

'And you tell me how I can contact Masson.'

'OK.'

The Greek held out his hand and Chapman laughed. 'I've only just arrived, will sterling do?'

'That's fine.'

Chapman counted out fifteen ten pound notes which he handed to Synodinos who examined them carefully, turning them over, holding them up to the light and flicking them with his finger before stuffing them into his shirt pocket.

'Now. What do you want to know?'

'Tell me first about Masson and the aircrash.'

'It was a genuine crash. All the bodies were burned beyond recognition. Masson was ill with dysentery or he would have been the pilot. When he realised that everybody thought he was dead he left Bangkok that night and went to Saigon.' Synodinos grinned. 'He wanted to be clear of his wife in France. He was living with a Thai girl and he took her with him. He'd got more papers in a different name.'

'I thought you met him in Bangkok.'

'He'd left in a hurry and when things had settled down he'd gone back to get his cash and other things. He was only there for two days. He'd grown a beard but I recognised him.' Synodinos grinned. 'He'd been running a small brothel on the side in Bangkok. And he was a pilot for a lousy little airline with a couple of Cessnas. He was pimping for the girl in Saigon. When his wife in France died he came out in the open again but with the new identity. Then the Americans got out and Masson got out just before the Congs came in.'

'Where is he now?'

For a moment Synodinos looked as if he wasn't going to keep his part of the bargain. Then he said, 'He's living in Berlin.'

'Have you got an address?'

'No. I just know he lives in Berlin.'

'Under his own name?'

'No. He's got a German passport.'

'How did he get that?'

Synodinos shrugged. 'I guess some Kraut owed him something.'

'What's his new name?'

'Rutke. Hans Rutke.'

'What does he do for a living?'

'He runs a few girls. He's partner in a club.'

'When can you let me have the first stuff on Masson's court case?'

The Greek shrugged. 'A couple of days. I'll phone you here.' As he got up to leave he smiled. 'You sleeping with her?'

Chapman looked puzzled. 'Sleeping with who?'

'The lady of the house. Anne-Marie.'

'You must be out of your mind.'

Synodinos smiled. 'She thinks a lot of you and there's always been plenty who'd have liked to share a bed with that one.'

'I'll look forward to hearing from you about the court case, Mr Synodinos.'

He waited up for Anne-Marie to return and as they drank a hot-chocolate night-cap she said, 'What did you think of Synodinos?'

He shrugged. 'A creep. But a useful creep.'

She smiled. 'He's had a very tough life and was probably Reuters' best man in the Far East.' She paused. 'More important is, was he any use to you?'

'Yes. He was. I've asked him to put together what he can find on Masson's court case.' He paused and looked at her. 'Did you know that Masson was still alive?'

'Good God, no. Is he? What about the plane crash and the funeral?'

'According to Synodinos he wasn't on the plane. The bodies were so badly burned they were unidentifiable and Masson took the opportunity to disappear.'

'Where is he now?'

'He's in Berlin with a new name and a German passport.'

She smiled. 'Still the same old Masson. Several people said they didn't believe he was dead but that was just because he was a born survivor. Are you going to talk to him?'

'If I can find him.'

She laughed. 'I'm sure you'll find him.'

11

After sleeping overnight on the information he had got from Synodinos, Chapman knew that he had arrived at a vital stage of the investigation. If he could trace Masson and if he could get him to tell him the truth the whole thing would be settled one way or another. Finding Masson in Berlin wouldn't be easy and persuading an incorrigible liar to tell the truth would be more difficult still.

He left another two thousand francs with Anne-Marie to keep Synodinos going and headed for the airport. There was no Berlin flight until the afternoon but he phoned Temple in Berlin and then phoned Mary at home.

'I'm going to be away for several days, honey. I'll be in Berlin and I'll be staying at the Remter. You've got the telephone number. I'll be there about seven tonight.' He paused. 'All OK with you?'

'I'm OK but Judy's a bit upset.'

'What about?'

'You remember the girl she was mixed up with. The one they call Dolly?'

'That was the one you thought was a bad influence.'

'That's the one. She's been taken into care by the local authority.'

'On what grounds?'

'I gather it's a lot more than just neglect.'

'Like what?'

'I've only heard the gossip but there's talk of enforced prostitution, incest, the lot. The mother chucked her out

273

and she got picked up by the police. A policewoman talked to her and she told her everything.'

'What's Judy's reaction?'

'Terribly subdued. And surprised of course. She just thought the girl was a rebel against her parents, nothing more. She's very sad for the girl and I think it's been a lesson to her on what life's all about for some people.'

'Is there anything we could do for the girl?'

'You mean for Dolly?'

'Yes.'

'That would mean being in contact with her and I don't want that. There but for the grace of God goes our Judy.'

'Don't talk rubbish.'

'What do you suggest we do?'

'I don't know. I'll think about it.' He paused. 'Don't fret about it, I understand what worries you. But there'll be something we can do that helps but doesn't involve any of us beyond the doing.'

'Shall I tell Judy?'

'Absolutely not. Not a word. I've got to go, Mary, I've not booked in yet. OK?'

'OK. Take care.'

'You too. And don't worry. Do your best to console Judy. See you.'

The plane was on time but when he had got through immigration and collected his bag there was no sign of Temple. Chapman walked to the cafeteria and bought a coffee and a sandwich and waited. When Temple had still not arrived an hour later Chapman took a taxi to the Remter and booked in to a double room.

It was ten o'clock that evening when the call came through.

'Is that you, Harry?'

'Yes. What happened?'

'Something came up. Something official. Do you want to leave it until tomorrow?'

'Do you?'

'Maybe it would be better. We'd have more time.'
'OK. Where? And when?'
'I'll come to the hotel about ten, OK?'
'Fine.'

Temple had worked with him several times in the past. They were about the same age and were level-pegging on the SIS league table. Temple wasn't married but had had several affairs that looked like heading for a permanent thing but something had always seemed to get in the way. But Temple wasn't the kind of man who grieved over lost loves. He soon found a new one.

Temple sat on the spare bed looking amiably at Chapman.

'What are you after in Berlin this time?'

'I want to trace a man who uses a German passport and the name Rutke. Hans Rutke. So far as I know it's a genuine passport but he's not German, he's French and his real name is Masson. Henri Masson.'

'What's he been up to?'

'I can't tell you. Let's just say he was a naughty boy during the war.'

'And what's he done now that makes you want him?'

'Nothing so far as I know. It's just the war-time stuff that interests me.'

'My God, we must be hard up if we need to dredge up that old stuff all over again. Have you contacted the War Crimes Commission?'

'No. So far as I know he didn't commit any war crime.'

'You got a picture of him?'

Chapman reached over to his briefcase, unzipped it and took out a faded photograph, handing it to Temple, who looked at it carefully.

'Who's the bird with him?'

'She was his wife. She's dead now.'

'Not bad.' Temple looked up. 'Can I take a copy of this?'

'Yes. But I want it back, it's my only print.'

'What's he do? What's he likely to be doing here?'

'Most of his life he was an airline pilot but I was told that he's a partner in some kind of sleazy club.'

'Sleazy? D'you mean a brothel?'

'I don't know. That's all I was told.'

'There's hundreds of girlie clubs in Berlin. Literally hundreds. They fold and spring up again. They get knocked off by the police for going over the top. Live shows or kiddy porn. But they come back. New address. New name.'

'Maybe he's on some voting list or tax records.'

Temple laughed. 'Those boys aren't interested in politics and they sure don't pay taxes.' He paused. 'Why don't you get our chaps to circulate it for you?'

'I'm not allowed to. That's why I can't talk about it. Especially to our people.'

'Why specially to us?'

'There's a vague connection back to us.'

Temple grinned. 'Some skeleton rattling in some cupboard, eh? So what do you want from me?'

'I thought maybe you'd front for me. Put this through the normal search machinery and see what you come up with.'

'Unless he's doing something naughty here in Berlin, or West Germany, there won't be anything on our computers about him.'

Chapman smiled. 'I can remember hearing Nichols say at a talk last year that we'd got Berlin sewed up.'

'That's true. But it only applies to our stuff. Agents, subversives, commies, left-wingers and cross-overs.'

'Would the *Kriminalpolizei* help you?'

'For God's sake. You've worked with them, you know them better than I do. Why not talk to them yourself?'

'I can't. There's a German connection.'

'How long are you here for?'

'As long as it takes.'

Temple pursed his lips. 'Like that, is it?'

'Yeah.'

276

'Leave it with me. Let me have a think about it. What are you doing tonight?'

'Nothing so far.'

'I'll take you to a meal and then we'll look at a couple of clubs and see what inspiration we get.'

'OK. That's a deal. What time?'

'Here at eight. OK?'

'Fine.'

They had taken a taxi to Café Wagenknecht on Olivaer Platz. Café Wagenknecht was for locals, not tourists, and served an excellent Wiener Schnitzel and a mouth-watering array of patisserie. They had talked desultorily of past operations as they made their way to *mille-feuilles* and eclairs. But when the hot chocolate *mit Schlag* was served Temple came back to the reason for their meeting.

'What else do you know about this chap Rutke?'

'He's a real con-artist. A kind of Walter Mitty. Tells tall stories of being the illegitimate son of a French count. It usually serves no purpose, it's just fantasy stuff to make him seem important or glamorous. His parents were just servants in fact.'

Temple smiled. 'You know, you've just described half the pimps and ponces in Berlin.'

'By the way, I don't think he speaks much German. French of course and some English.'

'None of them speak much German. Most of them are foreigners, here on false papers. So-called *Gastarbeiter* who come in to work on building sites, head for Hamburg after a couple of months, find Hamburg all sewn up and end up here. And as long as they aren't violent or playing espionage games I doubt if they ever get looked at.' He paused. 'There's too much international fun and games going on here for anybody to worry about prostitution as long as they aren't spreading disease. And the street girls are only the tip of the iceberg. By the way, that old photograph, how old is the guy now?'

'I'm guessing but he must be in his middle or late sixties.

The only date of birth I got from anyone was obviously wrong.'

'Where did he operate before?'

'When he was in the girl business it was in Bangkok and then Saigon.'

'Now that's interesting.'

'Why?'

'Thai girls are very popular here. Very pretty, very submissive and very obliging. There are half a dozen clubs that specialise in Far East girls. Let's have a look at a couple.' Temple signalled to the waitress for the bill, checked it and paid and then they left.

The first club was called The Lotus Blossom and was in one of the small streets off Lietzenburgerstrasse. It was down a flight of steps to a basement and a large man looked them over, knocked on the door and when it opened he waved them inside.

The single room was dimly lit except around the bar that extended the whole length of one wall, where the lights were bright so that the girls on the bar-stools were well lit. The atmosphere was heavy with smoke and most of it was not from tobacco.

As they were shown to a table the curtains drew back on a small stage and a spotlight beamed in on a naked girl. She looked more Chinese than Thai but she was very pretty and her dancing to the taped music was to display and titillate rather than entertain.

They paid an exorbitant price for two beers and looked around the tables. Several topless girls came to the table to ask if they would like to see the room upstairs and then Temple signalled to a girl standing by the bar.

She came over, smiling. 'Hi, Johnny. Where you been?'

Temple smiled and patted her backside. 'Get yourself a drink and sit down.'

The girl waved to a girl wearing only a small apron and made a sign for a drink before she sat down. She looked at Chapman as Temple introduced them. 'This is my pal,

Tom. Tom this is Lena.' He smiled at the girl. 'It's still Lena, isn't it?'

She laughed. 'Of course.'

Temple went on. 'Believe it or not this young beauty is not from Bangkok or Hong Kong but from darkest Cardiff.' He looked back at the girl. 'And how's your mam these days?'

'She came over for two weeks in early summer. She's OK.'

'Who runs this joint, honey?'

'A Kraut named Hermann and a Turkish chap.' She laughed. 'I can't pronounce his name.'

'Ever heard of a chap in the business called Rutke. Hans Rutke. He's in his sixties.'

She laughed. 'They're all in their sixties. What's he look like?'

Temple slid his hand inside his jacket and took out the photograph, passing it to her. She looked for a long time. And Chapman said, 'I think he's got a beard now.'

The girl looked at Temple. 'This work or private?'

'A bit of both.'

'He's a bit like a chap I worked for last autumn. But he called himself Heinrich. He had a club round the corner in Bleibtreu Strasse. There's a girl here called Mai Lin who was there at the same time. Shall I ask her?'

'Can you do it very discreetly?'

She grinned. 'You know me, I'm always discreet.'

She stood up, walking away to the bar, her hips rolling provocatively.

Temple said, 'I ought to have thought of her straightaway. She knows everything that's going on in these dumps. Her father was an American negro and her mother was a Filipino. Totally immoral the whole family. And as happy as skylarks.' He smiled. 'And she owes me, does that little girl. And she knows it.' He glanced towards the bar. 'If Mai Lin is the one she's talking to I wouldn't mind an introduction.'

It was nearly ten minutes before the girl made her way

back to them, stopping to chat and giggle with men at three or four tables.

Temple smiled and said softly, 'You'd think she'd been on a surveillance course, wouldn't you? Making sure that she talks to those guys before she comes over to us. Very neat.'

As she sat down she said, 'You'd better order more drinks, Johnny.'

When a girl had brought back two beers and a glass of mineral water that was supposed to be champagne she said softly, 'It's him all right. She hates his guts. Seems she was his girl-friend in Bangkok then he put her on the game when they went to Vietnam. Some dump called Ho Chi Minh City. Then he moved to West Germany and pimped for her in Hanover. Then he brought her here about two years ago. She left him last Christmas. He wanted her to do live-shows and beat her up when she refused. She's living with some Polish guy now and the other fellow, Heinrich or whatever he calls himself, has got half-shares in a club by the Zoo Bahnhof called The Mimosa. Mostly teenage girls on drugs.'

Temple said, 'The Kripos generally hit them hard if they're into drugs at a club. How's he get away with it?'

She shrugged. 'The usual way. Seems he's got some sort of protection.'

'Where?'

'Not in Berlin, was all she could say. She thinks it's in Bonn.' She shrugged. 'Somewhere in West Germany anyway.'

Chapman said, 'You're sure the protection is German, not French.'

'That's what she said.'

'Where does he live?'

'He's got a flat over the club.'

'Does he own the club or just have an interest in it?'

'So far as I know he's been sole owner of all the clubs he's had.'

Temple looked at Chapman, then at the girl. 'Thanks Lena. Just forget what we've talked about. We're just gossiping.' He looked at Chapman. 'We'd better go. It's getting late.'

As they walked back to the Ku-damm, Temple said, 'D'you want to do a recce now?'

'It's a bit late, isn't it?'

Temple laughed. 'It's only 2 a.m. Most of these dumps are only just coming alive.'

Chapman stood thinking and then looked at Temple. 'I need time to think about how to tackle this chap. The people I've talked to so far have all cooperated because they didn't have anything to hide. But if I announce myself to this guy as being an SIS officer looking into what happened in the war he's either going to refuse to say anything or he's going to do a bolt. I've got to work out how to approach him and how to persuade him, or pressure him, to talk.'

'Was it something he did himself or what somebody else did?'

Chapman shrugged. 'Probably both.'

'If all this is official, why don't we just lift him. Take him back to London and interrogate him properly. Why pussy-foot around?'

'Well, it's official all right but it's very complicated.' He shrugged. 'I'm sorry but I can't say any more.'

'Think about it overnight and I'll contact you again tomorrow about six. OK?'

'OK.' He looked at Temple. 'Could you get me some sort of credentials as a journalist if I needed them?'

'No problem. What nationality?'

'I don't know. Probably German or something neutral like Canadian.'

'Let me know what you want when we meet tomorrow.'

Back in his hotel Chapman lay in the warm bath, his mind trying desperately to settle on a plan of action. And because of his contact with Temple the solution seemed even more distant.

Temple reminded him of the attitude he would have had himself if the assignment had not been hedged around with vague but onerous restrictions. If they really wanted the truth why couldn't he talk with the MP? He must have had something to go on to raise the question in the House. They said that there were no SOE records left, that they had all been destroyed by mistake by SIS. Why were those records destroyed? And why had there apparently been no court of enquiry about the mistake? If it was a mistake. And his mind went back again and again to the talk with Jack Boyle in his suburban garden. And his warning about not keeping the people in Century House informed. Jack Boyle was obviously sure that they knew what had happened and that he had been sent out deliberately on a white-washing job. And Boyle's clear hint that if he found out the truth and told them what he knew then he would be considered expendable.

His mind went back to Dampier and Hughes and Forsyth. Dampier's body had been washed up at the foot of the cliffs at Beachy Head, Hughes had been killed by a hit and run driver in Rome and Forsyth's body had been found in Epping Forest with multi stab wounds. Each had been described in the brief four line press reports as Civil Servants and all three inquests had ended with open verdicts. But people inside had been aware that in each case they had seriously offended against the unwritten rules of SIS. Pensions had been paid in full to next of kin but the letter of regret had been formal and cool. He couldn't really believe that such things could happen to him. But Jack Boyle was no scaremonger, and no fool. And Philip Maclean had been sure that it couldn't happen to him either.

It was getting light before he fell asleep.

12

Chapman woke mid-morning and walked to the Tiergarten and had a snack at the cafeteria. His mind was clearer now. Not that he had a plan but because he knew that the only way was to play it by ear. If the man was Masson he was going to be very suspicious of anyone who talked about the war. Tonight would be just a recce and nothing more. It had got to be one step at a time.

It was well after midnight when they got to the club. There was a ramshackle wooden staircase that led to the first floor and a stockily built man stood outside the door marked 'Club Mimosa'. He looked them over and patted the bulge in Temple's jacket that was only his wallet.

'Ten marks if you're not members. Each.'

Temple smiled. 'How much to become members?'

The man looked more relaxed as he said. 'We don't have members. It's ten marks per head.'

Chapman gave him a twenty marks note and the man pressed a button at the side of the door and spoke into an entry-phone. There was a pause and an electronic buzz and as the man pushed against the door it opened and he waved them inside and said, 'You want privacy with a girl you get it inside. No girls can leave with customers.'

'What time does the club close?'

The man shrugged. 'About four or five, depends on how busy we are.'

Inside, the place was bare brick walls, and massive oak posts supporting heavy beams that held up the plasterboard ceiling. The first room was open plan with a bar and a dozen or so tables with red and white checked table-cloths. Through two wide archways they could see a larger room where the tables were set in small alcoves.

There were a dozen or so young girls clustered round the bar. The taped music was *Two Timer* by Frankie Goes to Hollywood followed by Billy J. Kramer and the Dakotas. Most of the girls would be pretty if they had a wash and a few square meals but their purple hair-dos and garish make-up made them look pathetically vulnerable rather than sexually appealing.

A young girl came up to them, smiling, 'Would you like some company, gentlemen?'

Chapman looked at Temple who smiled at the girl. 'How about you?'

She laughed. 'If you want some action you'd be better with two of the other girls. That's what they're here for.'

Temple shrugged. 'Come and have a drink with us.'

The girl smiled. 'OK. Let me show you to a table.'

She led them into the further room to a small alcove with a table and a lamp with a red shade. Most of the tables were occupied. The customers were dressed rather better than they had expected from the description that Lena had given them.

The girl sat down and signalled to one of the waitresses. They ordered two beers and the girl asked for champagne. The drinks came almost immediately and Temple raised his glass to the girl and said, 'What the hell is that stuff you're drinking?'

She laughed. 'It's the house champagne. We have to ask for it but I'll drink it slowly. Do you want a girl for your friend?'

'No. We're quite happy with you.'

'It's only a hundred marks for a girl, including the room.'

'Don't worry, we're quite happy with our beers and you. What's your name, honey?'

'Renate. What's yours?'

'Mine's Jack and my friend's Tom.'

'Are you tourists or something?'

Temple grinned. 'Mainly something.' He looked around at the other tables and said, 'The girls are very young here.'

'That's our speciality. They're all very pretty.'

'How long have you been working here?'

'About three months, it's a fairly new club.'

Temple held up his glass. 'I guess the customers don't come here for the beer, this is lousy.'

She shrugged. 'Nobody comes to a club for the drinks.' She smiled. 'Except you two.'

Temple said, 'I was thinking of investing in a club. Do you have to have a licence?'

'I don't really know. I think you do but I guess you just pay the right guy.'

'Who owns this one?'

'An old guy and a woman who owns an art gallery.'

'She his girl-friend?'

The girl laughed. 'No. She's just an investor. He doesn't need a girl-friend.' She waved her hand in the general direction of the girls at the bar. 'He's got all the girls he wants right here.'

'We'd better order some more drinks to keep the boss happy.'

They had tried whisky that time and the girl had stuck to the so-called champagne.

She looked at Temple. 'Why do you come here if you don't want a girl?'

'Like I said. I'm interested in investing in a club. I want to see how they're run.'

'You don't look like a guy who'd run a club.'

Temple laughed. 'I'd get somebody experienced to actually run it. Give him a share of the profits. I want to check out how he could rip me off.'

'Are you serious about this?'

'I could be.'

'Would you be interested in having a stake in this place?'

'Does it make money?'

'It makes a lot but the woman doesn't get on with the boss. She thinks it should be further away from the Zoo Bahnhof.'

'Why?'

'The Zoo Bahnhof is the main area for drug pushers and the girl addicts tend to come here to make money for their habits. She thinks the drug police will come down on us. We've had two warnings from the *Kripo*. She makes good money but she runs a reputable gallery and if it got around that she was connected with drugs she'd lose her reputation and her business too.'

For the first time Chapman spoke. 'What's the owner like?'

She shrugged and smiled. 'They're all much the same. He's older than most of them. I guess he makes some pay-offs. Likes the girls and he's putting plenty of cash away. I think he'd like a new partner.'

'I'll bear him in mind. How much do the girls make?'

'It's a hundred marks. He takes sixty, the girl takes forty. But he squeezes some of them. The drug girls are always desperate for money. They'll be lucky to keep thirty.'

'So why don't they hustle on the streets?'

'They've got no rooms to take men to. They live in squats. Some even live in cars. They need a place and they need one that's near the station and the pushers. This is the nearest.'

Chapman looked at his watch and then at Temple. 'We ought to be moving on.' He gave the girl a hundred mark note and she walked with them to the door at the top of the stairs.

As they walked back to the Ku-damm, Chapman said, 'That was a brilliant piece of thinking. It fits beautifully. Let's go back tomorrow night and see what happens.'

'She'll tell him about us and he'll want to look us over. You'd better pick up the ball tomorrow. I'll back out on the grounds that I've got some other club proposition I'm considering. Agreed?'

'OK. What time tomorrow?'

'I've got a date tomorrow evening. I'll pick you up at the Remter round about midnight.'

Temple had phoned just after midnight to suggest that they met at the Zoo Bahnhof in half an hour. Chapman had got there first.

No big railway terminal has ever managed to look welcoming, except perhaps for the main station in Milan, but the Zoo Bahnhof was incredibly grim. The building itself had no redeeming features, was overpowering in size and lacking any touch of humanity. It seemed almost to have been designed solely as a monstrous shelter for petty criminals and drug pushers. The people matched the buildings. Even the young girls who stood in the shadows of stone buttresses looked pale and lethargic, the prey of the pushers and the sleazy looking men who beckoned to them from their cars. It seemed incredible that men could be aroused by the sad young creatures who stood there, stoned by drugs and hopelessness.

Temple arrived and brought his usual aura of confidence and normality. A normality that insisted that if people didn't stick to the ground rules they should expect to get hurt, or knocked off.

The man outside the door took the money and let them in and when their eyes had adjusted to the dim lighting they saw Renate at the far end of the bar. As they headed towards her she turned and saw them and she looked pleased.

'Hi. We don't often get customers coming two nights running. D'you want a table or just a drink at the bar?'

For a moment she hesitated, then she looked at Temple. 'I mentioned our talk about clubs last night to the boss. He said if you came in again he'd like to talk to you. It's more private in the other room.' She laughed. 'He said if you came in to give you a drink on the house.'

They followed her to a table in the far corner and when a girl came for them to order a drink Renate told her to bring the old man's private whisky bottle.

'I'll go and tell him you're here, OK?'

Temple nodded. 'Why not?'

The bottle was Bell's and Temple poured drinks for them both and said quietly, 'Looks like we've clicked. You take over as soon as you can. I'll leave when you've got going.'

'OK. Here he comes.'

The man who walked along with the girl looked nothing like an older version of the photograph he had of Masson with his wife. It was hard to imagine this bloated face as ever having been mildly handsome. The man held out a pudgy hand to Temple and then to Chapman before he nodded to the girl in dismissal as he sat down, his paunch against the edge of the table.

'Renate said one of you's thinking about setting up a club in Berlin.'

Temple nodded and pointed at Chapman. 'It's my friend who's interested. I was only asking the questions.'

'So,' the man said, turning to look at Chapman. 'Are you genuinely interested?'

'I'm interested in hearing if it's a good investment.'

'Depends what you're looking for.'

Chapman shrugged. 'A good return on my money.'

'There's a lot of pay-offs in this sort of business.' He smiled. 'We don't keep books or accounts. We see we make no profits on paper so we don't pay taxes. It's a cash business and you need some way to get it out of Berlin.'

Chapman nodded. 'That wouldn't be a problem. What kind of money are we talking about?'

'My lady partner put sixty, seventy thousand marks in at the beginning and she had that back in four months.'

'Would she sell?'

'If I say so she's got no choice. I guess she'll sell.'

Temple stood up. 'I've got to leave you two.' He looked

at Chapman. 'Don't forget the proposition we've got from Thailand. It's worth considering.' He smiled. 'See you tomorrow maybe. Let me know what we're in for.'

'OK. I'll call you tomorrow.'

The man nodded and watched Temple head for the door, chatting to Renate on the way. Then he looked back at Chapman.

'Are you serious?'

'Yes. If it's a sound proposition.'

'You got funds for that kind of investment?'

'Whatever it takes.'

'What currency?'

'US dollars, sterling, yen.'

'Let's go up to my place and talk.'

The man walked slowly to a door at the far corner of the room and when Chapman was inside, the man turned the keys in two locks and slid a large bolt across.

There was a small hallway, bare of any furniture or decoration and then a red door that the man opened and stood aside for Chapman to go inside.

The inner room was surprising. Spacious and well furnished and with none of the vulgarity of the club itself. The only decoration on the walls was a framed black and white photograph of an odd-looking World War Two aeroplane.

The man waved him to a leather settee and sat down, panting from the walk.

'Tell me what you want to know, mister.'

'The main thing so far as I'm concerned is you. I'd have to trust you to give me a square deal.'

'The present lady's got no complaints on that score.'

'But she probably knew you already, I don't.'

'So ask me.'

Chapman smiled. 'I'd rather you tell me. I don't even know your name.'

'You can ask anyone about me. The name's Rutke, Hans Rutke. For some goddam reason most people call me Heinz. I've been in this business a long time. Your pal mentioned Thailand. I had my own club in Bangkok. You'll make more money here in Berlin.'

'What did you do before the clubs?'

'It's a long story, my friend.'

Chapman smiled. 'I'm sure it's an interesting one.'

'What makes you think that?'

'You're obviously an unusual man. I imagine you've had an interesting life.'

'When you look at me now you'll hardly believe that I was born to great wealth. The illegitimate son of a very wealthy man. A landowner. A titled man. I was his favourite son. My own servants, my own horses, my own plane. I wanted for nothing. When he died he left almost everything to me. But the family contested the will because I was a bastard. They hired the top lawyers and I ended up with nothing but the clothes I was wearing.'

'Please go on. I find it fascinating.'

'I started my own business, built it up. I had my own air-line. Nearly as big as Air France.' He smiled. 'You wouldn't guess I was originally French would you?'

'I don't know. You've got that French flair. When did you change your nationality?'

'When the Germans took over in France. They came straight to me. They had problems with Lufthansa. They wanted me to put it right. But they would be embarrassed by needing the expertise of a Frenchman. It was a condition that I changed my nationality.'

Chapman smiled. 'And I'm sure you sorted out Lufthansa.'

'I did, my friend, I did. They showered every kind of reward on me. Money, honours, a magnificent estate. Everything a man could want.' He shrugged. 'And then came the end of the war. And the Germans had lost. And I was technically a German.' He paused. 'But my talents for organisation had not gone unnoticed by the French. I was asked to take over the running of Air France. I kept my German nationality with their approval and Air France today owes, let us say, just a little to my fine-tuning.' He smiled and shrugged. 'Of course I built up a very good team around me. Scientists, engineers, economists. All of them devoted to me – wonderful men – and women of course.'

'You must be a little disappointed with your present situation – this club and a tough life.'

The man smiled. A knowing, amused smile. 'You might be surprised to know that there are men of top rank in French, German and British intelligence who owe their success to "Club Mimosa" and its predecessors.' He paused, smiling again. 'I am trusted with some of the world's best hidden secrets. We are a band of brothers, we old warriors. A club of like-minded men who strive to guide the futures of Europe into the right direction.'

He paused and let his hands fall onto his fat thighs as if he were a lawyer saying, 'I rest my case, Milord.'

Chapman said, 'You must be very tired, Herr Rutke.'

'We have to make sacrifices. All of us. From each according to his talents.'

'Could you see me again tomorrow evening?'

'Of course. Of course. I find you very *simpatico*. Come whenever you wish. I am always here.'

It was 4 a.m. when Chapman got back to the hotel. He was tempted to ring Temple at his flat. For the first time in the assignment he felt an excitement. A flow of adrenalin that made him eager to move in and settle the issue. It seemed strange to hear the man's fantasies first-hand after hearing them described by so many other people. The fantasies were less credible now. As if Masson himself was bored by their repetition and the need to find new variations to impress different people for different reasons.

Masson was a sad figure. Obviously suffering from some glandular problem that was the cause of his gross obesity. As he had listened he had tried to see in the old man's face the face of the dashing pilot and the charmer of young women. But it wasn't there. The heavy jowls and the flushed almost purple complexion dominated his appearance. He was conscious of the effort Masson had had to make, to make his story credible. Then finding encouragement when it seemed to be working, piling one impossible dream upon another, like a marathon runner making one last desperate effort to win the lifelong race. He felt almost guilty that it had been so easy to lure the old man into the revelations that established his identity.

13

Chapman phoned Temple's number at Security just before lunchtime but there was no answer. He called again in mid-afternoon but again there was no reply. In the early evening he rang Temple's home number but there was just a standard piece on an answering machine.

He was early at the club. Around 9 p.m. and the bruiser on the door had obviously been told to expect him. He spoke into the entry-phone and when the light came on he took Chapman inside.

As they walked the length of the bar Chapman noticed that the club was almost empty. A few teenage girls stood leaning against the bar, chewing gum ostentatiously, as if they were defying their mothers but not enjoying it.

Masson came out of his security door and put his arm round Chapman's shoulder.

'Welcome, my friend. I was hoping you'd call in.'

There was a Jacques Brel cassette playing on the hi-fi and Masson waddled over to switch it off before inviting Chapman to make himself comfortable on the leather settee. He poured them both a glass of red wine and as he handed a glass to Chapman he said, 'Did you have a busy day?'

Chapman smiled. 'A bit of shopping.'

'I had a visit from my doctor today.' He laughed. 'Just keep taking the pills.' He sat down heavily in an armchair. 'I've been looking forward to seeing you again.' He waved his hand dismissively. 'Nothing to do with business. You don't meet many civilised people in this business.'

'How long can we talk tonight?'

'As long as you want.'

'There's something else I want to talk to you about.'

'Anything you want.'

'I want your help. Your cooperation.'

Masson put his glass on a side table and leaned back with his hands clasped across his paunch.

'If it's money the answer is no. If it's a girl we can make a deal.'

'It's neither of those things.' Chapman took a deep breath. 'I want to talk about war-time. In France under the Occupation. When you were working for the British. For Special Operations Executive.'

Chapman saw the shock on Masson's face but he was taken aback for only a few seconds before he recovered and said defensively, 'What's wrong with working for the British?'

In a few seconds the man's elaborate fantasies of yesterday were left behind as if they had never been said. No excuses, no attempts to deny that they were lies. And, as with all psychopathic liars, no guilt.

'Nothing wrong at all. The RAF people said you did a very competent job. But I've been asked to find out what really happened with the Scorpio network.'

'They were crazy. Started a wild campaign against the Germans and the Germans picked them all up.' Masson shifted uneasily in the armchair. 'Who *are* you? How do you know about all this?'

'I'm a British intelligence officer from SIS. I think you know about SIS. A man named Palmer. Clive Palmer.'

'You work for Palmer?'

'No. He died some years ago. Tell me about him.'

'Oh sure. And then we have another court case or stuff in the newspapers. I've got enough troubles already.'

'I can promise you that nothing will happen to you. All I want is the truth.'

'About what?'

'About your deal with Palmer and your deal with the German, Westphal.'

294

'Why don't you ask Westphal? He's still alive.'

'Was it Westphal who got you your German passport?'

'Yes.'

'You worked with him before the war, didn't you?'

'I carried letters and so on for him when I was a pilot. That's all.'

'And then you went to England and you met Palmer. Tell me about that.'

'I escaped to England. I wanted to be a pilot in the RAF. There were many interrogations and then Palmer interviewed me. Said he'd got something special for me to do. I would be working for him direct but I would be with SOE as their air controller. He said he didn't trust the people in SOE. They were amateurs. Doing great damage to SIS. I was to say nothing about him or working for him but I was to report to him on everything they were doing.'

'How did you report to him?'

'I had a contact. One of his men.'

'Where?'

'In Paris. I gave him verbal reports and photo-copies of the Scorpio mail to London when the Lysanders came. Twice I had to go over to London without SOE knowing.'

'How did you do that?'

'Palmer's SIS people in France had their own Lysander flights. I went with them.'

'Now tell me about Westphal. He told me that you gave him photo-copies of the Scorpio communications to SOE in London. Why?'

Masson shrugged. 'I wasn't sure who'd win. One lot was insurance for the other.'

'You didn't care who won?'

'It wasn't a question of caring. I wanted the English and Americans to win but I wasn't sure they would. I'm not a hero, mister. I just worked to survive whichever way it went.'

'How were you funded?'

'The three SOE networks I looked after gave me money. And I got money from SIS.'

'And from Westphal?'

'Yes.'

'Did you ever have anything written from Palmer?'

Masson shook his head. 'No. He was too clever for that.'

'Why didn't the Germans wipe out Scorpio right from the start?'

'Westphal said they were doing no harm and it gave them an insight as to how a network was controlled and operated.'

'What happened to you when the Germans surrendered?'

'One of Palmer's men got me over the border into Switzerland. He gave me money and some gold and that was the last I heard from them.'

'You never tried to contact Palmer after the war?'

'No. He was a tricky bastard. I thought he might have a go at me. If I kept quiet he'd forget me.'

'What about Carlton, the SOE officer who testified for you at your trial?'

'I never knew why he did that but he hinted that he'd had pressure put on him in London to save my skin and bring the trial to a quick end.'

'Pressure from whom – Palmer?'

'I assumed it was him. Worried in case I talked too much.' Masson sighed heavily. 'You know, I thought there was something odd about you. I didn't know what.' He nodded. 'If you tried to use this against me I'd swear you were lying.'

'I told you. I just want to clear it up. Find out the truth. And who would want to make it public anyway?'

'God knows, but there's always some bastard who wants to stir up trouble.' He paused. 'You know, in a way I'm glad to have got it off my chest. It didn't worry me, what I'd done. But everybody wouldn't see it the same way.'

'I appreciate your cooperation. There won't be any come-back, I promise you.'

Masson said, 'The bastards are all dead except Westphal, and he won't talk.'

Chapman stood up and held out his hand. As Masson took it Chapman said, 'I'll leave you in peace, Herr Rutke.'

Down in the street Chapman looked around for a taxi. He could see two with their lights on in the distance by the Zoo Bahnhof. As he headed towards the station a figure moved out alongside him from a shop doorway.

'Keep walking, Harry, and don't look round.'

'Temple. What the hell's going on?'

'Turn right and you'll see a black BMW. Jump in the passenger side.'

As they got to the car Temple said, 'Not that side you bloody fool.'

As soon as he was in the car Temple drove off towards the Ku-damm and as they crossed the main street Temple threaded his way through a maze of side streets and finally pulled up at the Hubertus sports ground. As he switched off the engine Temple said, 'Just tell me what you're playing at, Harry.'

'I don't understand. I told you what I'm doing.'

'Don't play silly buggers with me, my friend. Remember – if you'd forgotten – I'm in the business too.'

Chapman looked at Temple. 'I don't know what you're on about. If you've got some complaint then make it. If not I want to go back to the Remter and get some sleep.'

Temple looked at Chapman for long moments and then he said, 'I got a coded tele-message from London this morning. It was waiting for me on my desk when I got in. It was very short and very simple. It asked me to try and trace a Kraut by the name of Rutke. Hans Rutke.'

'I've never given them the name. They don't even know I'm here.'

'I sent back a coded Fax asking for more details and I got a reply back an hour later that said that was all they knew except that he was possibly a Frenchman named Masson. Henri Masson.'

'Then what?'

'Then, my friend, I phoned an old mate of mine at

297

Century House, Chalmers, and asked him what was going on. He said he didn't know but he'd see if he could find out.'

'Go on.'

'Have you heard of a guy named Synodinos?'

'Yes, he's a Greek living in Paris, ex-Reuters in Hanoi.'

'Well, while I was waiting for Chalmers to come back to me there was another message from Century House.' He paused and stared at Chapman. 'The message said that agent Chapman H might be heading for Berlin. He was to be picked up on arrival at Tegel and sent under escort back to London.'

'What about Synodinos?'

'When Chalmers got back to me the saga went on. It seems a man named Synodinos had gone to the Embassy in Paris and asked to see somebody senior. He saw a junior Third-Secretary or some such title and spilled a long story about treason during the war and he knew who the culprit was. He'd given the story to a chap called Chapman who was a British intelligence officer who'd promised to pay him God knows how many thousand francs and then he'd done a bunk. He said the traitor was a guy using the name of Rutke and he was running a sex club in Berlin.' He paused. 'Is all this hogwash true?'

'I didn't promise him any money but the rest of it's true. As you know, we've found Rutke . . .'

'*You've* found Rutke, not me, sonny boy. You ain't heard the rest.'

'So tell me.'

'The orders to me are that Chapman H must on no account be allowed to search for Hans Rutke and all measures will be taken to prevent it. And no contact is to be made with Rutke himself.' He paused. 'And those orders came right from the top, Harry. If you make a wrong move you'll go in the mincer. Believe me, I know the smell of panic stations.'

Chapman sat looking straight ahead. 'What are you going to do?'

'Do they know you were staying at the Remter?'

'I told you. They don't even know I'm in Berlin.'

'I don't know whether it's you or those bastards at Century House who've made this giant cock-up, but I suspect it's more them than you. So here's what you do. I've paid your bill at the Remter and I've got your kit in the boot of the car. There's an early flight to Paris tomorrow morning. I'll get you a ticket in my name and I'll lend you my passport. As soon as you get to Paris you stuff it in a sealed envelope and hand it in to the Embassy to come back to me in the diplomatic bag. When you've done that you take a deep breath and put on your most stupid voice and phone whoever gave you your orders at C.H. You tell him about Synodinos, everything he told you. You say you don't believe him, that he's conning for money. You've had a couple of days off and you propose returning to London unless they want you to go on this wild goose chase to Berlin. OK, comrade?'

'They can check the manifest of the plane I came in on from Paris.'

'They won't. I've followed out their orders and I've reported that unless you came in under a different name you've not been to Berlin in the last seven days. I've put out a local routine search order on you. And they're so dumb they couldn't find Brigitte Bardot if she walked naked up the Ku-damm.'

'Do you want to know what I found out from Rutke?'

'You must be out of your bloody mind. And I suggest you tell yourself it was a dream. We'll have a coffee somewhere and you can sleep in the car. We've got three hours before we need to go to Tegel.'

As Temple started the car Chapman said, 'Do you think Travers will believe me?'

'Jesus, is it Travers you're working for?'

'Yes.'

'He'll believe you, sunbeam. You're telling him he's off the hook. It'll be music to his ears.'

* * *

Temple stayed with him until the Paris flight was called. Watched him go through Immigration and went up to the observation level and watched him board the plane. There was a slight ground mist but that was only to be expected. It was mid-October and autumn always came early in Berlin.

He looked at his watch. It was going to be a long day and a rough night.

14

Travers sat looking across the Thames from the window seat in the cafeteria at the Festival Hall, two coffees on the table in front of him. One for Crowther and one for himself.

When Crowther came back from the toilet he reached for the sugar as he said, 'Where are we at now?'

'Chapman phoned me mid-morning. Told me about what the Greek had said and went on to say that he thought he was conning us for money and the lead wasn't worth following up.'

'Why so long before he contacted you?'

'It was only three days. Said he'd taken a break for a couple of days. He'd done out a report and his conclusion was that while there was a lot of pretty damning hearsay evidence against both Masson and our friend Palmer there was no point in pursuing it because there was no actual evidence that either a civil court or a court of enquiry would accept.' Travers smiled. 'He was very apologetic that he had had to come up with such a negative report.'

'And the chap in Berlin that the Greek said was Masson, what about him?'

'I've had a word with Berlin and told them to check thoroughly and if he exists and they are satisfied that he's Masson then they should deal with him expeditiously.'

'Who did you speak to?'

'First to Richards and then his specialist, a chap named Temple.'

'You think they understood what's wanted?'

Travers smiled. 'I'm sure they do.'

'And the Greek?'

'He was dealt with yesterday.'

'Not those fools of yours in Paris, I hope.'

'No. I sent somebody over from here. He came back the same day.'

'We've sweated on this all these years and now there's nobody left whose evidence would be more than suspicion.'

'That's so.'

'Draft me a short memo that I can give to the D-G to pass on to the Minister.' He paused. 'When does the House sit again?'

'In two weeks' time.'

'What about Chapman?'

'In fact he's done a very good job. He wasn't suited to that job – that's why I chose him. He deserves a break and I'm giving him an active field job based on Amsterdam.'

'When shall we know about Masson?'

'I expect to hear tonight. Where will you be tomorrow?'

'With the D-G.'

'At Century House?'

Crowther smiled. 'No, at Wentworth. You can patch in to the line through my girl.'

He had bought her a KPM fruit bowl in Berlin, and she sat on the bed surrounded by wrapping paper, still holding the bowl in her hands watching him unpack.

'Do you really have to go in this afternoon?'

'Yup.'

'Surely they could wait when you've had a tiring flight.'

He looked at her and smiled. 'I've got a meeting with Travers.'

'Is that the smarmy one who wears brown suits?'

For a moment he looked taken aback then slowly he relaxed and laughed. 'I suppose you could call him smarmy, although I'm sure he'd prefer to be described as diplomatic.'

'Same thing. I bet his wife hates him.'

'Why on earth do you think that?'

'He just looks that sort of man. All smiles, with little beady eyes searching for a chink in your armour. Big on men's clubs where women aren't allowed.'

'For Christ's sake, you've only met him once.'

'So?'

He laughed and then said, 'Changing the subject, what's happened to the wayward girl, Dolly or Polly whatever her name was?'

'She's in some kind of half-way house for young girls. I went along to see if there was anything we could do to help.'

'And?'

'You know I envy other people who seem to be able to sort out what they think or believe in and know which side they're on. I never seem to be able to do that.'

He nodded and she went on. 'I went there terribly sorry for the girl. Incest and all that. What a bastard the father must be. And I thought it might upset me seeing such a sad young thing. But in fact she was very pretty and incredibly self-confident. And – I'd guess – totally promiscuous. Tight sweater, fantastic boobs for fifteen, and she knew it. I'd say she knows more about men than I do.'

He smiled. 'What did you do?'

'I gave the warden fifty quid but I'm damned if I know what it was supposed to be for.'

'Danegeld, because you were thankful that it hadn't worked on Judy.' He smiled. 'Anyway we showed that we cared.' He paused. 'I'm going to have a bath.'

He stood in his bathrobe at the bathroom window, looking at the people in the street, and wondered what it would be like to be like them, having decided views on politics, religion, sex and what was right and wrong, instead of having a mind that was never decisive. Where incest was totally wrong and the fault of the male concerned, and no wandering side thoughts about whether the growing sensuality of a young girl might not have tempted her to see if the machinery worked, even on her father. And if promiscuity might not just be a desperate distorted need for affection.

Travers was sitting at his desk, talking on the phone and he waved towards the leather armchair as he went on talking. And Chapman realised that Travers *was* wearing a brown suit and a shirt with brown stripes. He saw the file with his final report on Travers' blotter.

Travers hung up and pointed at the file.

'That was a first-rate report, Harry. No padding, but fully informative. Just what we needed.' He leaned back in his chair. 'A lot of careful work that shows that maybe there's no smoke without fire, but in this place, suspicion may arouse our curiosity but it's facts that are our life-blood. Like you said in your report. Plenty of opinions but nary a fact.' He smiled. 'Nothing a court would give credence to anyway. But it's a relief to be able to say – if the matter is raised again – that we've turned over all the stones but there was nothing to substantiate Price's scurrilous claims. The D-G said it was a judicious report – his own words.' He paused, 'But that's not why I arranged this meeting. It's been suggested that this business has meant losing a first-rate field agent for far too long and I'm inclined to see their point. Provided you agree I propose posting you to Amsterdam to head up our field operations throughout Holland and Belgium. It means putting you up a grade and . . .' he smiled '. . . that's well deserved. So – how do you feel about that?'

'Is it a married posting?'

'Of course.'

Chapman smiled. 'When do I start?'

'You'll need some leave, so I've pencilled in December one as your start date. Gives you a chance to sort out the domestic side.'

Travers stood up to show that the interview was over but paid Chapman the classic Whitehall courtesy of walking him to the door.

Anne-Marie Duchard had wondered why the Greek didn't come back for the translation that she had done for him. She was not a newspaper reader or she would have seen the brief paragraph in *Le Figaro* that reported that an elderly journalist named Panayotis Synodinos had been found hanging from a pipe in the toilet of his two-roomed flat. The police had discovered the body after the concierge had reported that he had not collected his mail for several days but had not left the building. There was a suggestion that the dead man had had psychiatric treatment at some time.

The fact that she had heard no more from the Englishman had disturbed her. Not that she expected him to have unravelled the convoluted strands of what had happened all those years ago. She had lived with her sadness at Philippe's death for too long for the details of how he had been betrayed to matter any longer. All that mattered was that he was dead. But she had liked the Englishman, Harry Chapman, he was a breath of fresh air and a sympathetic listener. She had looked forward to his visits because she felt at ease with him.

She was surprised and, despite herself, pleased, when she received a letter from the Ministry of Defence in London, just before Christmas. It said that certain facts had been drawn to the Ministry's attention regarding the status of her late husband and it regretted that a mistake had been made in classifying her entitlement to a widow's pension. It was quite clear that in fact he was a war-substantive captain in the Intelligence Corps and she was entitled to the pension applicable to that rank. The apology for the mistake was unequivocal, and a substantial payment for nearly forty years of underpayment had already been authorised and would be despatched to her in a few days' time.

Epilogue

As always on Remembrance Day there were groups of people at the high Foreign Office windows, watching the ceremony at the Cenotaph. For several years Chapman had brought his wife and daughter. It was the only perk that he could offer them from his job in SIS. He watched the people in Whitehall; the politicians, some of them wearing medals; the old soldiers, the honour guard, and the crowds of civilians lining the pavements. Some of them would be the widows and descendants of men who had not come back.

For most people the ceremony evoked memories of the last war. Dunkirk, the fall of France, the Battle of Britain, D-Day and the landings in Normandy, and the battles that led up to the German surrender.

He had learned a lot in the past few months and he knew now that all those military things were no more than the superficial wrappings around reality. For the vast majority of ordinary people in all the belligerent countries, life went on despite the war. When the Parisians watched in silence as the Germans marched down the Champs Elysées they were conscious of France's defeat but their minds were mostly on more mundane things. Young men wondered if the girl would still turn up for their date. Men with responsibilities wondered what would happen to their jobs. How they would pay the rent and keep up the payments on the insurance. Some shrewder men already selling their cars and looking for a bicycle. Nobody knows what happens when you lose a war. The headlines in *Le Figaro* or *Le Matin* about Vichy and Pétain were meaningless. Part of another world. What mattered was surviving.

And as the months went by, ordinary people settled into their new roles, which were not all that different from what they had been before the occupation. Maybe you were cold because the Germans had all the fuel. You may be hungry but it was unlikely that you would be starving, because there was always the black market and distant relations who lived in the country. Men and women still fell in love, and out of it. You worried about money but you had always worried about money. You cheated on taxes and food and clothing coupons but that was just part of the game.

When, in 1945, it was all over, then the old world came back with a rush and the politicians took over again. Chickens came home to roost. Girls had their heads shaved because they'd slept with a German. Girls even had their heads shaved for falling in love with a German and marrying him. Well-loved entertainers, singers and cabaret stars were put on black-lists. Writers, artists and musicians who had been favoured by the Germans were ostracised. There were different prisoners in the cells in Fresnes, and suddenly there was nobody who hadn't been a member of the Resistance. Things went back to normal.

It would be difficult to decide whether the next two years were more miserable and depressing for the French or for the Germans. For it was the Germans' turn to be vanquished. The game of international musical chairs had gone on and now it was the Germans who were left without a chair when the music stopped.

The Germans' Bayeux tapestry was the bombing of Hamburg and Dresden, the surrender in the tent on Luneburg Heath, the suicide of Adolf Hitler, Russians in Berlin and conquering troops all over Germany. And it was the Germans' turn with the same old losers' currency of cigarettes, bread, and pretty girls' bodies. Recrimination, revenge, greed and selfishness ruled the vast sprawl of Europe, and nobody was going to cry – 'Enough'. There was always a lot of people who liked what was happening. Always plenty of people who'd never had it so good.

Chapman was well aware that a year ago, or even less, his thoughts would have been very different. Or to be more exact he would have had no thoughts or opinions on such things at all. They were far outside his experience. But for the last six months he had been living back in those grim days and it had taught him a lot. Mainly that it wasn't possible to blame whole nations for the evil that men did. Not even the Nazis or the Vichyists. It was men who did those things. Just men. He remembered something that Mendes had told him. That more Frenchmen had been killed by Frenchmen after the liberation than had been sent to their deaths by the Germans as hostages, deportees and slave-labourers during the occupation.

And all that he had learned had left a haunting question in his mind. A question he didn't want to answer. How would our lot have behaved if we had been defeated? Would there have been Brits ready to resist and others to betray them, architects and builders to set up the gas-chambers? Politicians ready to do their new masters' bidding, entertainers who were happy to appear at the Palladium for the *Wehrmacht*. Girls ready to open their legs for cash or coupons and girls who fell in love with a soldier from Dresden or a sailor from Hamburg.

His mind was far away when Mary tugged at his sleeve and he realised that the parade was over and the room was empty except for them.

'Where were you?'

He smiled. 'A long way away.'

'Your little man in the brown suit said there's a buffet in the ante-room if we want it.'

'What d'you think?'

'I'd rather we all went and had a pub lunch if that's OK with you.'

Chapman put his arm round her shoulder, smiling as he said, 'Let's go to the Café Royal and see what Oscar Wilde's up to.'